BORROWER QUEEN

RAVYN FYRE

Disclaimer

Names, characters, events and incidents are either the products of the author's imagination or used in a fictitious manner. Any resemblance to actual persons, living or dead, or actual events is purely coincidental.

Author's Note

To my readers I hope you enjoy reading this just as much as I did writing it. Visit my website to find out what's coming next.

www.Ravynfyre.com

If you are looking to connect with me, find me on Facebook under Ravyn's Readers.

Happy Reading!

Chapter One

I should have paid more attention to those stupid tabloids ranting and raving about alien abductions and the like when I had the chance? I guess my first-hand experience trumped anything they would have taught me. Considering I awoke to find myself aboard a spaceship, just like something you'd see in the movies, only I am most definitely NOT an actor.

My last memory before waking was reaching my car in the parking lot at work when suddenly an intense-blue beam enveloped me. Before everything faded to black, I watched my body disintegrate into atoms as it floated up into the sky. I'm not sure why they picked me out of the billions to choose from on my planet, but I'm here, nonetheless.

I had a hunch; it had something to do with my ability, since the others aboard the ship with me were not exactly normal either. Luckily for me, I was born with the unique ability to sense when anyone within a one-mile radius of me possessed a unique gift, and then I could borrow that gift as my own.

The room was made mostly of metal and glass and was full of cryo-chamber beds of some sort. Besides the one I was on there were nine others. The five across from me were empty, but the ones to my left were filled with others, like myself, just waking up.

To my right, a person with his back to me was standing near a computer panel. Based on size alone, I wagered he was male. Dressed in a one-piece military uniform, he resembled a human, although slightly larger. Oh, who was I kidding? He was huge and looked nothing like the little grey men the tabloids featured.

The guard was tall and broad-shouldered, and the uniform he was wearing fit him perfectly. His long black hair was tied back with a leather hair tie, and he wasn't green, grey, or hairless. When he turned around, I knew he wouldn't have large black eyes either. His ability to read minds and feelings when touching someone would prove useful, though, but only if I suddenly became everyone's new best friend and made touchy-feely my new thing.

I turn my attention away from my captor and take stock of my fellow captives, three females and one male. They appeared to be in the same state of dress as me, and by that, I meant the lack thereof. If I needed more proof of the existence of aliens, the four in captivity with me were all the confirmation I needed. They were human-like in most ways, with some added physical and mental attributes.

The black-haired male appeared utterly normal except for three significant differences: his ears, tail, and manhood. His ears and tail were similar to a horse, and his manhood was almost as long. A penis that large would shred any human female, and I cringed just thinking of him anywhere near me. His unique ability to teleport looked promising and interesting.

The redhead was beautiful and alluring. Her eyes were a mesmerizing blend of orange and yellow that reminded me of the molten sun, only not as bright. Her ability was seduction through song. I believe mythology referred to her as a siren. She had the appearance of a fiery spirit with a don't fuck with me attitude. However, my mom said to never judge a book by its cover, and I'd wait to pass judgment until I at least spoke with her. But I wanted it noted that I didn't think becoming besties was an excellent idea.

Next to her, a black beauty of a lady with glowing fluorescent green hair and eyes, stretched to her toes, before gracefully flipping backward in a move so fluent it appeared, she never left the ground. Her ability was shapeshifting into a panther, and the ease of her mobility showcased it. Her skin was the color of midnight, which offset her bright hair and eyes perfectly. I'd never shifted into another being before and feared it would be painful. I prayed my fears were unjustified and I wouldn't need her ability anytime soon.

The blond woman beyond her was tall with pointed ears. Her eyes were silver and spaced slightly further apart than usual. The difference in her facial features didn't take away from her beauty in the slightest. Her affinity with nature gave her many abilities that ranged from growing plants to communicating with animals. Still, her gift to camouflage with her surroundings was the first thing I would borrow when we landed.

My gaze returned to her eyes, and I almost choked when her gaze found mine just as the silver clouding her eyes bled away to reveal violet eyes rimmed with the silver that once covered her vision. She must not have noticed my reaction or chose to ignore it, since she shrugged with an infectious grin—acting like she expected my response. Her smile was genuine, though, and made me feel I might have an ally in this crazy new world I found myself in.

Leaving me, a 5-foot 4-inch brunette with green eyes and olive skin. I'd consider myself average, cute, but not hot. I'm not a large girl by any means, but I have curves. Some where they should be and others where they shouldn't. My disgust of anything related to exercise would be the cause. I'd been lucky for most of my life with a high metabolism that made not working out a possibility, but the older I got, the less that played into effect. I'm just not as toned as I used to be without even trying, and my bad habits don't help either. Enough so that standing around nude made me blush.

The guard approached my bed as I stood up and looked at me without an ounce of appreciation in his, every day, I might add, stunning aquamarine blue eyes. He stopped within two feet of me and started speaking in a language I'd never heard before. It looked like he expected me to answer him, so I threw up my hands and scrunched my shoulders in the universal signal of "I don't know" and hoped that relayed my confusion.

He reached for my neck, and before I could think to move away from him, he flipped a switch on a necklace I hadn't noticed I was wearing. The feeling of being enveloped was instantaneous.

"My name is General Jaelel. We expect to arrive in port within the hour. Dr. Triste will be along shortly to prepare you." With that, he moved on to my neighbor.

Woah! I understood everything he just said! His speech went from gibberish to English just like that, it was amazing! My jubilation didn't last long, as the loss of my gift settled over me. Feeling disconnected that I could no longer sense anyone's talents, I tried unsuccessfully to remove the trinket around my neck. I gave up with a huff and used my hands to cover myself instead, as goosebumps rose on my skin. I had bigger things to worry about besides the loss of my gift.

My thoughts revolved around what type of prepping the doctor would do and how I could defend myself without the use of my gift. I was definitely at a disadvantage. My mind was going into overdrive and started remembering all the tabloid headlines of little grey men with large black eyes and medical experiments they performed on the abductees. I never believed we were alone in the universe, but that didn't mean I was ready to be probed for the sake of science.

I always thought the people who told their stories to magazines like the national enquirer were just attention seekers and never bothered to read more than the front cover. There could have been honest suggestions or helpful hints that would be wonderful in this situation, and I vowed that if, I mean, when I returned home, I would keep an open mind towards anything out of the ordinary in the future.

I hadn't seen anyone other than the guard; Maybe the aliens abducted him and made him their slave, and I was about to meet the real aliens for myself. Were they something out of *Star Wars*? Or *Avatar*? Were they all human-like? Did the ancient astrophysicists have it right? And we were just descendants of an ancient alien civilization, and lost our history?

The infamous doctor who sashayed into the room was a far cry away from looking like a little green man, and the only tool she seemed to be wielding was an electronic notepad in her arms. Dr. Triste was a tall willowy woman with long black hair that shimmered in the overhead light. Her heart-shaped face, delicate nose, and pink lips gave her an air of royalty. She was also wearing the military uniform, but everything about her screamed perfection.

She had the same color of blue eyes as the guard, and had me rethinking my theory on the General's abduction. They appeared to be related or, at the minimum, at least from the same species. Both were extremely beautiful, tall, and well-proportioned, which made me wish I didn't loathe exercise. With the necklace blocking my gift, I had no clue what type of power the woman might have, but I could only hope her profession had something to do with healing.

The doctor approached swiftly and genuinely smiled at me before speaking, "It is a pleasure to meet you, miss; my name is Annalise. I want to confirm our records and do a quick run of tests before we land. Would it be alright if I begin?" Too shocked to even begin to know how to speak words, I nodded my agreement.

"Very well," she says, "My records indicate your name is Jade Marcene Cordel."

When I nodded again, she continued, "You were born twenty-five years ago in Deer Park, Washington, to a mother whose name was unknown. Peter and Kathryn Cordel then adopted you. Is that correct?"

My jaw dropped at her statement, but I somehow managed to stammer out, "Yes, b..but how do you know all of that?"

"Believe it or not, your arrival on this ship is not by chance. You were one of five candidates submitted by your planet to be a representative of your species at the next All Hands Gathering, which happens to be in three days on my home planet of Strixton," Annalise answered with a smile.

Twirling a lock of hair around my finger to restrain myself from screaming, I calmly asked, "How is that possible? I've never even been out of the country, let alone to another planet. I . . . I mean . . . I wouldn't know the first thing about representing my planet. There must be some mistake, is there someone in charge that I could speak with on this matter?"

Annalise's smile faltered slightly before she quickly disguised it. "Of course, once we land, you can take your concern to Lord Kalen. I have just a couple more questions before you can head out for a shower and get some clothes on."

"I'll answer as long as I can ask one more of my own?" I paused for a nanosecond and, before she could deny my request, asked, "Who is Lord Kalen?"

She graced me with a brilliant smile and answered, "The king of my people, but don't let that scare you. He is very kind, generous, and compassionate in all that he does." Dropping her eyes to her clipboard, she nibbled on her bottom lip before she continued, "We show that you are a level one Sixer, with a gene mutation on the 6th chromosome."

"Come again?" I stammered out. How the hell did anyone get a hold of my DNA? Mutation, like in X-men? I always thought my gifts were supernatural. Who knew?

"Are you saying I'm a mu..mutant? How do you know any of this? What's a Sixer?" I rambled.

"In layman's terms, anyone with an ability beyond the five senses is a Sixer. You can borrow the gifts of those around you, which means you are considered a level one Sixer, the highest rank

12

assigned. The gene mutation on your sixth chromosome is the reason you have that power. We identified the mutation using our technology the moment you boarded our ship."

"I have no idea what you're talking about. How do you expect me to respond?"

"I would expect you to respond with an affirmation or declination of that ability," her tone of voice was indicative of her annoyance.

There was no use in denying what was already known, so I straightened my shoulders, looked her in the eye and replied, "Yes, that is the nature of my gift. Might I ask why my ability appears to be blocked?" I fought not to break eye contact with her as I waited to see how truthful she would be with me. I didn't want her to see how intimidated she made me feel.

"All gifts are muted with the necklace in the beginning. It also aids us in being able to communicate bi-directionally without language barriers to the many planets that we protect."

I was on the verge of a mental shutdown from all she revealed and needed time to regroup, but my curiosity got the better of me. I sat up and blurted out my next question without a filter, "Protection from what?"

"From the evil Mengh, nasty little grey men that have notoriety on your planet for alien abductions involving probes. Please lie back so we can finish. You no doubt will be interested in a shower, and this should only take a moment."

I couldn't believe she just confirmed that probing is an actual event, and little grey men exist. I laid back before I fell. Once reclined, Annalise slowly ran her hands from the bottom of my toes to the top of my head, stopping every so often with more concentration. I could feel the warmth of her hands spreading tendrils of contentment, though she never made direct contact with my skin.

"I am a healer by gift. The warmth you feel is the healing your body required from the abuse you have put yourself through. Might I suggest a healthier lifestyle?" Her look of disappointment was enough, and I nodded my submission. It was over before I wanted it to be, and I stared at her profile as she scribbled more notes on my chart.

"Please excuse me. I must see to the others." Patting my hand, she turned slightly before saying, "Lord Kalen will answer the rest of your questions during the banquet. Your quarters are down the hall, first door on the left. You will find all that you need in the attached bathroom and something to wear."

I made my way to my quarters quickly and was elated to discover a gorgeous green silk dress and underthings laid out for me. The space was small and only furnished with a bed and nightstand that jutted out from the wall. It looked uncomfortable, with barely enough room to turn over. Sitting down to test how soft it was, I was happy we weren't staying long.

The room had a private bathroom that wasn't much bigger than an airplane lavatory. Standing in the cramped shower, I was delighted to find my usual shampoo and conditioner stocked and ready for my use. When real water cascaded over me, I grinned despite my circumstances. The shower did wonders for my alertness level, and I felt better prepared to accept my new reality. I still had no idea where we were going or what my real purpose was from here on out, but I'd find out soon. Clothed and feeling semi-normal, I joined the others and awaited my meeting with Lord Kalen.

Chapter Two

Landing the alien spacecraft was nothing like I expect the astronauts of Earth experienced. There was no turbulence or resistance while entering the planet's atmosphere; it was as if the ship split the very air in front of it, creating a pathway meant just for us. I expected jarring and heat, but it was smooth with no temperature fluctuations, despite the flames licking the window.

So far, I had yet to see anything but the inside of the craft. A few times since waking, I found myself hoping that I never left Earth but had been kidnapped by psychopaths and I would find myself home in no time. But once I approached the exit, it was apparent - we were not in Kansas anymore.

The sky was violet instead of the blue sky I was used to, with not one but two suns just over the horizon. They appeared smaller and further away, which would explain why it didn't feel scorching hot. The air was humid, with a slight breeze. I could hear the sounds of an ocean in the distance to my left. There was no mention of their air not being compatible, so with my first steps on alien soil, I took a deep breath and noted a faint smell of the sea with a hint of something sweet like a flower yet masculine as well.

The ship had landed inside some sort of walled-off enclosure, close to water. There was an impressive palace to the right. What drew my attention were the many hangars for the multitude of airships that lined the tarmac. Dozens of small-crewed ships like ours were also landing with people such as myself. Behind that were fighter planes and the carriers that could transport them to other worlds.

If the display in front of me was any indication, it looked like they were preparing for war. I remember Annalise had said they protected planets from the Mengh, but I didn't make the connection to how serious it could be until I saw the firepower in front of me.

A commotion to my right caught my attention. General Jaelel was striding toward a company of soldiers, and as my eyes reached his apparent destination, it felt as if the ground shook beneath my feet. All of my senses jumped to life as my vision tunneled to the man, I could only assume was Lord Kalen, and boy, was I in trouble.

He was the most beautiful man I had laid eyes on. Over seven feet of pure masculinity. He had the same characteristics as the general, black hair, tanned skin, and aquamarine eyes, but his face rivaled Adonis. The uniform he was wearing revealed he had the body to go along with the look. Everything I'd seen thus far was beyond lickable for sure, and I couldn't imagine it being anything other than perfection.

Stop that right now! I needed to focus on more important things, like getting off this rock and back to my old life. There would always be time for fantasizing later, and I had every intention of using this eye candy in front of me as the star of my next fantasy. He had an air of authority about him, and the fact that everyone stood just behind him, as the general stopped in front of him and bowed was another indication. I gasped out loud at the intense wave of desire I felt for a man I had never met before.

Lord Kalen's head snapped in my direction at the sound of my gasp, and his aquamarine eyes mesmerized me even further. Instead of acknowledging the general, he side-stepped him and instantly appeared directly in front of me. How did he move so fast? One moment he was there, and next, he was in front of me in the blink of an eye. My heart fluttered at his nearness, and I was sure I would hyperventilate at any moment. I'm short, but I felt tiny in his presence. Staring down at me, he reached out to caress my cheek, and the second he made contact, I let go of the breath I hadn't realized I was holding with a long shudder. I couldn't bring myself to look away and nuzzled into his hand in encouragement.

The connection was unlike anything I had felt in my life. I only had one word, completion. My heart rate declined the longer he touched me, leaving me feeling warm and electrified all over. His searching eyes touched the bottom of my soul and made me want to fall even faster toward this man who reached into areas I had no idea were lacking and waiting to be filled. It was as if we were the only two people in existence until Dr. Triste cleared her throat loudly from behind me. Lord Kalen dropped his hand, and the connection I felt disappeared, leaving me feeling adrift inside myself.

As he took a step back, I shook my head and lowered my eyes. What in the hell just happened? I'd never felt so out of control in all my life. I had no doubt if the doctor wouldn't have rudely, I mean kindly interrupted us, I would have thrown myself into his arms whether he wanted it or not.

Lord Kalen masked his expressions well and appeared to be in complete control, showing no sign of being affected. Whereas I felt anything but in control, and there were parts of my body still standing at attention. I wasn't usually the type of woman to drop my reservations after mere moments and go all in, but he made me want to reconsider. You always wish that someone, somewhere, will take your breath away and be the star of your dreams. I just didn't realize finding Mr. Right would require space travel. Romantic notions aside, I needed to control my thoughts and figure out my next plan of action.

Dr. Triste interrupted my wayward thoughts again when she said, "Ladies and gentlemen, let me introduce you to Lord Kalen, ruler of our people."

Kalen smiled politely, bowed to the crowd before he addressed them, "Welcome distinguished guests, proper introductions will need to wait until later, but I hope you like your accommodations. Please make sure to let someone know if there is anything you require while staying as a guest in my palace." His voice was like molten chocolate, delicious, dark, and left me wanting more. He turned to me when he was done and added quietly, "I have pressing matters that I must attend to. Until tonight."

Bowing once more, I blinked, and the next thing I knew, he was standing next to Jaelel, like he never left them. With their heads hunched together in conversation, they moved in the direction of the palace, with a full armament of guards following after them. An older gentleman and a young woman approached them as they neared, but Kalen waved them off as he continued inside.

The added distance cleared my addled brain like a bucket of cold water. I mentally kicked myself for not getting the answers that Annalise stated he would provide and vowed the next time I saw him; it would be the first thing out of my mouth. I needed to find a way to resist the pull he had on me if I expected to make coherent sentences in his presence.

The group I was in moved forward in waves, and I struggled to keep up. The palace entrance was enormous and made me feel small and inferior in comparison. Two guards, posted on either side, held the massive doors open for us as we passed through. The grandeur of the place was breathtaking. As my eyes took in the floor's glistening black stone, I noticed a multitude of rainbows shimmering on the surface from the clear crystal ceiling above.

Walls made of a granite-like stone with veins of opal gave the foyer a bright, whimsical feel. The giant staircase leading to the balcony on the second floor was on the left of the entrance, and a comfortable meeting room with a large fireplace was to our right. The hallways were a bustle of activity as servants flitted about carrying platters of drinks and food to the new arrivals.

Another tall lady in a dark skirt suit descended the staircase, cleared her throat, and addressed the gathered crowd, "May I have your attention. My name is Cenara, and I'll be your hostess for today's informal meet and greet. Please make your way into the Great Hall. Enjoy the drinks and hors d'oeuvres going around. I'll go over a few rules before each of you will be paired up and shown to your accommodations."

We filed in like cattle, and several groups gathered into huddles discussing the palace's grandeur in hushed whispers. As I looked about the room, a definite pattern of stereotypical cliques started to form, dividing the beautiful and strong from the ordinary and weak.

Cenara stood at the front of the room and clapped her hands to get our attention before her voice projected over the area like it was magnified, "As we wait for everyone else to arrive, please take a moment to introduce yourselves. Once the last stragglers come in, we'll get started. We have a lot to cover, so pay attention. Otherwise, you'll find yourself lost in the upcoming trials."

It didn't take long for the room to erupt into conversations, and from what I could gather, everyone was here of their own free will, which made my situation even more bizarre. The number one topic of discussion was the All Hands Gathering banquet in three days, as well as the coming trials leading to the selection. I needed more intel if I was going to survive and decided to assimilate myself into a group of women that looked like they knew what was going on.

The moment I entered their circle, all conversation stopped. The majority of the crowd were staring at me, but a few shy ones only had eyes for a tall black-haired woman mastering the group like a puppeteer. Following the others' line of sight, the haughty woman tossed her plated hair over her shoulder as she turned to face me. It was the young woman Kalen brushed off earlier.

She plastered a fake smile to her lips before she spoke. "Hello there," she purred while looking me over with mild disgust. When I didn't respond, she sighed dramatically and said, "And you are standing here because?"

The hairs on the back of my neck raised when her cronies snickered at the jab. I felt like I was back in high school and had to remind myself I couldn't control what happened around me, but I could control my actions toward the snarky bitch. Taking a deep breath, I ignored her rude comment and said, "You looked like you might know what was going on around here."

"Clueless and homely are not a winning combination, but seeing as I'm in a giving mood, I'll cut you a break. These trials are where the weak and strong are separated. The elite move on to be above peasants like you. Maybe if you're lucky, I'll let you be my maid when I become the ruling lady."

Was she referring to me as weak? The nerve of the woman! I tugged at the necklace and rued the loss of my power as I narrowed my eyes at her. I wasn't going to show how much her direct attack was affecting me, so without thinking, I opened my smart mouth, "Anyone who picks you would most likely shrivel up and die from your icy snatch."

With a gasp, the bitch's face became a snarl before she cleared her throat and said, "My planet, Marni, has produced more Sixers and mates than any other. Considering our union was prophesized, it is only a matter of time before I take my place by Lord Kalen's side."

"Ha! Must have been foretold by a magic eight ball! Not sure who your source is, but I think you're delusional and should seek help soon," I replied with a shrug and then turned on my heel, showing them my backside like I had nothing to fear. In reality, I was shaking from the encounter and was wondering what I had gotten myself into. From my peripheral vision, I watched her turn her sickly-sweet attention back to the others and breathed a sigh of relief that the confrontation hadn't escalated further. Truth be told, I'd never had to fight with my hands and had no idea how scrappy I could be, but my instincts screamed that I could take her.

I saw a familiar face in the crowd and headed that direction, hoping my women's intuition regarding the blonde was accurate. I could use an ally in this rat race. Being the only one in the room caught off guard was wreaking havoc with my inner peace. I showed up to the game without knowing the rules and wasn't sure what we were playing for. A part of me wanted to sit back and let them play it out amongst themselves, but the bitch in me wanted to win first prize and rub it in their faces. Who were they to judge me?

The blonde smiled at my approach, held out her hand in greeting, and said, "Hello, my name is Beatress, from Garrone. We arrived together, but with all of the hustle, I didn't have the chance to introduce myself."

I smiled softly, "I'm Jade, from Earth." I shook her hand and released it quickly. "I seem to be at a disadvantage."

With a lopsided grin, she said, "How so?"

"Well, for starters, I'm not entirely sure why I'm here. Kidnapped from my home planet with no warning or knowledge seems unfair when everyone else appears to know what's going on.

To them, nothing is out of the ordinary. Not to mention, I seem to have made some enemies already." Nodding my head toward the in-crowd.

"I wouldn't worry about them. The trials are quite competitive, so it doesn't surprise me they would single you out. They're just jealous because you are so pretty. I'm sorry you feel lost. This experience must be weird for you. Where I'm from, every eligible man and woman prays they are the next selection. I can't imagine how I would feel."

Blushing, I stared at the ground and muttered, "Thanks. I think. On the ship, they told me I would be representing my species at the All Hands Gathering, but everyone is talking about a selection. What does that entail?"

"Men and women from across the stars compete for certain positions in the Strix army over the next few days. Their performance at the trials will determine which role they will end up with. Lord Kalen announces the selections at the culmination of the trials."

"What are the different roles and levels required for each?"

"There are many roles, but the major categories would fall under warriors, scholars, or mates. Mates can be any level; fate's not finicky. Whereas warriors are usually level one or two Sixers, scholars are rarely higher than level four. The rest will fill more menial jobs."

"What if the person selected would prefer to go home?"

"I have never heard of someone asking to leave. The selection is final, and there is no reversing the decision; I couldn't imagine anyone rejecting immortality."

"Immortality?"

"Yeah. It's part of the job description, which depends on which role you get assigned. For instance, there is a ceremony for warriors, and they exchange blood. The exchange gives them added abilities and strength and grants immortality. But if you're talking about a mate, a bond is forged after consummation. The bonded pair maintain it through the consistent exchange of blood."

"In both instances, you referred to blood. What am I dealing with here? Vampires?" I jokingly asked.

Beatress chuckled, "I haven't heard that term in a while, but yes, that is one of their many names. They prefer Strix."

She must have seen the fear written all over my face because she quickly added, "Not to worry, though. They are a very peaceful species unless provoked." I nodded and swallowed the lump in my throat. It was just my luck, finding out that not only aliens and vampires were real, but they also happened to be the same thing. I started hyperventilating and saw Beatress's concern just before I hit the floor, and all went black.

Chapter Three

For the second time in a day, I awoke to strange surroundings. I was lying upon the softest canopied bed in existence with curtains surrounding all sides in differing shades of aquamarine. I wondered what happened. The curtains swayed softly from a slight breeze, and I peeked out from behind them to see balcony doors to my right slightly ajar. Looking around the room, I took in the opulence and sighed.

The king-size bed barely began to fill the room and sat directly across from a large stone fireplace. There were three doors in the room—two on either side of the fireplace and one to the left of the bed. I ventured out of bed to explore when curiosity got the better of me.

Gaining my memory back, it dawned on me I passed out and missed the rules. I had no idea who I'd be partnering with for the coming trials. I was surprised to be left alone but figured someone would be by shortly to check on me and that I should use the time now to review everything I'd learned thus far. It was still light out, so I hadn't lost much time. Unless I slept through the night, which had me thinking about Lord Kalen again. He said until tonight.

I started to question the room's ownership as it dawned on me; there was only one bed. Didn't they say we would have roommates? Where was the other bed? It was then I noticed somebody changed my clothes. I was no longer wearing the silky green dress I had on earlier, instead I was wearing a thin nighty. As thoughts whirled through my head, a tingling sensation along my spine alerted me I wasn't alone. I turned around and found Lord Kalen standing in the doorway of the balcony staring at me. Squealing, I darted for the bed and dove under the covers. He let out a delightful laugh in response.

Lowering the blanket to my nose, I peered over the top to find my captor at the foot of the bed, with a predatory grin on his face. Stalking forward, he whispered, "I mean you no harm, Jade. Surely you must feel that."

Ensuring my voice was no louder than his, I whispered, "I feel overwhelmed and confu-" He grabbed my hands at the front of the sheet and caused my brain to short circuit. So when I finished my sentence, it ended up sounding like a question instead of a statement. ". . . sed?" More than anything, his touch grounded me. It caused my body to hum to a frequency, so foreign in and of itself, yet so right at the same time that the only I desired was to explore it more.

"Your beautiful body shows no sign of confusion. I suggest you follow that line of thought." His confident smirk is just the reminder I needed to snap out of lala land. Regardless of how wet he made me, I needed to start thinking with my brain and concentrate on getting some answers if I wanted to escape. Clearing my throat, I pulled my hands free of his hold and tried valiantly to keep my libido in check while I stared into his beautiful aquamarine eyes.

"Lord Kalen, believe me, my body is every bit as confused as my body, I mean m..my head! I think there has been some kind of mis . . . mistake. Nothing about today makes sense. I mean, I'm on another planet speaking with a gorgeous alien in his bedroom dressed in practically nothing. At least this time, after waking up in a strange place with other men, I have some sort of clothing on!"

My little rant seemed to catch his attention. Although, from the growl emanating from his chest, I wasn't sure which part had him on edge. Leaning forward and capturing me with both hands on either side of my body, he said, "I assure you, my pretty, nothing about this is a mistake. Though in the future, I would advise you not to speak of men from your past." I could feel the heat of his body surrounding me, and if I were thinking more clearly, I would have taken that moment to shut my mouth but instead, I let him have it.

"Excuse me! Where do you get off telling me something like that? I realize you are something of a hotshot here but waking up naked on one of YOUR spaceships with YOUR general this morning is not a man of my past. I was referring to it because for the second time today, I woke up in a strange place, not knowing how I came to be here or why. Is it normal for your people to kidnap unsuspecting humans? No one asked me. I didn't even get the chance to say goodbye." I finished on a croak.

His expression changed instantly to one of tenderness. Leaning closer to the point that I could feel his breath on my cheek, he sighed, "I forgot you were from Earth. It is the one planet we protect where the government refuses to acknowledge the existence of aliens. Of course, they had no problem accepting our protection, and it has always been easier not to make waves. We need their cooperation because in the end, if they are not with us, they are against us. The Mengh would conquer your little planet faster than even I could imagine and would give their meager forces many needed supplies and soldiers that we cannot afford to let happen."

Without even seeing his eyes, I could feel the truth of his words in my soul and struggled to piece together the latest news.

"Dr. Triste said that I was one of five presented to you by my government. Where are the other four from my planet?"

Scooting back to be able to look me in the eye, he said, "We rejected the other four presented. We only require one from each planet every five years to maintain our treaty, and for whatever reason, they did not make the cut."

"Why me?"

"DNA samples are collected from each state in the United Nations. Either at the time of birth in a public hospital or during their first doctor appointment. We scan the samples looking for obvious gene mutations that we can use to our advantage. We also look for descendants of our race on your planet as possible mates for our people. You happen to have both qualities, which is rare. We selected you above the other four candidates for those reasons. I will forever be grateful because I have been waiting for you for millennia."

What do you say to someone when they drop a bomb like that on you? I knew it had something to do with my ability, but to hear that I wasn't entirely human was a definite surprise. The conversation I had with Beatress earlier came rushing back in. The selection as a mate was what he was talking about.

"Wait a minute. Did you just say that I was your mate? Isn't that decided at the All Hands Gathering? That's not for another three days!" My voice ended on a high squeal. I was quickly going to find myself blacking out again if I didn't get control of myself and soon. Concentrating on breathing, I tried to move outside of his arms, and before I knew it, I was in his lap.

"The All Hands Gathering is just a chance for my people to meet all of the selectees. A chance to find out if their mate is amongst those present. Nothing is left to chance; if one of my people meets their mate, they will know instantly. The moment your scent reached me, your future was guaranteed to be entwined with mine because I will never let you go."

As soon as our bodies made contact, my breathing normalized, and that same calming effect came over me. "How do you know? Could there be a mistake?" I whispered, remembering the black-haired beauty's claim that he was hers. "I'm not sure what's going on. I feel different when I'm around you. I should be freaking out, but I'm not, and it scares me even more because I'm not." I continued to stare at his chest as I waited for him to answer my question.

Kalen nudged my chin up with his long fingers until our eyes met. His beauty took my breath away. "Jade, you feel different around me because your body recognizes its mate. Fate does not make mistakes." I opened my mouth to protest, but he moved his fingers to cover my lips. "My people have enhanced senses, and when they smell their mate, it is a tremendous experience. The missing piece our soul needs is like a beacon in the dead of night. I could find you from anywhere by following that light. When our souls merge, it will be a sight to behold." While he spoke, I couldn't help but lean closer to him as though pulled by an invisible string. When he finished his statement, his eyes locked on mine as he closed the short distance between us.

The kiss was unlike anything I had ever experienced. The gentle pressure of Kalen's lips over mine felt so right. I melted into his embrace as he deepened the kiss with a growl. My confusion faded the longer the kiss continued. How could something that feels so right be anything but? I pulled away, gasping for breath, and Kalen followed, scorching a trail of kisses along my jawline toward my ear. He paused and took in a large breath, releasing it over my heated skin. I shivered in his embrace. Aching for something more, but not knowing what that might be. I whimpered as he pulled away.

"Oh, sweet Jade, your desire smells divine, and knowing it's just for me is even better. I know you do not yet understand this longing, and believe me, it will only get worse the longer we prolong our mating. Normally we do not meet our intended until after the trials, during the banquet, so the longing never becomes a problem." A look of concern briefly crossed his face at the mention of the trials before he blinked and schooled his face to a look of determination.

Lifting me off his lap, he began to pace in front of the bed, forcing his fingers through his hair roughly. He stopped and nodded to himself before he faced me and said, "There is no reason for you to compete, as far as I am concerned. Instead, I will have a lady's maid assigned to you tonight, and she will prepare you for the ceremony over the next couple of days. You will stay here where I can be sure of your safety." My heart rate increased at the mention of staying in his room, and I watched as his eyes dilated with his increased breathing.

"There is more than one bedroom in my quarters. I will be staying in the main bedroom while you reside here. Although I would thoroughly love for you to join me there, I will await our union."

"You mean . . .? I mean . . . Why would I not be safe?" Choosing not to bring up where I'd be sleeping in an effort to keep my thoughts more PG. I mean, why would I want to think about whether he chooses to sleep in the nude or not? I mean, I wouldn't, right? Right. I just needed to keep telling myself that.

When he didn't answer I pushed for more, "What are you protecting me from? I mean obviously the Mengh, but here on your planet surrounded by your army and weaponry, what are you protecting me from?"

His smile dropped, instantly sobering his expression. "I have waited my whole life for you, Jade. You are the soulmate I cannot wait to cleave with, and nothing will take you away from me. I refuse to take anything to chance. You are lucky I haven't claimed you already." He growled, stalking toward me.

"What's stopping you?" I have no idea where that blurted from, but the longer I stared at him, the more I needed him. I wanted to be selfish and have him all to myself. I found myself no longer wondering what my future held as long as he was a part of it.

Chapter Four

His aquamarine eyes pulsated with unleashed lust. He opened his mouth to answer me, but a knock at the door interrupted him. Kalen's head whipped around, and he growled as he repositioned himself within his fatigues. Stomping towards the bedroom door, he snarled, opening the door to find General Jaelel with an amused expression.

Bowing in deference, Jaelel straightened and whispered something in Kalen's ear before promptly turning and gliding away. Kalen turned, and the look on his face was that of a chastised child in a candy store. Clearing his throat, "Excuse me, darling, but my friend just reminded me of my pressing duties. I will send Selene up right away. You are never to go anywhere alone. I've assigned two of my most trusted guards, Rom and Kiso. You'll take them with you wherever you go." Turning abruptly and blinking from the room left me no time to argue, and I stared at the spot he had left in awe.

A yearning like no other left me exhausted and strangely hungry, but for what I wasn't sure.

I didn't have much time to ponder my state because the next breath was followed by a squeak when two giants, who I could only assume were my guards, stormed into the room to announce my handmaiden. My hand flew up to my chest in surprise at the intrusion. They both seemed to realize their mistake as they scrambled backward, mumbling apologies over each other on their way. "Sorry, my lady," the taller of the two stammered at the same time the slightly shorter guard uttered, "We didn't mean to frighten you. Next time we'll knock."

"No reason to be sorry. Your entry took me by surprise, is all. I'll hold you to the knock, though. I'd hate to see what the king would do if you walked in while I was indisposed. He seems like the jealous type to me. Anyways. Where are my manners? Since we haven't met, I think an introduction would be appropriate. My name is Jade," I replied, holding out my hand. I dropped it to my side when they looked at it with fear and said, "Sorry. Where I'm from, it's customary to shake hands when introducing yourself. It must not be the norm around here. No worries. I'm sure it will be one of many things that are different from where I'm from. Let's just start with names. Which one of you is Rom?"

The taller Strix nodded his head towards me and said, "I am your lady, and this is my brother Kiso. We'll be right outside your door if you need us."

"Thanks. Was there a reason you stormed in Rom?" I asked with a smile to show them I was at ease.

His resulting grin was infectious as he nodded yes to my question before he replied, "Yes, my lady. Your Handmaiden has arrived." He stepped to the side as a beautiful black-haired gem appeared in the door with a broad, genuine smile.

"Hello, my lady. My name is Selene, and if you require anything, I am to ensure that you are not left wanting." Dropping into a large curtsey, she remained on the floor, appearing to await my command.

I stared at the fair beauty in front of me, waiting for her to rise. When it became apparent she wasn't moving, I cleared my throat and said in a slightly annoyed voice, "Thank you, Selene. I do not require anything at the moment."

Selene rose quickly from the floor and exclaimed, "I meant no disrespect, my lady. Please forgive me."

I smiled, and my defenses fell slightly, "You weren't disrespectful. I'm just not used to having anyone serve me. Seeing as I am hardly a lady, it would please me if you would drop the formalities and call me Jade."

She nodded, slowly losing her smile. "Lord Kalen had suggested you might be interested in a long bath before dinner," I wasn't sure if she had agreed to my request or not because she hadn't referenced a title in her last statement, so I decided to give her a break and acquiesce. "I would love a long bath. Thank you, Selene."

She curtsied again and led me to the door closest to the balcony. Opening the door with a flourish, she indicated to enter in front of her. I walked into luxury and stood in wonder. The bathroom was bigger than my apartment back home and had a mini swimming pool directly in the center, sunken into the middle. The same black marble I had seen in the foyer was throughout the room, and the water flowed into the tub from the ceiling continuously, never quite filling to the surface.

The tub was lit from within, giving the water an iridescent glow, sparkling in green, purple, and blue hues. The scent of the water was pleasing and drew me forward; before I took a plunge into the water, Selene spoke up. "My lady, might I help you with your garments?"

"Um . . . Please don't take this the wrong way, but I wasn't born of privilege. Being waited on hand and foot is not something I feel comfortable with, I can do it myself."

Selene bowed yet again, "My job is to serve you in whatever capacity you need me in, and I take pride in my job. Many of the women I serve in the palace prefer not to lift a finger and enjoy the life of a royal. I did not mean to offend you, my lady. I am here for you. I will heed your wants and needs. If you prefer more space, I will be just outside the door getting your outfit ready for dinner."

I immediately felt like shit. I had a lot to learn about this place and my new life. I might need her help in the future, and it wouldn't be smart to burn any bridges this soon in my tenure. "Thank you, Selene. It's a lot to take in at first and I could use the privacy to regroup. You did nothing to offend me, I assure you. I just need time to adapt and assimilate." Selene grinned slightly and shuffled off to the right, slamming drawers and cupboards in what I could only assume was the closet in the next room over.

Not waiting any longer, I made quick work of the lingerie and slowly melted into the water step by glorious step. The water was fluid, like home, but aquamarine instead of clear. Sinking to my shoulders, I laid my head back to relax and closed my eyes. I took a deep breath and congratulated myself for handling the day relatively well, despite fainting twice. The heat of the water and warm stone beneath me was magic to my tense muscles. So much had happened in a day. The fact that I wasn't in hysterics was a noble feat in and of itself. I was on another planet, about to be mated to a vampire, who happened to be a king of some sort, all because I was gifted and not entirely human. I should be commemorated or get an award or something.

Without Kalen by my side, the weight of how quickly my life changed in an instant was hard to bear. In less than 24 hours, I discovered we were lied to about aliens' existence for many years. So many people on Earth were more than ready to embrace the unknown, and I could only hope that I would have the chance to expose the truth one day.

My thoughts drifted to my ability as I wrapped my hand around the necklace. I felt adrift without the connection and the only time I completely forgot that it was absent was in Kalen's presence. His ability to calm me with just the slightest touch was an enigma. The feelings he stirred within me were out of this world; literally, pun intended. Fighting the attraction I felt for him would be insane, and if I were to be truly honest with myself, I don't think I have it in me to try. Swirling thoughts of what was coming, and the journey I was about to embark on, had my eyes springing open, willing myself to stay in the moment and take life one step at a time.

The ceiling's waterfall was surrounded by a circular skylight that allowed the waning light from the two suns to cast tiny rainbows onto the walls and ceiling. I was entranced at the dancing light and, before long, found my eyes closing in exhaustion.

"My lady, I don't think it's a good idea to fall asleep in the bath. As far as my knowledge extends, humans do not breathe underwater, milady Jade."

I opened my eyes and, noticing the concerned look on her face, smiled. "I'm not asleep. Although this water feels to die for, I have no wish to end my life when it has hardly just begun."

Selene leaned down behind me, softly stroking my strands of hair, and quietly said, "It would be my pleasure to wash your hair, my lady. Some say that a good head massage is all that is needed to melt your worries away." Moaning my agreement, she carefully scrubbed my scalp with a relaxing lavender-scented shampoo. Covering my forehead with her hand, she washed the soap from my hair with such gentleness it was almost reverent.

"Over the next couple of days, you will be under a lot of pressure to . . . what was the word you used? Oh yeah, assimilate. I just wanted you to know that you can count on me to be here for you. I will instruct you in our traditions and educate you on what to expect at the Gathering. At least you will not have to worry about competing in the Trials. Do you have any questions?"

Did I have any questions? She was a regular old comedian; of course, I had questions. I'm just not sure where to start. "When will I be allowed to use my powers?"

"Usually only during the trials and then after the selection. You might have to wait until the ceremony since you are not participating in the Trials. I will discuss it with Lord Kalen."

"Why do your people require a tribute from the planets they protect?"

"Many centuries ago, the evil Mengh invaded our home planet, hoping to conquer and control our people. Their invasion greatly reduced our numbers over the years, and when we fled our planet just before they destroyed it, Lord Kalen vowed it would never happen to another race. Using our technology, we reached out to the other known planetary systems outside of the Mengh's control and made treaties. He found this abandoned paradise and built our army from nothing with those tributes, carefully selecting those with the greatest power to join it. We were a peaceful people, and someday I hope we return to our roots."

Grabbing a towel, she motioned for me to get out of the tub and wrapped it around my body as I emerged from the water. "Why do the Mengh attack? For what purpose? If they eventually destroyed your planet, it couldn't be for the resources. What purpose does it provide?"

Selene stared in wonder, perhaps at my naivete, before she spoke. "Their resources are the people of the planet. The gifted become slaves in their army. They eat the rest."

Wow, nothing like being blunt. I was beginning to be sorry I asked. What was that saying, what you didn't know wouldn't hurt you, but perhaps that wouldn't be the case this time because the thing I didn't know about could actually eat me. What was the other saying? Something about knowledge is power? I think that should be my new motto.

"Well, by all means, tell it like it is, Selene because I want to live from this point forward with the wool pulled away from my eyes."

"I have your dress ready, my lady. A gorgeous green to match the color of your eyes. Once I finish with your make-up, you'll be the talk of the night. I know you are uncomfortable with my help, but the dress is quite difficult to put on, so if you would allow me the honors."

"Thanks, Selene. I think I am ready to see what the night will bring, but I thought we agreed you would call me Jade?"

Selene dropped her eyes to the ground, folding her hands in front of her demurely before she answered, "You are the Lady to my Lord. It would not be proper for me to address you as so."

"We haven't tied the knot yet. Until we do, I insist you call me Jade. Gives me a sense of normalcy."

"How about a compromise? I will call you Jade if Lord Kalen gives me the right to do so, but only in private."

Shaking my head, I smiled and said, "That's not a compromise in my book, but I will talk to Lord Kalen at dinner to make my wishes known."

"Perfect! He will be expecting us shortly. Let's get a move on, my lady."

Chapter Five

The person staring back at me from the mirror is a thing of beauty. If I don't consider the wide-open mouth staring back at me. It makes me look like a largemouth bass. Snapping the offending object closed, I pinned my gaze on the miracle worker standing behind me with a beaming smile on her face and asked, "What did you do to my face?"

Dropping her shoulders in defeat, her smile melted like ice cream in an incinerator. Her lower lip slightly wavered as she replied, "I applied makeup, my lady, as is customary to our traditions. I am sorry you do not like it. Do you want me to start over? We will be late, but I will gladly take the blame."

"Like it? I love it! It's just; I look nothing like myself. Are you sure you didn't change my face to make it this way?" I cocked my head to the side as a small grin slowly replaced Selene's grimace. Admiring myself one more time, I turned to face her and wished for the umpteenth time I had control of my gift. Never one to hold back on my need for knowledge, I contorted my face in what I hoped was a silent apology, and I blurted out my next question. "What abilities do you have?"

"I'm an artist, my lady. I can draw a perfect circle without instrumentation, even with my eyes closed."

"That ability must qualify you for a different position. How in the hell did you end up here?"

Selene averted her eyes when she murmured, "I don't do well in crowds. I failed miserably during the trials. They determined I work best alone."

"Why didn't you go home? Didn't you have a choice?"

She slowly raised her eyes to meet mine and, with a look of defeat, sighed, "I couldn't face my family. They think I am a cartographer with the scholar group because I was too ashamed to admit my failure. It's too late now. I've taken the oath granting me immortality." The tears she managed to avert from my earlier stab fell freely this time when she closed her eyes to escape my sympathetic gaze.

I couldn't help my empathy, but if I was going to be the lady of this establishment, I should use that authority to help her. "Well, I'll say something to Lord Kalen at dinner. There must be something we can do to get you moved to the right team."

"Please, my lady, I beg you to forget what I just said. I am honored to be your maid, and if you say something now, they will assume you deemed me unworthy of serving you. I doubt I will ever be allowed in the castle again. Please." Selene seemed to be holding her breath as she waited for my response. The look of terror on her face was not what I expected when I offered to talk to the king. Her statement had me questioning the morality of the man fated to be my mate. The saying till death do us part had a whole other meaning when one could live forever.

My anger at her reaction had nothing to do with her and everything to do with Lord Kalen and his archaic hierarchy.

I forced myself to tamper my outward appearance as I coerced a smile to my face, despite the fire brewing in my gut, before I answered her. "Forget what?"

When she smiled in return, I promised myself I would do everything I could to protect the girl in front of me, regardless of whether the problem happened to be the girl standing in front of me. With a half shrug, I added, "Besides, I doubt just anyone could make me look the way you do. I guess that means you're stuck with me. Unless you're sick of me already, that is?"

"Oh no, Lady Jade! On the contrary, this is where I should be."

"Good. Now freshen up while I go relieve myself, and then you can fill me in on the proper table manners that'll be expected of me while we make our way to the dining room."

She gave a slight nod, which had me rushing into the bathroom to give her a sense of privacy. Closing the door quietly, I leaned against it, closed my eyes with a sigh, and stewed. Struggling to get control of my racing thoughts and heart, I tried to meditate and failed miserably as my brain tossed ideas around my head like a tornado. The more I thought about the injustice Selene and others like her endured, the angrier I got. I schooled my expression to hide my anger and opened the door with a flourish. After I assured myself Selene was once again in control of her emotions, I gestured towards the door and said, "No time like the present. Shall we?"

Selene bowed and, with a nod of her head, she glided forward and pulled open the door to reveal an enormous hallway devoid of light. The second she stepped foot outside the bedroom, the opal veins running through the granite walls lit up from within. The soft glow reminded me of Himalayan salt lamps; only instead of a warm orange glow, the opal emitted a rainbow of colors. I stepped out into the hallway, and my guards Rom and Kiso filed right behind me.

I listened as Selene listed off a stream of the do's and don'ts of dinner etiquette along the way, though they only vaguely registered in my conscious thoughts as panic set in the closer we got to the king. His presence was like a lighthouse that guided me in the darkness. Even without Selene's help, I had no doubt I would have been able to find the dining room independently. I needed to stay as far away from the king as possible if I intended on confronting him later because every time he touched me, I lost all logical thought and forgot about anything other than his touch. Selene pulled on my arm as she stopped abruptly and looked at me. "My lady? Did you hear what I just said?"

Squirming in place, I raised my eyebrows and rattled off some of the stuff I remembered from her speech from the corner of my mouth. "I . . . might have missed the last thing you said, but I got the stuff about how to act at dinner. Like no slurping and sit up straight during the whole meal, etcetera. Something about no one likes a slumpy queen. Although, in my defense, I'm not the queen yet."

Selene chastised me with her eyes before she relented and repeated herself. "I told you to watch out for the Marni. Their latest representative, Princess Onyx, is spreading rumors she is Lord Kalen's true mate."

"What a bitch!" I muttered under my breath. "I guess that means dinner could get ugly when he announces I am his mate."

"I doubt Lord Kalen will make a statement in words, but when he places you next to him, that act will be all the statement anyone needs. I will point her out, but if you feel someone shooting you with daggers from their eyes, it is probably her."

"No need. I believe we already had the pleasure of meeting this morning in the great room, but I appreciate the forewarning. Always nice to put a face to your enemies." Taking a deep breath, I steeled my shoulders and looked straight ahead before I continued. "No sense in delaying this any further. I can feel Lord Kalen growing anxious from our delay. Let's get this over with before he thinks I'm going to run."

Plastering a smile on my face, I followed Selene into the room and looked about in wonder. Large totems carved with intricate designs bordered four silk-covered arched doorways across from the entrance. Silhouettes of naked men and women could be seen dirty dancing together behind the veil. The erotic scene ignited the flames smoldering inside of me.

When my thoughts drifted to Lord Kalen, and the sensation intensified, I averted my eyes to the domed cathedral ceiling above me and counted to five under my breath. Taking in the beautifully painted scenes of a foreign landscape centered me enough to let out the breath. I didn't realize I was holding and lower my gaze to the occupants of the room.

I was under the impression I'd be walking into something quaint; instead, I found a giant banquet room capable of seating hundreds. Leveling my gaze, I scanned the tables in front of me, looking for friendly faces. Onyx made no attempt to cover her contempt at my presence. I turned my nose up and pretended she didn't exist as we started forward once again.

I noticed how quiet the room was as all eyes followed my movement through the room. People whispered as we passed by the tables on the main floor until the place went silent once again when Selene led me to the open seat next to Lord Kalen. His overbearing presence commanded the room while his lust-filled gaze commandeered my libido. The second my ass connected with the chair, waiters filed in serving the first course.

The zing coursing through my body tempted me to forgive the king for any wrongdoings. At this point, I felt like I would do anything to ensure the feeling continued. Grinding my teeth, I focused on my anger to ebb the pleasure his proximity did to my female parts. Once I felt I had a modicum of control, I spared a glance in his direction and politely smiled before I hissed, "Please tell me you didn't make everyone wait to eat until I got here." I found my gaze focused on the dimple his smile produced from my statement and made myself focus and look away.

"Mere coincidence, I assure you. Your maid has impeccable timing and taste. You look beautiful, Jade." Leaning closer, he traced my ear with his finger before his breath sent a shiver down my spine as he whispered, "Although I must be honest, if I wanted to make everyone wait until you graced us with your presence, no one would be able to stop me. Tell me, mate, what has you on edge. Do I need to cut off someone's head?"

I gasped at the suggestion of violence and pulled back to look him in the eye and crumpled in relief when I saw laughter in his eyes. Shaking my head at how easy my emotions were swinging from side to side, I took the easy way out and stalled. I needed more time to steel myself against the man if I had any hope of winning. Moving the food around on my plate, I deflected, "What is on my plate?"

"An ailnot petal salad with kalenberries and pealegumes, drizzled with a citrus vinaigrette. Delightful on the taste buds. Try it." Kalen stabbed a petal and held it to my lips as he waited for me to open my mouth.

The only ingredient I understood from his description was citrus. Being a picky eater, I almost declined until he lifted my chin with his finger and practically begged me to acquiesce. The intensity of his stare made me question if opening my mouth and accepting food meant more than it appeared, but the moment the aroma reached my nose, I opened my mouth willingly and closed my lips around the most delectable bite. Closing my eyes, I moaned in approval. Opening my eyes slowly, I looked up at him with a smile. My whole body buzzed with desire, and when he offered me a glass of wine, I didn't hesitate to part my lips as I greedily waited for him to bring the glass to my mouth.

A horrible scream filled the air, breaking the trance I was under. I whipped my head towards the sound, a mere millisecond from accepting the king's offering, to find a petite pixie from Onyx's table writhing in pain as she toppled over to the floor in convulsions. The king and most of his guards jumped into action. Coming to a halt, they formed a circle around her as her cries cut off on a gasp.

Flopping onto her back, she arched off the floor as she took a shaky breath and let out a silent scream. The crowd backed away in a panic as the veins and arteries in her face turned black. With every beat of her heart, the inky blackness spread to the rest of her body until whatever was preventing her from making noise let loose, and she let loose a dead curdling wail that rattled my bones.

Chapter Six

The room erupted into chaos as people pushed and shoved their way towards the guarded exits. Lord Kalen's voice roared above the crowd stopping everyone in their tracks. "No one is allowed to leave until I have had a chance to question each person individually. Since the majority of you have an early day tomorrow, the faster we accomplish this, the better."

I climbed onto my chair for a better view, only to wish I hadn't, as the poor girl's body turned into black goo like time was on fast forward. Steering my eyes away from the scene, I found something even more alarming. Princess Onyx was glaring at me until she realized I was watching her, and she flashed me a triumphant smile that disappeared almost as fast as it appeared, making me question if I ever saw it in the first place.

I wanted to be wrong about my suspicions. I wanted to believe Onyx wasn't capable of killing an innocent person. My hackles rose at her possible involvement as I struggled to find a motive or what benefit the girl's death provided her. Staring her down, I raised my eyebrows in a silent challenge to her and gave her an evil smile when she glared back with acceptance.

I lost her as the guards corralled everyone to the back of the room, and a team of men and women wearing biohazard suits filed into the room. They worked quickly to contain and sanitize the area using a multitude of powers, as Kalen interviewed everyone with General Jaelel at his side.

I jumped down from my chair and moved to step forward to get a closer look, only to be stopped short by a large guard. Shaking my arm to get loose, I was surprised when the guard folded me into his arms and whispered into my ear, "The king has instructed me to take you back to your room."

I would have struggled or spoken up if I had the time but, as I drew in a breath to scream, the room tilted and faded out. For a second, I feared I was passing out for a third time that day, only to puff up my cheeks and let out my breath slowly when my bedroom came into focus a second later. The guard dropped his arms and stepped back as I swung around and pointed my finger at his chest.

"The next time you transport me somewhere, I want you to have my permission! I almost peed myself!"

After a guffaw at my outburst, he hung his head in defeat when I narrowed my eyes at him and gave him my best "don't fuck with me" look.

"I only take orders from Lord Kalen, my lady." I opened my mouth to voice my displeasure but snapped it closed when he added, "But I promise to warn you next time before we flash. If it makes any difference, you handled your first flash very well."

His praise had me standing straighter for a moment because it felt great to be good at something without trying for once. Usually, if I set my eyes on something, I had to work for it. My gift being the only exception. However, I did have to work hard at learning how to control it.

The high didn't last long when I remembered why we flashed in the first place, and I deflated, both physically and mentally, into a pile on the floor. The guard rushed forward, and I held a hand up to stop his progress. Lifting my gaze, I cleared my throat and said, "I'm okay. Drained, discombobulated, and slightly delirious."

My answer didn't seem to appease him as he crouched to my level with a panicked look on his face. With a sigh, I closed my eyes and counted to five before I answered him. "I'm not broken or injured, just human. Please give me a moment to break so that when I build myself back up, my fractures will make me stronger, not weaker."

Opening my eyes to plead my case, the guard saved me the trouble with a firm nod and a tight smile. He stood up and moved towards the door to the hallway. Stopping with his hand on the knob, he locked the door and looked back at me. Pulling myself together, I looked about the room for a weapon in a panic.

The guard took notice, and with his hands out, he shook his head, licked his lips, and swore under his breath. "Shite. I have no idea why I got stuck watching you. I'm no good with females." Taking a knee, he bowed his head and spoke calmly.

"I mean you no harm, Lady Jade. I locked the door because I can flash out of here and didn't want you to have to get up. You needed a moment, and I gave it to you, but your safety will always be my priority. Please accept my apology for scaring you; it was not my intention."

The day taught me if I wanted to survive, I needed to adapt faster to my environment. There was no limit to this new world, and whether I asked for it or not, this was my new reality. Strengthening my core, I forced myself to stand, using the bedpost like a lifeline. Taking a deep breath, I pushed my fear aside and walked toward the guard on shaky legs. "Apology accepted as long as you stand up."

Raising his head, he flashed me a wicked smile and straightened his six-foot-three muscular body with a grace that shouldn't be possible. I admired his form, and as I studied his face, I admitted he was handsome. Immediately upon thinking about him, he winked at me like he was reading my mind. I quickly added I thought his features were too feminine for my tastes. His frown was enough to confirm my theory; he could read minds, and I smiled wickedly back at him.

I missed my gift more than ever and fingered the necklace with longing. Refusing to dwell on what I had no control over, I dropped my hand and decided to accept my circumstances, but under my terms. The first thing on the list was to establish allies in this rat race. The guard standing in front of me was as good as any.

Wiping my hands on my dress nervously, I waved awkwardly and introduced myself properly. "Hi. My name is Jade Marcene Cordel. Supposedly the king and I are mates. It's a pleasure to meet you." I held my hand out and was a second away from dropping it in embarrassment when he shook it firmly and answered.

"The pleasure is all mine. My name is Tanen Soltan, and I am a royal guard and the king's best friend. Seeing as you are his mate-to-be, that duty now extends to you as well."

"Thank you, I guess. Do you know when Kalen will be back?"

Tanen paused for a moment with a far-off stare. Shaking his head, he chuckled softly before he answered. "He says he's over halfway done and can't wait to hold you in his arms. Oh, he's got it bad. The man is spoiled and isn't used to answering to anyone. I look forward to watching you put him in his place often. Whatever you do, promise me you won't go easy on him."

I highly doubted I would be putting anyone in their place, least of all the king. That fine male specimen did something to me. Every time I was around him, all logical thought ceased to exist, and thoughts of sex overruled me. My body acted like it was putty in his hands. I panicked when I remembered Tanen could read my mind and risked a peak to gauge his reaction to my one-track mind. He seemed uninterested, which perplexed me until he arched an eyebrow in question.

Throwing my hands up in frustration, I growled. "Argh, this stupid necklace is driving me crazy. Can you read my mind or not? And if you can't, what is your gift?"

"You guessed correctly. I can read minds, but I have to be listening and focused on the person. The exception to that would be thoughts concerning me. Those thoughts I hear whether I want to or not. It can help or hinder my performance. What is your talent?"

So used to never speaking about my gift, I avoided the question. "How could something that awesome be considered a hindrance. You must be unbeatable during a fight if you always know your opponent's every move. No wonder the king selected you to guard him."

Tanen blushed, despite his dark coloring, and cleared his throat before changing the subject. "The king shouldn't be much longer. I'm to inform you of the exits in case of my demise before he arrives."

When I guffawed, he gave me a look that spoke of how serious he was before he continued. "No one has access to this wing besides the king's most trusted guards and your maid. His quarters are enchanted only to allow the king and myself flash access, but it never hurts to be prepared. Kalen instructed Selene to stay away tonight, so do not answer the door for anyone. Rom, Kiso, or I will flash in if we hear the slightest of struggles, but there are two other exits from this room besides the hallway if we are too late. Let me show you."

Following behind him to the bathroom on autopilot, I noted the button he pointed out but snapped out of my daze when he mentioned how it worked.

"Hold up! My bath turns into a water park theme ride if I push this button? Where in the hell does it spit me out? Better yet, where would I go once I got there? I have no idea where I'm at or who I can trust. You guys have not thought this out! I don't even have my powers! How am I supposed to defend myself?"

Tanen looked chastised as he shrugged his shoulders in defeat. "This secret passage leads to a safe room. Trust no one besides the two of us for now. Lock yourself in and wait for word from Lord Kalen. As for defending yourself, I hope it doesn't come to that, but if you permit me to approach, I will turn off the power blocker on your necklace."

"Thank you! I would very much appreciate that."

Tanen stalked forward and asked me to spin around and lift my hair. I complied and was surprised when tingles ran down my spine as he messed with the device until I realized the sensation for what it was. Spinning around to face Lord Kalen, I realized my mistake a second too late when Tanen's arms wrapped around me in surprise, making the scene look less than innocent.

Chapter Seven

The king's growl shattered the silence as he tossed Tanen away from me like he weighed less than a feather. Pushing me behind him, Kalen flashed to the location Tanen was headed and huffed out his frustration when his friend had anticipated the move and flashed, mid toss, to a different location as far away from me as possible. Holding up his hands like he was facing off against a rabid dog, Tanen started talking in a calming tone. "Easy big guy. I'm not trying to steal your woman. Besides flashing her here and unlocking her necklace, I haven't touched her! Do I need to remind you? You're the one that asked me to keep her safe. If something happened to me, she wouldn't have been able to protect herself."

"I will be the one to protect my mate!" Kalen growled, stalking toward Tanen with murder in his mind.

Afraid the confrontation would turn brutal, I stepped in between the two men and pushed my arms out, using a fraction of my mate's telekinetic power to force them both back a step. Turning to look at Kalen, I put all of the anger I was feeling into my voice. "Enough! I shouldn't have to defend myself to you when I didn't do anything, but since you've given me no choice by acting like an alpha asshole, I'll make this quick. Nothing happened here, nor does your lack of faith in me bode well for anything happening in OUR future with you acting like a jerk!"

Kalen pulled up short and, with a look of astonishment, pinned me in place with his smoldering stare. I watched in fascination as his fangs extended and shivered with desire as I imagined what it would feel like to have those embedded in my flesh. Growling out a curse, Kalen ordered Tanen to leave. "You and I will discuss this tomorrow, but if you know what's good for you, you will get out now!"

The king didn't wait for his order to be followed before he prowled forward against my feeble attempt at using his gift. I gasped when his thoughts invaded my own, showing me his fangs penetrating my swollen clit as I climaxed all over his face. I groaned at the image and then surprised myself when I growled as Tanen flashed away, taking his mind-reading gift with him.

I kept telling myself if I were in real danger, I would protect myself, but the truth was I was dying to find out what other sinful things the Strix had in store for me. Not wanting to appear desperate, I backed away slowly in a feeble attempt at playing hard to get. I barely managed to stop a squeal when Kalen flashed forward, catching me off guard.

Flames of desire pulsated through my body as I stared up into his ocean-colored eyes and found myself drowning in them. Feeling faint, I gulped in some much-needed air and choked on my saliva with as much grace as a great dane puppy who had yet to grow into his massive paws. Wishing I could crawl under a rock after demonstrating my less than stellar seduction skills, I covered my face with my hands in embarrassment.

After a short pause, Kalen closed the short distance between us until the only thing separating us were our clothes. His taut muscles left nothing to the imagination when he rotated his hips, giving me a tease of what he had to offer. I shivered with need as his breath cooled my skin seconds before he peppered kisses along my neck. Pulling on my hands, he brought them to his mouth and kissed them one by one. I closed my eyes like a petulant child, squirming as he proceeded to kiss my forehead, eyelids, and nose seductively. I was seconds away from melting into a puddle on the bathroom floor.

I bit my bottom lip, preventing a sigh from leaving my lips when he didn't continue his downward trend of kisses. I wanted his mouth on mine, but I didn't want to beg. It wasn't ladylike. Refusing to be the only one affected, I shimmied my hips in a slow seductive dance against his erection and lost myself to the feeling. I didn't want to be the first to make a noise but failed miserably when he traced my bottom lip with his tongue. I released my lip with a moan and hissed when he sucked it into his mouth and nicked it with a fang.

His answering growl was like gasoline to the slow-building fire in my loins, igniting the moment I tasted the coppery tang of blood in my mouth. My eyes fluttered open when he pulled away; at the same time, my arms reached out to pull him back to me. Feeling needy, I ignored the warning signs going off in my head that we were moving too fast as I threw myself into his arms and wrapped my legs around him. Thrusting my fingers through his inky black hair, I brought him closer and sucked his lip into my mouth as he carried me out of the bathroom.

Driven by a force larger than myself, I bit down until I tasted blood and felt a rush of adrenaline as his need and desire flooded my senses. All sense of rational thought fled my body as he pulled his lip away from me, and I lurched forward for more. Shaking his head, he lowered me to the floor slowly, ensuring I had plenty of time to feel every ripple and indent of his powerful body. With a wicked smile, he licked the lingering drop of blood from his lip and said,

"Fuck protocols. I wanted to give you more time to get used to us, but you sealed your fate with that love bite."

When he bent forward, I whimpered as I imagined him lifting my dress and pleasuring me with his tongue. Instead, he surprised me when he ripped the beautiful garment and my undergarment in half. Pouting slightly, I lowered my arms and let the remnants of my dress flutter to the floor as I thought, *Damn! I liked that dress.*

"Your turn." Moving forward on instinct, I looked for a way to relieve him of his clothes with as much ferocity as he showed me. I searched madly for a zipper or seam around the collar and waist of his fatigues only to find it impenetrable. Too far gone to be embarrassed by my wanton actions, I begged for his help. "Argh! Please."

Kalen stilled my hands and brought them to rest over his heart; it beat at the same rhythm as mine. I questioned the meaning and looked up at him in wonder. The look of hunger in his eyes promised this mating would not be gentle, and I shivered with anticipation. I squealed when he picked me up and tossed me onto the bed behind me. Raising myself to my elbows, I blinked in confusion when he flashed forward six inches, and his clothes fell to the floor behind him.

My eyes devoured every inch of his naked flesh. Dear Lord, save me. The man was the epitome of male perfection. Strong, masculine, virile, and sexy all rolled into one package. I had a feeling he would be a handful but lost my train of thought when a light trail of black hair beckoned my eyes south. His V-cut abdominals made me want to run my hands across them as I counted an eight pack giddily. But the piece de resistance was his enormous cock. It bopped to the flutter of my eyelashes and beckoned me to touch it. I needed him inside me. I licked my lips as I imagined him fucking my mouth and practically purred when he stalked toward the end of the bed, ready to claim his prize.

I felt cherished when he climbed onto the bed and crawled towards me, trailing his fingers along my skin, leaving goosebumps in their wake. His mouth wasn't far behind as his lips worshiped each leg before he settled between my legs. With each touch, the heat in my pussy turned up a notch until I felt like I would explode like a supernova. Throwing my head back, I mewled like a kitten as his breath teased my sensitive nub. Arching my hips forward, I begged him to touch me and sighed in gratitude when he slid his tongue in between my soaked folds. When he latched onto my clit and sucked, my sigh turned into a full-blown pornstar moan.

I was seconds away from the fastest and most explosive climax of my life. I was almost afraid to fall off. It felt like I'd be falling over more than a cliff. My impending orgasm was more like falling into the event horizon of a black hole. I was afraid if I went over, I'd never come back.

Squirming to escape the onslaught of emotions and sensations, I grabbed onto Kalen's head. Unsure if I wanted to hold him there or push him away, my choice was removed the second he pushed a finger or two inside me and increased the speed of his tongue. I had no idea how it was physically possible for him to suck and vibrate simultaneously, but the combination of his mouth and fingers pushed me over the edge.

The orgasm that consumed me was euphoric and mind-blowing. It felt like I was floating in a sea of endorphins that were constantly refueling the high of the orgasm. Kalen was relentless as well. He lapped up the essence he had a hand in making and growled into my flesh, sending delicious tremors through my core, like ripples on the water.

I could hear myself beg him to stop while I anchored his head to me, confused as to whether I should chase the feeling he stirred within me or push him away. Kalen, sensing my indecision, increased the tempo one more time and added another finger. Giving myself up to the sensation, I screamed when another orgasm ripped through me as his fangs pierced my swollen clit.

Each pull he took of my blood intensified the convulsions pulsing through my body, taking me to pleasures I never knew existed. As I came down from the high, my eyes closed in a dreamy state. His resultant growl centered me, ensuring I didn't check out and miss out on what happened next. Retracting his fangs, he sat upon his knees, flipped me over, and positioned me with my ass in the air.

With the urgency in his movements, I braced myself for a rough entry, only to sigh when he rubbed my juices all over his cock like he had all the time in the world. He entered me with a restraint belying his need. I reveled in ecstasy as he slid slowly into my quivering pussy one inch at a time. His complete control over me should have thrown me into a panic attack; instead, I craved a similar reaction in him. Taking action, I pushed back until I felt his balls against my clit. His resultant moan was music to my ears. Capitalizing on my moment, I proceeded to squeeze his shaft over and over again until his control shattered. His loss of control when he roared was all the encouragement I needed.

Grabbing my hips, he pistoned in and out with such savagery that I lost myself to the rhythm. A fleeting thought that I'd be sporting a few bruises in the morning crossed my mind until he reached around and thumbed my clit in circles, in sync with his hips, making me oblivious to anything but the sex god behind me. I dropped my head to the bed with submission, only to be yanked up by my hair until my back was flush with his chest. Guiding my mouth to his, he slowed the tempo of our joining, sealing his mouth over mine.

The new angle brought an onslaught of sensations to my overstimulated body as he slid over my g-spot with each penetration. As I ascended to yet another precipice, I struggled to reach the top, hovering between pleasure and pain. Unsure what I needed to push me into nirvana, I deepened our kiss, savoring the way his tongue dueled with mine. At the hint of something metallic on my tongue, I turned into a zealot hellbent on finding redemption.

Devouring his mouth, I searched for more until the loss of it sent me into a panic. Frightened by the intensity of my need, I pulled my head away from him in a haze. Grasping for a modicum of sanity while he continued to move within was challenging. I took deep breaths willing my racing heart to slow down. I needed to come back to reality. Wanting to drink someone's blood like my life depended on it was not natural.

I didn't understand what was happening, but a small part of me knew that there would be no taking it back if I let this continue. I was seconds away from pulling away, but Kalen was having none of that. Moving my hair to the side, he trailed his fingers up and down my neck, bringing me back to the moment. The movement was hypnotic. Kissing my ear, he purred his approval when I melted back into him like I was in a trance. "That's right, my sweet. Stay here with me. Accept me as your mate, and I will spend eternity worshiping you. You'd like that, wouldn't you?"

"I don't know what I want when I'm around you."

"Do you want me to stop?" Kalen growled, stopping mid-stroke over my g-spot. When he swiveled his hips, jostling the sensitive area in the most sensual way, I lost the battle to resist him and practically wailed out my answer, "NO! Don't you dare!"

Stalling his assault on my pussy he nibbled on my ear and added, "I'll only continue if you agree to be my mate."

"You're blackmailing me?" I huffed out. Trying my best to fuck myself on his cock but failing miserably.

"I call it a trade-off," Kalen replied, resuming his slow but delicious moves. "I get you, and you get what you want as well as what you didn't know you needed."

Closing my eyes, I sighed and let go of my reservations, deciding to follow my heart and not my head. Ignoring the voice in my head that reminded me it was my body, not my heart, that was the player in this game, I nodded my agreement. I could feel him smile against my neck before he snapped his hips forward, holding himself deep, and said, "I need the words, my sweet."

"Unh." I whispered, which was all I could manage at first, before I found my voice, "Y . . Yes."

"Yes, what?" He replied by pulling out to the tip of his cock, like he was teasing me he could take away my new favorite toy.

"Oh, for fuck's sake. Yes, I agree to be your mate. Now finish what you started and fuck me!"

With a growl, he bit his wrist and placed it next to my mouth before he whispered, "Anything for you. Blood of you, blood of me. Forever mine, forever yours. For all eternity. Drink, my sweet. Make it so."

The second my lips touched his open wound, I latched on like a newborn babe wholly lost to the connection forming between us. Overwhelmed by the feelings his body and mind wrangled from me, I barely heard him praise my enthusiasm before he sank his teeth into my neck, pushing me into sweet oblivion.

Chapter Eight

For the third time since my abduction, when I opened my eyes, I was not in the same place as when I closed them. A mirror above the bed proved I looked as thoroughly used up as I felt and confirmed my mate had a kinky side. I smiled as I recalled the night before and blushed at how uninhibited he made me feel. My hair resembled a rat's nest, and my makeup made me a close runner up for Pennywise the Clown's doppelganger. Stretching like a cat, I purred in contentment. I fingered the bite marks on my neck and sighed when the act incited a flush of warmth in my core. Scissoring my legs to create friction, I moaned at the delicious sensations coming to life.

Thinking I was alone, a drawn-out grunt from across the room had me grabbing the sheet to cover myself. Holding the soft fabric against my naked skin, I raised up on my elbows to find Kalen standing in the doorway of his bathroom, stroking his cock with a mischievous grin. "I was afraid you would be sore this morning, my sweet, but I can see now your ache for me matches my need for you." Motioning me with his free hand, he beckoned me toward him. "Join me in the shower."

Shaking my head 'No' playfully, I smiled seductively. Patting the bed next to me I said, "Why don't you come back over here. I'm not ready to get up." Biting down on my bottom lip, I trailed my hand down my stomach and sighed when my hand cupped my swollen sex.

Expecting to get my way, I closed my eyes with a sigh and was seconds away from inserting a finger, only to gasp when Kalen's mouth replaced my hand. He growled into my flesh and sent delicious shivers up my spine. There was nothing gentle about his approach as he nipped and sucked until I was writhing beneath him in a matter of seconds. Kalen tore himself away from me with a snarl and said, "I want all of your orgasms, but I want it in the shower!"

I didn't have time to answer before he scooped me up and flashed us to the shower in the bathroom, joining our rooms. Growling down at me, he guided me onto his stiff cock and didn't stop until he bottomed out. Holding me in place, he moved me against the wall and ground against me. He teased my nub with just enough pressure to drive me mad, but not enough to finish me before he whispered with barely contained lust, "If we had stayed in our bed, we would have never left. Soon we'll have time for a true merging of our souls when I plan on keeping you in bed for weeks. Right now, though, I need you quick and hard."

With a snap of his hips, he reminded me who was in charge in this coupling as he pushed me to new heights. "Yes. Yes," I moaned as small tremors rippled through my pussy in a slow-burning orgasm, only to climb even higher when he sank his teeth into my flesh and exploded inside of me. The coupling was sensuous compared to last night's explosive union and had me yearning for more. I wanted everything he had to give me, and if last night and this morning were anything to go off of, this man, Strix, whatever he was, should be known as a god in bed.

I shuddered when he removed his fangs slowly—sighing in pleasure when he licked the holes and kissed each mark lightly before he nuzzled my neck just below my ear. I was surprised I enjoyed the whole biting and blood thing, but the act was erotic, pleasurable, and intimate. I had no idea how much blood he required daily, but if we continued at our current rate, I'd be drained dry before the end of the week.

The thought brought me up short. If Kalen didn't drink from me? Who was he drinking from? I didn't want to imagine who he used to drink from, but once the thought entered my mind, I couldn't let it go. Even though we had only been together a short time, I felt possessive, and there was no way I would be able to handle another female's, or a male's, scent on him.

Pushing against his chest, I scrambled off of him frantically, and fled from the shower. Placing my head between my knees, I gulped in some needed air as a panic attack threatened to consume me. My breathing increased, and the sound of my heart reverberated through my head to the point I barely heard his frantic words, "My love, what's wrong?" When I didn't answer him, he dropped to his knees in front of me and pulled my head up so he could look me in the eyes, "Are you ill? Talk to me!"

Focusing on his eyes, I swallowed the lump in my throat. Welcoming the calm his touched wrought, I whispered, "What are you doing to me?"

Kalen dropped his hands to my knees and gave me a steamy smile. "I think you know what we've been doing. Don't tell me you didn't enjoy it. I could feel your pleasure through my bite."

I hmphed with exasperation while I shook my head. "I do not deny it, but maybe I'm enjoying it too much. I'm . . . I'm feeling things way too soon . . . things that shouldn't be possible. I mean, I barely know you. It's like sex is launching our affair into overdrive, and suddenly you mean everything to me! All of this is happening so fast, and I don't know all the rules. Not like you can't tell, but I'm quickly becoming addicted to what you do to me. To the promise I feel in your bite. I'm addicted to the taste of you . . . to . . . to you, and it scares me."

A panicked expression was the last thing I wanted to see on the man I had just poured my heart out to. Dropping my head in embarrassment, I was stunned when he grabbed my chin and forced me to look at him a second later with a look of acceptance and love.

"What makes you think you are the only one affected? I'm dreading my daily obligations because they take me away from you. You became the center of my universe the moment I caught wind of your presence, making me question my position as the leader of my people because, for the first time, when I think of the future, I only see you. I'm not scared for you or me. I'm scared for anyone or anything that gets between us, seeing as I will stop at nothing to keep you."

The truth of his words did wonders to soothe the possessive bitch dominating my thoughts but did nothing to assuage the fears threatening to consume me. If anything, his confession confirmed the complexity of our union and made me realize our feelings would only grow over time. My bottom lip quivered as I voiced my concerns. "The thought of you touching someone else moments ago pushed me close to an anxiety attack. How are we supposed to breathe, let alone function as individuals with the feeling that I will die if I lose you? It's too much. What if humans can't handle that kind of connection?"

Kalen puffed out his chest during my confession and looked on the verge of laughing until he saw my reaction and quickly covered his smile with his hand, "Oh my sweet. It only feels overwhelming because it is so new, but your jealousy is music to my ears. Let me try and put some of your worries to rest. I can't say I'll never touch another being. We're immortal, and forever is a long time. But I can promise the only touching I do will inflict pain on the other party. After all, I am a warrior."

"What about your need for blood? Will my blood be enough to sustain you? I don't want anyone else to experience your bite. I'm trying to ignore the fact that there was anybody before me."

"My need for blood? I forgot about the ridiculous stories rampant on your planet concerning my species." Pulling me to my feet, he leaned down and brushed his lips across mine, once, twice - before he stopped to nibble. The act elicited a groan from me, giving him access to deepen the kiss. My mouth flooded with his essence a moment later. I sought out the source and sucked on his tongue without inhibition. Just a few drops were all I needed to feel complete, which proved he wasn't the only one suffering from the ailment.

He yanked his tongue free with a groan, and with a knowing smile, he continued, "I crave our blood bond because it solidifies our union, gives us access to each other's emotions, and grants you immortality. I do not require blood to live, nor do I consume it as food. Blood holds power and is shared in my world but not as you would expect. You are the first person I've drunk from, and the first to drink straight from my vein. There was no one before you; there will be no one after you. Drinking straight from the source is saved for your mate because it offers the drinker access to thoughts and memories. We use my blood to grant our warriors immortality, but they drink it from a golden chalice, never from the vein. It helps maintain a loyal army if you can tell when a person is lying or if they harbor ill will toward you or yours."

I felt like an idiot for assuming any of the myths I'd heard held any truth but considering the amount of weird and supernatural stuff happening around me, who could blame a girl for overreacting?

It would appear I had a lot to learn about my new world if I intended to keep my dignity and save my sanity.

I smiled with a shrug and felt the beginnings of a full-body blush when he tapped my lips playfully and said, "While I love the direction of your thoughts, any action we take will have to wait until tonight. I am late for a meeting with my special forces team to discuss what they uncovered about the murder last night before the trials, which are scheduled for this afternoon."

He chuckled at my groan and then groaned himself when I sucked his finger into my mouth and nipped it lightly. I smiled with victory only to mewl with disappointment when he flashed to the opposite side of the room. "Damn it, woman, you're making it extremely hard for me to concentrate. Get dressed. I'll be back to collect you after my meeting."

"Unless there is something in my closet that doesn't require assistance, you might find me naked when you come back."

"What on Earth are you talking about?"

"You sent my maid away last night. I'll be flying solo until you return her."

"Until I know how the pixie died, no one will be allowed near you. Pick something out, and I'll be in to help you after I get dressed."

"Do you have a favorite color?"

"My new favorite color would be every shade of green your eyes emit in the sun," Kalen replied with a wink before flashing out of the room.

Chapter Nine

I stood in the middle of the large walk-in closet without a clue what to wear. I had no idea what was proper or what my duties would entail on a day-to-day basis. If Selene were here, she'd know exactly what I'd be facing, which made me appreciate her position even more. I made a mental note to find a way to speak to her today and make sure she was alright. Hopefully, they'll find the culprit soon because I'll earn the nickname "frumpy queen" or some shit if I dress myself.

Looking around at what was supposedly mine, I laughed. I still couldn't believe any of this was happening and laughed harder when I realized I didn't have time to ponder it either. I needed to find something to wear. Something along the line of business casual sounded good. Skimming my hands over the soft fabric, I noticed the only things on the racks was fancy evening gowns and flirty dresses.

I moved towards the built-in dressers, looking for something more practical, and moaned when I saw my reflection in the mirrors. The water in the shower had done nothing for my appearance. In fact, I looked worse. My makeup was all over my face. The water plastered my matted hair to my head. So much for taking a shower.

Next time I'd have to remember to wash up first before any kinky stuff, or better yet, after said kinky stuff.

I attempted to run my fingers through my hair only to make it a couple of inches before they got stuck. Shaking my head at the chaos looking back at me, I moved quickly to ensure I would have enough time to make myself presentable. I opened the first drawer roughly and gasped when it revealed nothing but earrings in every different gem and color under the rainbow. Closing it shut with greater care, I opened the rest of the drawers one by one and stood there with my mouth gaping open when each revealed another treasure trove of jewelry separated by type. I had a drawer of bracelets, one for rings, another for necklaces, and even one for tiaras.

My hand hovered over an emerald necklace with want. I was afraid to touch anything, but the desire to wear it was overwhelming. I had never seen anything so intricate and beautiful before. It was the color of my eyes, and oh so tempting to put on. "Damn, aren't you pretty!"

"I see you've found the small tokens I've been collecting for you since I was a young man," Kalen replied from behind me.

"Holy crap! You need a bell or something. You scared the shit out of me!" I screamed, snapping my hand back like he'd caught me stealing. I flipped around to face him, closing the drawer with my body as I flattened myself against the dresser in a slightly protective stance. I relaxed somewhat when the devastatingly handsome man smiled at me encouragingly. He was drool-worthy, but his ability to pop in and out would take some getting used to.

"I don't smell anything?" Kalen replied with confusion. When he started looking behind me for a mess, I was seconds away from dying of embarrassment until he buckled and started chuckling at my expense. Probably from the look of horror on my face.

"Ooh! You!" I replied by throwing my hands in the air when he gave me a wink. Fingering the dresser behind me, I asked, "Why aren't these under lock and key? Having them out in the open like this is practically an open invitation, asking for trouble."

Kalen approached me with a look of confidence. He caged me in with his arms before he replied. "Our quarters, in our personal wing, is hardly out in the open. I feel anyone walking in here without an invitation is asking for trouble. In fact, I dare someone to try and take the horde I've been building for my mate. Why aren't you dressed yet?" Kalen asked, eyeing me up and down before fingering a wet lock of hair and tucking it behind my ear.

"I didn't know what to wear. What am I doing today? Will my day consist of sitting in my room? Did you really say you've been collecting these trinkets for me? For years?" I finished in a whisper when I got the final question out.

"Thousands of years. Yes."

"How did you know what I'd like?"

"Do you like them?"

"Very much. They are beautiful."

"I'm glad. I didn't know what kind of jewelry you'd like when I acquired them, but they called my name. I hope you like them."

"What am I doing today?"

"I thought you could accompany me to my meeting, seeing as I don't want to leave you alone quite yet. How does that sound to you?"

"I would love to go with you, but what does one wear to a meeting like that? Are we doing anything afterward?"

"We usually wear our uniforms, but you can wear whatever you want. I recommend anything light that breathes. It's usually warm here. As for afterward, we must attend the opening ceremony of the trials." Perusing my closet contents, he grabbed a sheer green sundress and held it out for my review. "What about this one?"

"That would be perfect if we were on a romantic picnic, but not what I want to prance around in or go to important meetings in. I don't want people to look at me as just your arm candy. I have a brain and can be quite powerful when I'm in a room full of Sixers."

"You are my mate. Not my arm candy and, trust me, I am well aware of your powers. Impressive, but the thought of you being in a position where you might have to use them is causing me to see red. Tell me, Jade, if the room you are in is void of a Sixer, what will your gift do for you?"

I pulled up short at his comment, having never thought about it. "Good question. Well, shit. I don't really have a good answer. I've never been in a situation where my life was on the line, so it wasn't anything I worried about."

"Not the case anymore. Do you have any experience with hand-to-hand combat?" Kalen quipped while proceeding to pace in front of me.

"Not really. I took a small self-defense class when I got out of high school at my local community center. It mostly revolved around stabbing people in their private parts with anything I was carrying, but I did fairly well. Besides, my gift has a long radius; someone is usually nearby." I reasoned.

"We'll have to remedy that. I might not want you to be in danger, but I wouldn't be able to forgive myself if you were forced to defend yourself without your gift and had no way of accomplishing it."

"Could you stop pacing? You're making me nervous. I thought you said we were late."

Kalen stopped in his tracks and shook his head. "This bond is going to take some getting used to."

"I literally just told myself that same thing, but I was referring to your flashing ability!"

"We are late. I'm surprised we haven't been interrupted yet. Pick something out. You make it hard to concentrate without any clothes on."

"Can I get something like what you're wearing? All of your warriors have them."

"I wouldn't be able to concentrate with your curves on display."

"My curves and skin will be on display if I wear a dress. How is that not more debilitating to you? At least my bits would be covered with a uniform like that."

Kalen eyed me up and down and said, "You're right. It doesn't matter what you wear. I'll have some ordered for you, but until then, how about a compromise, and you wear this." Offering me the dress again.

"Fine."

When Kalen smiled with relief, I smiled mischievously in return. The look of confusion was worth it when I swiped the see-through garment from his hands and said, "Seeing as you rendered my undergarments to pieces, I guess the palace will get to see me in all my glory as we prance on by. I don't see any replacements in here."

"I beg to differ," Kalen replied with a growl. Walking towards the entrance, he pushed a button and held his arms out wide as a second set of drawers, hanging rods, and shelves emerged from behind the first set of racks forcing the pretty dresses to the back.

I spun in a circle with my mouth agape as rows of clothes of all sorts appeared before my eyes. Gathering my wits, I mouthed out a response that had no sound. Shaking my head, I cleared my throat a couple of times. "You could have just shown these to me in the first place."

Crossing the small distance between us, he cupped my cheek. "True, but I'm selfish and like the easy access a dress provides. Plus, I'm fairly sure you could have gotten dressed by yourself. I thought it was your way of wanting to spend more alone time with me, which I was happy to oblige. I was simply prolonging the rendezvous." He leaned down, kissed me softly until I couldn't resist, and melted into him, deepening the kiss. Pulling back on a growl, he looked down at me with desire and shook his head. "I need to check in with Tanen and Jaelel while you finish up. You'll find an assortment of lingerie in the drawers to your right. You have five minutes."

I laughed and pointed to my head, "Sometimes I think you are blind. I won't be able to fix what's going on up here in five minutes. You can't rush beauty."

He gave my hair a quick once over before he shrugged and asked, "Ten be enough?"

Pushing away from him, I waved him on with a grunt and turned around, grumbling to myself as I moved toward the dressers, "He better not expect a masterpiece."

"You are more beautiful than I imagined. Whatever you come up with will be perfect."

I looked over my shoulder to thank him, but he was already gone. Smiling at his compliment, I dropped the dress and pulled out the first set of undergarments I found, slipping them on with a sigh. A girl could get used to this kind of luxury. I contemplated the sundress, but knowing I'd feel more comfortable in something less revealing, I rummaged through the more casual outfits for something sophisticated yet sexy as a compromise. I ended up choosing a daring green silk blouse with a low neckline, paired with skin-tight black leather pants and a pair of emerald suede knee-high fuck me boots to round out the ensemble.

Rushing to the bathroom, I proceeded to wash my skin with care. The last thing I needed was a red face. Thankful for a clear complexion, I decided to go au natural, pinching my cheeks for a little color before I tackled the mess on my head. Figuring I had a little less than five minutes, I pulled it up in a bun, leaving out a few tendrils to frame my face. The end result wasn't anything spectacular, but I was proud of what I had accomplished in record time.

Surprised I was done before Kalen came to get me, I studied my reflection to see if I could do anything else with the time I had left to improve my appearance. When it hit me, I needed some bling. Heading back into the closet, I pushed the button to bring back the other half of my closet and waited patiently for the movement to stop before I grabbed my treasure. I was moments away from putting on the beautiful emerald necklace when Selene screamed at me from behind to stop what I was doing.

Chapter Ten

Startled, I dropped the necklace on accident and panicked as I watched it shatter to pieces on the marble floor. "No!" I yelled out, turning in Selene's direction to scold her for scaring me. The look of terror on her face confused me until she pointed at my feet and cried, "Move!"

From my peripheral vision, a plume of black tendrils spiraled up from the necklace. Surprised, I stumbled backward to escape its expanding radius and nearly fell over. Kalen caught me in his arms. Shoving me behind him, he pushed his arms out and closed his fists. The action caused the vapors and the necklace's remnants to contract on themselves until they imploded into dust.

Kalen spun around, frantic with worry, methodically inspecting me for injury, utterly oblivious to my astonishment. "Are you hurt? Did you breathe in anything? My men are on the way."

"Holy shit, you can control gravity! I thought your gift was telekinesis. Boy, I was wrong. I completely underestimated you!"

"Who the fuck cares about my power, Jade? Are you hurt?" Kalen bit out angrily as Rom, Kiso and Tanen crowded into the room. Making my large closet feel much smaller.

"I don't think so. I feel fine, Kalen. What the hell was that? I'm cringing over here thinking about what might have happened if Selene hadn't arrived in time to stop me from putting it on." Turning to face my maid, I was shocked to find her splayed against the wall grabbing her throat as she struggled to breathe. Kalen's guards brandished their swords and spread out in a circle around her.

"Selene! Wait! Don't hurt her!" I lurched forward to assist, only to be pulled back by my brute of a mate before I made it one step. I looked up at him in question and back-peddled away when I could practically see the rage rolling off of him in waves. He made that effort difficult when he tightened his grip around my waist. I knew Kalen was angry with Selene, but we needed to get answers, not revenge.

Stroking his arm with feather touches, I tried to reason with him before he killed her. "Kalen. Please let her breathe. If you kill her, we won't be able to find out what she knows." When Selene started turning blue, I tried a different approach. "Selene saved my life, Kalen. If she wanted to hurt me, then she wouldn't have stopped me from placing that necklace of death around my neck. I think we'll want to hear what she has to say. Please."

My final plea appeared to reach him when he looked down at me with a torn expression. His grasp around me loosened slightly, allowing me to turn around and face him. The gasp behind me was euphonic. Taking a deep breath in relief, I cupped his cheek and held his gaze before I kissed him lightly and whispered my gratitude. "Thank you. Can you let me go so I can check on her?"

He shook his head and snarled out a gruff refusal, crushing me to his chest. The one-word response was a bit alarming. His actions were almost feral and I was concerned he might snap. I smoothed my hands over his chest and acquiesced, leaning into him, letting him feel for himself that I was unharmed. I glanced over my shoulder and was relieved to see the guards give Selene some room to pick herself up off the floor, albeit delicately. At least she was moving.

When she raised her head, and bloodshot eyes stared back at me, I drew in a sharp breath. She looked horrible. I could hardly believe this was the same woman I met yesterday. I opened my mouth to apologize but stopped when she dropped to the floor in a low bow and blurted out an apology that made no sense. "Thank you, my lady, for your compassion and forgiveness. I am thankful I got to meet you finally and even more grateful I got here in time to save you."

Pushing against Kalen, I hissed at him when he proved immovable. "Let me turn around, you big brute. I just want to face her. I'm not going anywhere." Squirming in his arms, I managed to turn around. Blowing wisps of hair from my eyes, I studied the frail woman bowing before me with perplexity. Gone was our earlier rapport, nowhere to be found. She was acting as if we had never met.

I could feel her artistic gift at my fingertips, but a tingle of something foreign I couldn't identify confused me. I waited for her to get up, and when she continued to kneel, it finally dawned on me, she was waiting for one of us to give her permission to stand. Knowing the Strix behind me was incapable of rational thought at the moment, I cringed, feeling uncomfortable in my new role as I told her it was okay to stand. "I thought we'd been through this before, Selene. There is no need for you to bow in my presence. Please get up so we can talk."

Selene rose slowly with a look of gainsaying. "My lady, the woman you met earlier was not me. When I received the summons to report for duty as your maid, somebody ambushed me on the way.

The person you met yesterday was a replica of me. We've never had the pleasure of meeting before."

"Impossible! The only way into this corridor requires fingerprint analysis. Not to mention Rom should have been able to sense your approach and intercept you. Let's not forget Kiso either. The second his brother felt your presence, he should have locked this place down! I'll deal with the two of you later!" Kalen roared before turning to face Selene once more. "How did you get in here? My patience is wearing thin. Explain yourself!"

"I never saw who attacked me, but whoever it was, was a woman, and she was working with a doppelganger. I heard her tell the doppelganger as it was copying me to plant the cursed necklace and kill me after. I escaped before It came back. I knew the risk I took sneaking in here, but I headed this way as fast as I could once I was free. I used the secret passages to bypass the guards because I couldn't risk the delay. Making my way in the dark was a hindrance I didn't account for, but I was praying I wouldn't be too late. I had to do everything in my power to stop them from killing you and destroying my good name."

Kalen's posture went rigid before he asked Selene in a chilling voice, "Who showed you the passageways? I only decided to add a maid last week."

Kiso stepped forward and, with a shaky but loud voice, answered, "I showed her, my lord. I thought she should know how to help her charge if we were not around, my liege."

"No reason to cover for me, Kiso. I can defend myself against this ogre better than you can. Especially when he's not thinking clearly," Tanen replied, stepping in front of my guard, patting him on the shoulder as he passed.

"Did you forget your place? I am the king! How could you betray me?"

"Then act like it! I showed her the passage the day you hired her, and I would do it again. The girl needed to be able to save herself and the life of your mate. If you were currently in your right mind, you would realize my supposed betrayal is why you are holding your Jade now. The real issue is the doppelganger. If what Selene says is true, then it could be impersonating anyone at the moment."

A commotion in my room diverted my attention when General Jaelel flashed past the guards and announced, "There has been another murder, Lord Kalen. Your presence is required at once in the infirmary."

A snarl had me snapping my head back to the man behind me. I expected to find Kalen on the brink of losing it, like I was, but was happy to see him lucid. So much drama with so little time to process was messing with my mind. His hold on me didn't ease as he assessed the room methodically, looking at each of his guards before he bellowed out orders, "Jaelel, gather the council members. We must postpone the Trials. Rom and Kiso take Selene to see Praddix. She will determine if she speaks the truth. Tanen, follow me to my office."

I opened my mouth to question his motives and shouldn't have been surprised when he didn't wait to see if they obeyed his orders before he flashed us away. On touch down, I scrambled out of his arms. I whirled around to give him a piece of my mind but stopped short at the look of fury on his face.

Chapter Eleven

I knew he wasn't angry at me, but I was thankful when Tanen appeared milliseconds later, demanding action, "I hope you've come to your senses, my friend, because now is not the time to start losing your shit. Foul play is at work, and it's time you figure out who is responsible instead of getting your cock wet between the legs of your mate. No offense Jade."

"None taken," I answered automatically as I watched my mate approach a tall painting of a large sea creature to the left of his desk. The image was striking and so life-like, with a small lighthouse that seemed to strobe in the distance. I barely pulled my eyes away when Kalen looked over his shoulder with a devilish smile and replied. "I look forward to the day you find your mate and are forced to leave them when duty calls. Now apologize to Jade for your rudeness and help me summon Levi."

The look of astonishment on Tanen's face should have been a sign I was in for another surprise, but nothing could have prepared me for what happened next. Shaking his head in denial for a second as he considered his choices, he eventually dropped his head in respect before he replied with sincerity, "Sorry, Jade. I meant no disrespect. Please forgive me."

"Apology accepted."

Tanen nodded his head with acknowledgment before he turned to Kalen with a look of astonishment on his face, "Are you out of your mind? We barely escaped with our lives the last time you struck a deal with him. Not to mention, it took us forever to pay him off. Do you want to involve him? What are you going to promise him this time? Your firstborn?"

Kalen spun around and growled, "You go too far. I will stop at nothing to protect the woman in front of you, and if he can find the doppelganger before they have a chance to carry out their assassination, I will take that chance. No cost is too much in my eyes."

Tanen shook his head with disappointment but sauntered forward anyway. "I hope we don't regret this decision."

"Hold up! This doesn't sound good! Who the hell is Levi?" I asked, taking a step in their direction.

"An old-time acquaintance that has the power of true sight," Kalen answered hesitantly before turning back towards the painting, signaling the end of the conversation.

"And that means what to me?" I asked in confusion, tapping my foot impatiently.

When he remained silent, I marched forward, tapped him on the shoulder, and waited for him to look at me before reiterating my question. "I know you have a lot going on AND probably aren't used to explaining yourself to anyone, seeing as you are the king and all, but I asked you a question that I think deserves an answer."

Kalen looked up at the ceiling like he was searching for the right answer before he took a deep breath and let it out slowly, deflating slightly in the process. Lowering his eyes, he caught my gaze before he answered, "True sight is a rare gift that detects magic of all types. The innate ability of a doppelganger tends to be hard to identify by even the best sorcerer. Levi will take the guesswork out of the equation and let us stop this coup d'état before it starts."

"Sounds easy enough, but in my experience, nothing easy comes free of trouble. What aren't you telling me?" My simple question had him cringing, which caused my woman's intuition alarm to fire on all cylinders. Cocking my head to the side, I furrowed my brow and tried a different approach. Shrugging my shoulders, I acted nonchalant when I said, "Guess it doesn't matter. Summon Levi, and I'll just ask him myself."

The statement had a profound impact. Kalen grasped both of my arms, catching me off guard when he looked down into my eyes and pleaded, "I'll explain everything to you tonight. Just please don't initiate a conversation with him. He has a way of talking in riddles, and sometimes you find yourself caught in the middle, promising things you had no idea you promised."

I studied his face for any signs that he was just telling me what I wanted to hear. When it appeared he was genuine, I nodded my acceptance and said, "I won't start a conversation, but I expect a full explanation of what you are getting us into, or you'll find yourself in the doghouse."

Kalen's anxiety melted with my agreement, and without missing a beat, he replied with a sly grin, "On the assumption, I would not like the doghouse, I agree to your terms." Without waiting for an affirmation, he kissed my forehead and released my arms before resuming his position alongside Tanen in front of the oceanesque picture.

I braced myself for the bizarre, but nothing I imagined happened as Kalen stepped forward and knocked three times on the picture frame. His hand hovered above the sand in front of the creature like he was waiting for a signal. I barely contained a gasp when the sounds of the ocean filtered through the room. The moment

I heard a lighthouse horn, like in the picture, I barely caught myself from falling by grabbing onto a chair next to me.

I wanted to pretend that I was dreaming, but the rational side of me tended to be visual, and the old saying of seeing was believing was hard to overcome. As Kalen reached his hands into the painting, I let go of societal norms of what was real or fake and chose to accept what I saw as plausible. Tanen's sudden move to grab the back of Kalen's fatigues brought me back to the moment as I watched half of Kalen's body disappear into the scenic view.

As the smells of the ocean wafted past me, I grew nervous and braced myself to meet Levi. If I believed the painting was real, then the only thing missing would be the massive sea creature present in the center. I looked about the room nervously and had a hard time imagining how it would fit in here by itself, let alone with the addition of the three of us.

Stumbling back a few steps, I opened my mouth to express my concern and promptly closed it shut with a snap when Kalen backed out of the frame a second later, followed closely by a ten-foot-tall very naked man. His height ensured his penis was at eye level, and as it appeared to stare me down, I tried to look everywhere but at him. Averting my eyes to Kalen, I cleared my throat and said with annoyance, "What is it with this place and their lack of clothes! Umm . . . Could we get him something to wear?"

"It appears your female is unable to contain her lust in my presence. Are you positive she is your mate?" Levi purred in a gravelly voice.

My eyes snapped toward the giant at his comment, and with a snarl, I pinned him with a glare and said, "Never doubt my loyalty. It is my number one attribute. I simply would rather not converse with someone whose penis looks like a shriveling spiny sea cucumber. I'm rather fond of eating and would prefer not to lose my appetite before breakfast."

I steeled myself for some type of punishment from my outburst, but I wasn't about to back down from the smug giant. Much to my surprise, Levi doubled over on himself in laughter. I let my guard down slightly and looked to Kalen and Tanen for direction. Their baffled expression was no help as we turned our eyes to the elephant in the room and waited for him to stop. He was fully dressed when he finally came up for air. Wearing a long flowing robe, he had tears streaming from his eyes before he wiped them away and said between chuckles, "Thank you, dear one, it has been centuries since I laughed like that. I almost lost control of my form, and that hasn't happened since I was a wee little one."

My mouth might have dropped open from his comment if I hadn't been paying attention to my mate's emotion through our bond. It went from amused to angered and then back to amused again in the blink of an eye. Not wanting to ruin the modicum of peace my outcry brought about, I curtsied and said, "You're welcome. Glad I could help." With a wink to an open-mouthed Kalen, I waited for him to bring us all up to speed.

Tanen elbowed him in the side when he continued to look between Levi and me like a fish out of water. The jostle was enough to break the trance Kalen seemed to be in before he blinked, shook his head, and got down to business. "Levi, do I need to be concerned that you might lose control of your appearance?"

"I am in full control. You have my word."

Kalen quickly nodded his approval before he cleared his throat and continued, "As I mentioned on your home planet, we need your service. An assassination attempt was made against Jade tonight with the help of a doppelganger. I require your true sight in tracking the culprit down and the person who hired it. Nothing is off the table. Name your price."

Bracing myself for a steep offer, I expected Levi to ponder the question with calculated interest in his eyes. Instead, he surprised me again when he snarled in response and answered without delay, "I'll do it! Show me the accused!"

"I expected as much when you followed me here. I have no time for games. What payment will you require for this service?" Kalen demanded with annoyance.

"I've been paid. Show me the accused!" Levi roared as the air around him seemed to shimmer.

Tanen stepped in front of his king and waved his hands in the air as he took control of the escalating scene, "I'll flash you there myself, but who paid you? Forgive us for looking for a deeper meaning behind your words. Our dealings with you in the past have made us wary. What will you be requesting of us for this boon?"

"Jade paid me with a soul healing laugh, but if you insist on delaying any further, I will change my fee to something far more costly materialistically speaking," Levi replied as he popped his neck in waiting.

Kalen looked skeptical but shoved Tanen to the side as he addressed Levi with gratitude, "Forgive our hesitancy, but I hope you understand where we are coming from after our last encounter."

Without waiting for a response, he turned towards Tanen and spoke with authority, "Take Levi to Praddix. They should be in her quarters. When you finish, report to the council room immediately."

Tanen gave a quick bow to his liege before he approached Levi with an outstretched hand and said, "Shall we find ourselves a doppelganger?"

"We? There will be no "we" in this equation. You are merely my transportation assistant." Levi replied as he reached forward to grab Tanen's hand and winked at Jade before he added, "There's no use denying how awesome I am." As they flashed from the room, Jade could hear Tanen warn Levi he was playing with fire when it came to flirting with the king's mate.

"Less than a day ago, that would have been true, but seeing as we need his help, I'm glad it's one less thing I have to worry about," Kalen countered with noticeable relief. He took a moment to assess me like he was double-checking my mental stability was still intact.

I crossed the space between us and grabbed his hand to assuage him as well as me that we were still very much alive and present, ready to face whatever life threw at us next. Leaning forward, I pressed my lips to his and whispered, "What do you say we see what the council has to say before you make any more decisions for the day?"

"I think that's the second rational thing you've said today," Kalen responded by nibbling at the corner of my mouth.

Dizzy from his ministration, I barely registered his remark. As my mind circled back to reality when he pulled away, I asked, "What was the first rational thing I said today?"

"When you admitted you're addicted to me," Kalen replied with a smirk before he folded me in his arms and flashed us away.

Chapter Twelve

Even though it took less than a second to flash to the council room, I had a hard time stepping away from the comfort Kalen's arms provided. With my face buried in the crook of his neck, it was easy to forget the chaos going on around us. However, it didn't take long for the whispers behind us to remind me we weren't alone.

Through the bond, I could sense Kalen's need for my support. With a strength I wasn't aware I possessed, I pushed back so I could look him in the eye when I addressed him. "What do you say we go solve this mystery so we can pick up where we left off." Dropping my voice to a whisper, I added, "Blood of you, blood of me. Forever mine, forever yours. For all eternity. Did I say it right?"

The flash of lust that swept through our bond as I repeated the words he used during our mating ritual was potent. Delicious flutters of need settled between my legs, making me blush as I tried my best not to announce to the room how turned on I was by the Strix in front of me. The growl was the affirmation I said it right, but it didn't help my horniness when my nipples hardened in response. He looked at them with longing before he leaned forward and whispered in my ear, "Yes, you said it right." Taking in a deep breath, he nuzzled my neck before he finished. "Fuck, I love the way your arousal smells. This will be the quickest council meeting in history."

Grabbing my hand, he pulled us to the front of the room. Practically running to keep pace with his long strides, I barely had time to take in the place as I followed behind him in a sex-induced trance. It took my brain a couple of milliseconds to process his statement, and by the time we reached our seats, I was bright red and mortified; No one should know the state of my underwear!

Leaning over to voice my discomfort, he silenced me with a finger to my mouth as a shimmering bubble surrounded us like a security blanket. In an instant, I knew it was his way of ensuring only he would be able to enjoy my potent desire for him. His gentlemanly act was like an aphrodisiac and had me squirming in my seat to bring my swollen clit some relief. In a last-ditch effort, I turned my attention to the occupants of the room. I needed to quench my growing craving for the Strix sitting next to me. It didn't take long for the contempt of some of the attendees to make that happen. Three council members of the ten, to be exact, were all shooting daggers at us with their eyes. I made a mental note to question Kalen about their attitudes when we were alone.

Kalen leveled the occupants in the room with a death stare until the murmurs died down before he zeroed in on the crying woman next to us and spoke, "Clary, you have my deepest condolences. It is my understanding it was your niece, Anolla, that was taken from us last night. Natashia attempted to save her using a time jump, but unfortunately, every intervention she tried ended in her ultimate death. Jaelel informed me your sister requested to be present for the burial ceremony, and he wanted you to know he's on his way to pick her up personally."

The tiny pixie with pastel blue hair and eyes blew her nose into a handkerchief before she spoke, "Thank you, my liege. I want to be the executioner once you find the culprit." Rising into the air with see-through rainbow wings, she added, "My family will not rest until justice is served."

"That's a given, Clary, and I will do everything in my power to make that happen quickly." Cocking his head to the side, he furrowed his brow and asked, "What information do we have on the newest death?"

A red and gold bird-woman with black eyes answered, "It was my nephew Castice. Thankfully, he's a half-phoenix and has already risen." Nodding to the elf across from her, she added,

"Natashia was kind enough to send him home to his mother. No one wanted to handle a newborn phoenix pissed off that he's once again a baby. We questioned him before he left, and unfortunately, he has no idea how it happened."

"Thank you, Fansa. I'll make sure he's compensated and receives what would have been his normal wages for having to repeat puberty. At least until he can take his rightful place among us."

"I'm sure he'll appreciate the gesture, Your Highness. I wish my gift would have warned me. I was looking forward to having the young man around. His clairvoyant gift was just starting to wake up, but he was on track to bypass me in predictions."

An older gentleman with gray hair, a beak-like nose, and bushy eyebrows pounded his fists on the table before he exploded, "Compensated? Throwing money at a problem will not make it go away. What are you going to do to ensure the rest of us are safe? Two murders in less than 24 hours and what have you been doing? I'll tell you what you've been doing. You've been holed up in your chambers with your human harlot while the rest of us did your job!"

Murmurs broke out in response to the slimeball's outburst. The soon-to-be dead man ran a shaky hand through his oily, slicked back hair before he stood up, puffed out his chest, and added, "The people of Marni, whom I represent, move for a vote of no confidence! We should have a king that puts his people first!"

I could feel my mate's fury building through our bond and braced myself for an immediate explosion. Squeezing my eyes shut in anticipation of blood and guts, I was surprised when the room grew eerily quiet and still instead. Opening one eye, I jumped back with shock in my seat when I found a violet-eyed Natashia head poking out of a portal in front of me.

Peeking around the scene in front of me, I found her body in a chair across the room with her head inside the portal. Sitting back slowly, I returned my gaze to the inquisitive ethereal beauty in front of me. I opened my mouth to ask her what she was doing when she interrupted me with an apologetic look.

"I'm sorry this is a little embarrassing. No one's ever caught me peeping before. I figured it wouldn't hurt to take a closer look at our new queen after I froze you. I mean you no harm." Her pale cheeks took on a rosy complexion the longer I continued to stare at her unabashedly until I found my voice and rescued her. "No harm done. Just not used to seeing a live head without a body on anything other than a video call or television."

"Oh, I thought all timewards could travel via portals. I guess it doesn't matter. It will be useful to have another timeward around. Can you travel forward in time?"

I looked at Kalen in my periphery and pondered how much of my gift he'd want me to divulge. I'd always been so different that a part of me was jumping at the chance to be considered normal. Refusing to hide anymore, I opted to tell her the truth, "I've never tried honestly, seeing as it's your gift I'm borrowing, but it feels like we can."

"Are you saying you're a borrower?"

"I've never heard it called that before, but it's fitting. Are there other borrowers?"

Natashia got quiet for a moment before she spoke with sadness in her voice, "There's only been two that I am aware of, but they were both killed eons ago."

"What happened to them?"

"The first was a mystery and played off as an accident, but the second murder was at the hands of the Mengh when they found out how far her gift reached. Kalen and his father were devastated when they lost Queen Zandrea, and Kalen vowed revenge when he took the helm after his father lost his life in the First War."

"Kalen's mother was a borrower. Damn, how did they manage to kill her?"

"She was kidnapped and tortured in a room by non-Sixers."

"No wonder Kalen freaked out and wanted me to learn self-defense." Pushing back from the table, I got up and began to pace. "It sure didn't take the little fuckers long to try and take me out. The attack against my life today is all starting to make sense now! Well, they better believe I won't go down without a fight." I screamed and then yelped when electric lightning I wasn't expecting shot from my hands hitting the wall, barely missing Bastian. Closing my hands into fists to put out the blue fire, I looked at Natashia awkwardly and shrugged, "Oops!"

"Well, I'll be. Beatress was right! You are an extraordinary Sixer!"

Cocking my head at the bizarre and flattering statement, I chuckled before I said, "Not sure what Beatress was right about, but thanks for the compliment." Looking about the room at our frozen companions, I added, "Although I am very grateful for this little reprieve, mind explaining what the purpose of our time-out is for?"

Looking around like she forgot where they were, Natashia shook her head before she replied, "Yeah, we should probably get back to that. Just a second." Natashia backed out of her portal with a grunt. I watched it close in fascination, only to jump a bit at the end when it popped.

"Phooey, that was sloppy. Guess you should know it takes practice to enter and exit in silence. Where was I . . . oh yeah . . . revealing the purpose of our pause. One of my many jobs on this council is to hit pause if I think someone is about to do or say something they might regret."

"Well, don't you think you should have paused it before that asshat over there opened his mouth?"

"Normally, I would have, but I wanted to see how far Bastian would take his charade and how many of my brethren felt the same. During my attempts to save Anolla, I wasn't able to find any hard evidence on the killer's identity, but his niece was always in the vicinity on each of my trips."

"Would that be Princess Onyx?"

"The one and only. What do you know?"

"Nothing. Just got a bad vibe from her at dinner last night. I'd like to get close to her to feel out her gift, but I have a feeling that will be next to impossible now. Kalen will probably lock me in the safe room after this."

"I'll think of something. In the meantime, help me wake up Kalen. After Bastian's latest tantrum, I have a feeling Kalen will need more than reassuring words from an old friend to calm him down. We'll be lucky if he doesn't kill Bastian and start a civil war, even with our intervention!"

Chapter Thirteen

"How do we wake him up?" I questioned as I approached Kalen slowly. I knew he wasn't privy to our conversation, but I couldn't help feeling like I was waking a sleeping bear just coming out of hibernation.

"All we need to do is touch him, but I think it would be better if you do it. So your face is the first thing he sees," Natashia replied with a lopsided grin.

Considering my options, I decided to use some of my feminine power to control the possible loose cannon I'd be facing. Pushing Kalen's seat back, I straddled his legs, being careful not to touch him before I was ready. Snickering at how foolish I might look to my new friend, I looked over my shoulder and said, "Considering we might not make it out of this, I'd like to say it was a pleasure meeting you, Natashia."

"Likewise, Jade, but I think our king will have a change of heart considering his current viewpoint. Pun intended, of course."

"That's what I'm hoping for. Wish me luck." Leaning forward, I fell in love just a little bit more as I studied his face before I placed a kiss on his lips like he was Sleeping Beauty. I was pleasantly stunned when he growled, pulled me closer, and ravished my mouth properly. Proud of myself for distracting him from his original plan to kill or maim Bastian, I sank into his embrace and relished our connection. Promising myself, I would pull back after another second.

It didn't take long before he pulled back slightly and shattered my hopes that he was no longer going to kill Bastian. He nibbled my mouth once more and then said, "While I appreciate what you are trying to do, I need you to move away so I can show that sniveling elemental the meaning of respect and loyalty."

"Kalen, even though I would love it if you stood up for me . . . In fact, I can't lie, it would be a major turn-on. In this instance, however, I want us to do the opposite. Instead, I think we should focus on how a vote of no confidence would benefit him or any of his allies. He only brought me into it so he could rile you up and make you act rashly, seeing as you're a newly-mated male. He's playing you. Don't let him win! We need to appease him somehow so we can get to the true meaning behind his preposterous claims. Tell me the rational side of your brain agrees with me!"

Kalen's face fell in defeat before he picked me up from his lap and gently placed me to the side. I thought my plea landed on deaf ears when he exited his chair and approached Bastian on a prowl. Both Natashia and I scrambled to block his path but were too late as he flashed in front of us and pulled his victim into the air and let loose a cathartic roar in his face that chilled me to the bone. I expected his next move would be to end the pathetic male's life, but once again, he proved me wrong when he sucker-punched Bastian in the groin and then promptly placed him back in his chair and instructed Natashia to resume time as he strode to his place at the table.

"Are you sure you're calm enough to respond? I could give you more time, my liege."

"Time will not help my rage. Do it now so he'll feel a fraction of the pain he deserves because I won't be able to stop myself from ripping his heart out if I touch him a second time!"

Sitting next to him gingerly, I grabbed his hand with mine and tried one more time to reach him, "You won't have to touch him. I'll gladly knee him again for both of us, but I need you here with me AND in the right frame of mind. Which means I need you capable of making rational decisions that will affect the lives of all under your protection, including you and me. Can you do that for me?"

Kalen squeezed my hand tightly in response. Taking a deep breath, he blew it out slowly from his nose before his touch gentled and his shoulders sagged with the stress of his responsibilities. "I'm not sure I can ignore the instincts I feel as a mated male compelling me to defend you. Maybe it's time I step aside and let someone else be king."

Stunned at his confession, I grappled with a response that would motivate him to put me second, but nothing came to mind. If I were honest with myself, all I had ever wanted was to be someone's first, and I'd be damning that dream if I said anything to the contrary. For once in my life, I could have my heart's desire, but the weight of the decision weighed heavily on my mind. When I realized the world's possible demise would forever overshadow my happiness, my wants and desires seemed pale in comparison. Without second-guessing myself, I froze my mate once again and asked Natashia for advice.

"Call me crazy, but can we reverse a mating if we go back in time and ensure Kalen and I don't see each other until the All Hands Gathering?" When no response came, I looked over my shoulder, expecting to find an astonished elf, only to shake my head in disbelief when I saw a frozen statue in her place. Shaking my head, I laughed nervously, hoping to ward off the ominous feeling the silent room held as I crossed the short distance to wake her up.

Touching her shoulder gently, I almost had a heart attack when she vanished in front of my eyes, only to pop out behind me with a knife held to my throat. Going off pure instinct, I borrowed the stone ability from the silver-templed gargoyle in the room, making my skin impervious, and tried to reason with the frightened elf, "Um, I thought we were friends? Why are you trying to kill me?"

Natashia gasped at the sound of my voice and dropped the knife like it was on fire. "I'm so sorry. Did I hurt you?"

Turning around to face her in my stone glory, I held my arms out and replied, "No, I'm hard to injure when I'm in a room full of Sixers." Dropping the stone exterior, I shrugged impishly and added, "I didn't mean to freeze you."

"Is that what happened?" Natashia replied incredulously.

"Yeah. I wanted to ask you a question, so I used your gift and froze the room so I could. Did I do something wrong?"

A look of disbelief flashed across her face, followed by a look of wonder by the time she replied, "Timeward's are immune to time freezes. What you just did was unprecedented! I thought you indicated you were a borrower?"

"I am. At least I think I am. I can feel the different abilities at my fingertips, and I call upon them in times of need. On Earth, having abilities is something we keep hidden, so I didn't have a lot of practice, but if someone was around and I was in the comfort of my room, I played. It was hard not to."

"Wow. It must be a little overwhelming to have eleven gifts at your disposal. It took me years as a child to master my power. How do you know what to do?"

Snorting in response, I replied, "Try over fifty right now and I can't explain how it works. I just know what is near me. It's like my conscious brain knows what's available so I can make logical choices on what is necessary for a situation, but I believe my gift is what operates the abilities if that makes sense."

"What's the range of your ability?" Natashia asked in a whisper.

"Around a mile, give or take a few yards," I replied quietly.

"Fuck! Kalen's never going to let you out of his sight. You could be right about him locking you up in the safe room."

"Hence why I froze him again so I could run something by you."

"Unless it's something foolproof that guarantees your life, I don't think it would be wise for me to assist you. If something were to happen to the king's mate, my life would be forfeit. Regardless of my position on this council."

"What if he didn't remember that I was his mate? I mean, is there a way to reverse our bonding or make him forget it happened? Not forever, obviously, just until the All Hands Gathering. I would need to avoid him until the Selection, but that would hopefully give me enough time to find who's trying to sabotage my mate."

"Oh, I don't think that's a good idea. The Trials aren't exactly easy. We haven't lost anyone for centuries, but history has a way of repeating itself. Plus, I thought you said you already had one attempt on your life. How are you going to protect yourself when everyone is out for themselves and only themselves?"

"So, it's possible then."

"That's all you got out of what I just said! Gah!" Hanging her head in exasperation, she sighed before she added in defeat, "Yes, it's possible, but I want it known that I don't agree with this plan at all."

"Does that mean you'll help me?"

"There has to be another way. Talk to Kalen. He might have something up his sleeve."

"He's doing his part, but I need to do mine as well. I don't want to be the woman left at home who always needs to be protected. I need to prove to him that I am worthy of being by his side. I want his people to respect me, not for my title but my deeds!"

"If I don't, you'll just do it yourself." She replied as more of a statement than a question while she shook her head. Releasing a big breath, she added, "Damn, I hope I don't live to regret this. I'll help you, but on one condition."

"Name it!"

"We visit Adira and get you a potion to change your physical appearance. We don't need to take any chances that someone is immune to our time-travel or whatnot and remembers you somehow."

"Can she make me look like anything?"

"I suppose. Why?"

"No reason. It would just be nice to be tall for once. Athleticism would be nice as well for the trials."

"Be careful what you wish for, sometimes wishing for something you don't have can have unintended consequences."

"I'll take that into consideration."

"No time for goodbyes, unfortunately. If we're going to do this, we should do it now."

I allowed myself a final glance in the direction of my mate before I followed Natashia into a portal that would erase the best two days of my life.

Chapter Fourteen

Time-travel has a way of messing with your head. I always thought if someone went back in time, they would see a replica of themselves, but in reality, when I entered the same space and time as my earlier self, we merged into one being. Natashia and I concluded after our meeting with the alchemist, Adira, my best bet of pulling off the impossible would be to go incognito and start from the beginning.

My second trip into the light, or in my case, sucked up into a spaceship, wasn't nearly as awe-inspiring when I knew what to expect. I was a little uncomfortable in my new skin and anxious to land so I could satisfy the piece of my soul that was missing my other half. Nervous energy traveled up and down my spine as I wondered if my disguise would work. It was supposed to keep Kalen from recognizing me as his true mate.

Adira was insistent that I had nothing to worry about because the veil of concealment would alter my chemical nature, making it impossible for the king to pick up on my smell. To be honest, I was a little disappointed Kalen couldn't enjoy my new form. I felt like a blond bombshell, tall with ample bosoms and hips to rock any man's world. The only thing I kept from my previous form was my eyes.

I went through the motions with General Jaelel and Dr. Annalise Triste on autopilot while contemplating how I would prove Onyx was responsible for the murder of Anolla and the attempted murder of Castice. Oh, and let's not forget to mention me as a factor in that equation. Part of the problem was, I didn't know all the players in the game.

Onyx topped my list of suspects. I speculated she hired the doppelganger. I couldn't guarantee it would manifest itself as my handmaiden Selene again, which left me with a limited amount of people I could trust. Bastian's accusations also needed to be looked at carefully, considering he's related to my person of interest. I highly doubted those two were the only ones involved. I promised myself I'd use every bit of my power to uncover every last culprit engaged in conspiring against my mate. I needed more people on my side to do that.

Rushing through my shower, I quickly dressed so I could join the others and mingle. Isolating myself wouldn't bring me more allies, and I could use some. I was taking a gamble. Assuming Onyx employed the doppelganger, I deduced everyone on board was probably themselves and therefore safe. Going off first impressions, I avoided the siren and sidled up to Beatress as she conversed with the panther jovially. I waited for them to finish their conversation before I introduced myself.

Sticking my hand out, I plastered a smile onto my face and said, "Greetings, fellow trial participants. My name is Jade from Earth. Anybody else dying to get this thing started?"

"Who isn't! I've been waiting my whole life to be selected! I'm Sheridath from Icanton, but my friends call me Sher," replied the shapeshifter with a purr, shaking my hand in return.

"I'm Beatress from Garrone. I wouldn't die to get this started. Seems counterintuitive to me," responded the elf with a frown marking her confusion on my word choice.

"I didn't mean to die literally. Sorry, it's a figure of speech in my world; it means I'm excited for the trials to begin," I answered apologetically.

"Oh, that's a strange phrase. To answer your question then, I'm excited, but I'd be perfectly happy to let it unfold slowly. Three days will go by fast, and I want to relish every step of this journey. For instance, if we skipped things, I might miss out on meeting nice people like you," Beatress responded with a wink, grabbing my hand and giving it a firm shake.

Chuckling in response, I dropped her hand and added, "You've got a point there. I could learn a thing or two from you."

"Living life in the moment is the only advice I'd have for you. Everything else will fall into place if you follow that rule," Beatress stated matter-of-factly with a firm nod of her head. "I'll try and remember that," I answered with a shy smile. Clearing my throat, I looked about the room as I scrambled for a topic of discussion that wouldn't give away my ignorance. It'd be nice to be on the same playing field as some of my other opponents.

The Satyr sauntered into our group and introduced himself, saving me from coming up with anything. "Well, hello there, my beauties. Allow me to introduce myself. You are standing in the presence of Zoar, sex god to lads and ladies across my home planet of Trinton."

"I've heard of you!" gasped Sher while placing a hand over her chest in awe.

"You have? What system are you from? It's always nice to know where one's fans are located," Zoar pressed while puffing up his chest proudly.

Sher pranced toward him, seductively. She ran a finger down his arm before she leaned forward, giving him an eye full, and replied, "It's called in your dreams, pig."

Beatress and I couldn't hold back our laughter at the look of devastation on Zoar's face. He sputtered for a moment before he seemed to gather his dignity and leave our little circle with his tail literally between his legs.

The shapeshifter shrugged and said, "Sorry, I couldn't help myself. Nothing pisses me off more than egotistical assholes who think they are God's gift to women or men, for that matter. I don't think I'm asking too much for them to have a little poise and decorum when they speak to people. It's called common courtesy. Gah!"

I patted Sher's arm and said, "Nothing to be sorry about; maybe next time he'll think twice before making a fool of himself. We can only hope the rest of the gang will be easier to get along with. I wonder how many more assholes we'll encounter during the trials?"

"Considering there are only 25 participating, the possibility exists that we could meet 22 more assholes before the day is up. Everyone will have their own story to play out, but my Aunt told me the key to surviving is to find others you can trust. Every situation we face will require a different skill set. If we work together, we have a better chance of earning the position we desire," Beatress answered quietly. When she finished, her eyes darted to the siren in the room nervously before she added in a whisper, "Not everyone will want to be a part of the team. There are always those that prefer to go solo."

"Those that are out to prove themselves rarely do," Sher replied in agreement.

I stole a glance at the siren behind us and quickly averted my eyes when I saw her looking directly at us. I cleared my throat and was about to mention that tidbit of knowledge when I felt the hairs on the back of my neck stand up. The telltale sign someone was coming up behind me. Whipping around to face the threat, I found myself face to face with her molten colored eyes. A tiny squeak slipped past my lips before I swallowed the rest and stuck out my hand in greeting. I surprised myself when my voice came out strong as I introduced myself, "Hi, I'm Jade."

The siren rolled her eyes at my outstretched hand with disgust. I dropped it slowly while I contemplated throat punching her instead. She must have sensed my anger because she smirked before putting her hands on her voluptuous hips and addressing my group, "I'm Cynosis from Acelex, but you can call me Cyn. I couldn't help but overhear your naive little comments. Normally I'd let you figure stuff out yourselves, but I'm feeling generous today. EVERYONE at the trials is out to prove themselves, not just those of us who choose to go solo. If you're not . . . what's the point of even being here? Besides, those who can handle every trial independently have the first pick of the open positions during the All Hands Gathering. I don't know about you, but no one will ever have that kind of power over me! I'm in charge of my destiny, so don't stand in my way!"

The vehemence wafting from Cyn as she practically snarled out that last part was intense. It made me question what might have happened to her growing up that turned her into such a closed-off bitch as she stormed off. It felt like the word 'again' was implied or missing from her tirade. It almost made me feel sorry for her until she turned around and flipped us off as she continued to back up towards the outer wall of the loading bay.

"Damn, something must have crawled up her ass and died. Wonder what her power is?" pondered Sher quietly.

"My guess is it must be something special if she thinks she can take on the course by her lonesome. I've only ever heard of generals who made it through the course on their own." Beatress responded as she cupped her chin in deep thought.

I waffled on the edge of uncertainty about revealing my gift and decided the only way to earn their trust was to be as honest as possible. Swallowing past the lump in my throat, I threw caution to the wind and offered, "How solo could it be if the person's gift is to manipulate others to do their bidding?"

"Oh? Do tell," Sher purred evilly.

"She's a siren. Her only power is to lure men to do her bidding. I suppose some females might not be immune. Regardless, I'm not sure how that could be considered unassisted?" I replied with a raised eyebrow and a smile.

"And you know this how?" Beatress asked, studying me more carefully.

"My necklace wasn't on when I woke up. As a borrower, I scanned the room on instinct before the General noticed it was off," I replied with hesitation. My nerves were on edge as I watched both of their reactions, trying to gauge if my secret would be a deal-breaker or deal sealer. When they both seemed to regard me in awe, I counted my blessings and knew I'd made the right decision.

"Did you say, borrower? My nan told me they were a myth. What's my gift?" Sher asked with a nervous laugh.

"Shapeshifter. Panther, to be exact. Beatress has an affinity to nature. Zoar can teleport. The doctor can heal, and Jaelel is a mind reader if he's touching you. Although, I've never met another like me, I'm real. You'll have to let your nan know next time you see her," I offered with a wink.

"Holy Shit! Do you know what this means?" Sher challenged as she looked between the two of us enthusiastically.

"Of course. We're going to have an advantage with her on our side," Beatress gushed with praise as she hooked her thumb in my direction.

"Advantage? It'll be more than that if we ally ourselves with the right Sixers. Think about it. Who'd be able to top a borrower with multiple level one powers at her disposal? We'd be an unstoppable force!" Sher fervently raved before she caught my expression of confusion. Sobering quickly, she mumbled, "That's if you want to . . . um . . . uh . . . align yourself with us?"

I snorted in disbelief at my luck before I found myself smiling like a fool and answering just as rashly, "I don't know about being unstoppable, but I'd be honored to be a part of your alliance." On a shrug, I added, "Are you sure you want me? I can be quite a bitch."

"Look who's trying to be modest. Damn girl, you've got it going on. Not only are you rocking a hot bod, but you've got powers and the humility people tend to gravitate toward. I think I speak for both of us when I say the honor is all ours," Sher responded in admiration as she eyed Beatress to see if she would disagree.

Beatress didn't disappoint when she responded, "Oh, yes. Honor is a good description of what I feel and perhaps a dash of fate."

Their apparent acceptance of my uniqueness was a balm I didn't know I needed. A pang of regret crept into my thoughts as I tried to keep my smile genuine and not forced when the general announced our approach to the planet Strixton. The guilt I felt for hiding the reason I was attending the trials threatened my resolve. It'd be easy to forget the mission and just lose myself in the competition, but I knew a lot more was at stake than just my future.

Chapter Fifteen

Saying my nerves were shot would be the understatement of the century. I followed my newfound friends towards the exit. I couldn't help but worry if my disguise would hide me from Kalen. For the sake of the mission, my brain knew I needed it to work, but my heart didn't want to get on board with the plan. As soon as I cleared the hull, I brought my hands up to shield my eyes from the glaring suns as I looked toward the castle and sought out my mate among the crowd. The second my eyes latched onto him, it was just like the first time when the world faded away, and he was the only thing left in my line of vision.

My memory didn't do Kalen justice as I feasted on his male perfection. The dimple from his smile as he addressed Jaelel made me wish I could sprint into his arms and erase going back in time altogether. Making a conscious effort to ignore the calling of his soul, I took a deep breath to remember why I was putting myself through hell and instantly regretted it.

The second I inhaled his unique scent mixed in with the sea breeze, it brought me up short as I grappled with the desire coursing through my veins. It screamed at me that I was making a terrible mistake. The longing and grief it left behind made me feel shallow, empty, and had me questioning if I was doing the right thing. I was seconds away from giving myself up when someone pushed me from behind. I felt myself free-falling and snapped out of my daydream in time to hear Cyn announce, "Oops. I didn't notice that she had stopped."

Never one to be nimble on my feet, I was even more of a klutz in my new body. It all happened so fast, but I'm sure I made an absolute fool of myself as I toppled down the ramp like a tumbleweed. I had no idea how I managed to pull off not taking anyone else down with me, but as I laid sprawled out at the bottom of the ramp staring up at the violet sky, I couldn't help but laugh uncontrollably.

Beatress and Sher rushed to my side, fretting about incessantly, which made me realize my grand entrance was the opposite of staying under the radar. Slapping a hand over my mouth to stifle my outburst, I batted their hands to the side. Rolling over, I got to my hands and knees and froze when I felt Kalen's presence come over me.

His black combat boots came into my field of vision, and I held my breath to find out if Adira's potions would hide me from my mate. My heart felt like it was going to march right out of my chest as I raised my eyes to meet his gaze. Kalen looked stupefied as he studied my face before he offered his hand to help me up. Lost in the moment, I paused mid-reach as I drank him in. He smiled at my obvious attraction and met me halfway. Grabbing my hand, he pulled me to my feet as if I weighed nothing. Stepping forward into my space, he molded me to his body. I reveled in the zing our connection created.

I felt like I was drowning until I remembered I was holding my breath and let it go with a whoosh. I watched Kalen close his eyes in ecstasy and take in a deep breath through his nose. The look of turmoil when he opened his eyes after breathing me in almost broke my heart. Somehow, I knew a part of him recognized me as his mate, but when my smell didn't match what the rest of his body was telling him, he looked wounded and confused.

He searched my eyes one more time before he dropped my hand reluctantly and took a step back. The loss of his touch was almost painful. It took everything I had not to close the distance he'd created between us. Tearing my eyes away from his sorrowful gaze, I stared at his chest and dug my fingernails into my palms. I was mindful enough to stop before I drew blood, unsure if Adira's potion would mask it, and prayed the pain would distract me from the crushing feeling in my chest. Taking a deep breath, I gathered my resolve and whispered my gratitude, "Th..thank you."

I saw him nod in response; remorse evident in his posture before he turned to face Dr. Triste. Raising my eyes, I drank in his scrumptious backside and ached when I watched him run his fingers through his thick black hair. I wanted to be the one grabbing his hair as I brought his mouth down to mine. Slapping my forehead to put an end to my dirty thoughts, I groaned when my memories taunted me. I could almost feel his silky hair running through my fingers when I closed my eyes.

Opening my eyes to reacquaint myself with reality, I dropped my gaze and stared at the ground. Damn, this was going to be more challenging than I thought. Speaking of hard, my nipples were ready to cut glass. Ugh, I needed a cold shower. Kalen didn't seem to be faring any better when his voice cracked as he addressed the doctor. Aware my smell was like an aphrodisiac, I shifted uncomfortably, trying to cross my legs to hide my growing lust. He cleared his throat a couple of times, drawing my attention before he tried again, "Annalise, please escort . . . " he paused and looked back at me, clearly flustered that he didn't know my name.

The deep timbre of his voice sent delicious tremors through me, awakening all of my erotic zones in the process. No matter how hard I tried to contain myself, I was defenseless against my mate. A gasp escaped me when I felt my arousal soak my panties and I watched his eyes dilate in response. Kalen threw up a veil to shield us in a gravity cocoon, giving us a modicum of privacy, before he closed the gap between us and pulled in a deep breath. He growled in response to my arousal, which had a direct link to my libido. My core clenched, and my breath hitched as I lost myself to the sensation he pulled from me without even a touch.

Feeling overwhelmed, I averted my gaze and attempted to recall why I was tormenting myself like this in the first place. I couldn't help but feel like my presence was the catalyst that set the previous attacks in motion. I was crazy to think I could do this on my own, but until I knew for sure the pixie's death wasn't because of me, I needed to follow through with my plan. Thinking of Anolla helped douse the fire burning inside me.

My shoulders slumped and I let my head drop. I took a deep breath to harness the guilt building within me as I worked to control myself around the Strix in front of me. I promised myself if my going back in time didn't alter the events that ultimately lead to my time-travel, I'd drop the farce and beg Kalen for forgiveness. I'd known facing him would be difficult, but I hadn't expected it to be soul-shattering. My mate made an impatient sound threatening my resolve. He reached out slowly, giving me a chance to step away before he lifted my chin with tenderness and asked in a seductive voice, "I need your name, woman."

Knowing I was seconds away from giving myself up if he kept touching me, I raised my chin off his fingers and stepped back. I needed to change the direction our encounter was moving toward if I expected to pull this off. Squaring my shoulders, I gave him what I hoped was the best, back the fuck up glare I could before I layered my voice with annoyance and answered him, "Jade. My name is Jade, and I'd appreciate it if you kept your hands to yourself." I was shaking by the time I was done with my performance and prayed he would mistake my reaction for anger instead of the desolation threatening to devour me.

He cocked his head to the side at my sudden change in demeanor and took in several calming breaths. It felt like hours passed as he continued to drink me in before he finally shook his head and said in a gruff voice, "I'm sorry. I don't know what came over me."

Shaking his head, Kalen dropped the shield with a flick of his hand and mumbled under his breath as he stalked toward me, "Get a hold of yourself. She's not your mate."

Whether it was intentional or not, he ignored my request to keep his hands to himself and placed his hand at the small of my back as he directed me toward Annalise. His touch short-circuited my ruse and made me forget I was supposed to be mad at him as I glided forward in a trance. Kalen stood taller and assumed a more professional demeanor when he addressed the doctor like nothing had happened, "Please escort Jade to the medical ward and ensure she didn't sustain any serious injuries."

My mind was so focused on the tingles his touch granted that I almost missed his order to have me ushered away. There was no way I could afford to miss hearing the rules a second time. I needed to be at that meeting, so I knew what to expect in the coming days. Knowledge and a whole lot of luck would be the only way I'd survive the trials.

Shaking my head to clear the haze plaguing my thoughts, I stepped out of his reach again before I finally spoke, "That won't be necessary. Nothing was broken or hurting . . . Well, besides my pride, I guess." Proud of the strength my voice held, I risked a glance at Kalen before I shrugged and added, "Really, I'm alright. I'm just going to join my friends."

The look of astonishment when I didn't follow his command brought a smile to my face. I found I liked surprising the possessive male. I hooked my thumb over my shoulder and glanced in Beatress and Sher's general direction. Ensuring my path was relatively clear, I backed up slowly. I needed distance between us before my resolve completely broke down and my libido took over.

Kalen tensed and looked like he was seconds away from dragging me back to his side when Dr. Triste, bless her soul, placed a hand tentatively on his arm and broke the spell binding us. I knew she meant well, but I barely stopped myself from growling with jealousy as my eyes lingered on the hand, daring to touch my mate.

Either sensing her impending death or the tension rolling off me like a nuclear blast, she quickly removed her hand from my man. The primal part of me basked in her discomfort until I remembered myself and wished I could crawl under a rock with embarrassment. Never one to stake a claim on a male, my actions were doing a poor job of acting like the king's presence didn't mess with me on a personal level.

Annalise must have been a saint in her former life when she acknowledged my non-apparent claim with a nod and a knowing smile. Ensuring she had my attention, the doctor made sure her true intentions were on display before she addressed Kalen with caution, "My liege, she speaks the truth. Her fall didn't cause her harm. I highly recommend she joins her comrades and attends the festivities." Expelling the breath I was holding, I waited with bated breath for his answer.

Chapter Sixteen

Not showing an ounce of discomfort from his display of dominance over me, Kalen ignored the crowd around us and gave the doctor his full attention. I watched in awe as he shuttered all emotion in the blink of an eye, donning his kingly persona, pretending like our latest interlude did not affect him. Granted, His Lordship was something to behold. His very presence commanded the attention of those around him. He oozed confidence, and his power felt all-consuming. The loss of his attention had me wishing I had his ability and could shut off my feelings without a second thought.

I wasn't sure if he was trying to coat me in his essence or prove he was top dog, but it almost felt like he was flaunting his stuff like a proud peacock. Gravity, drenched in his spirit, caressed every inch of me. He was reminding me of what I was missing. Either that or he was trying to scare off everyone else that would challenge his authority or recent actions. I'd almost forgotten my original request to join my friends when his voice broke through my haze. "As long as she is capable of participating in the trials, her health doesn't matter to me either way. If you'll excuse me, Annalise, Councilman Bastian wanted a word with me."

I shouldn't have been surprised when Kalen flashed away without a second glance, but his total disregard for our connection flayed me open. He wasn't supposed to be interested in me for this to work, but his statement was like salt on an open wound. I cringed at the rejection evident in his words and then chastised myself for letting my feelings rule my actions. I couldn't take his brush off personally. He wouldn't be acting like an asshole if I hadn't chosen this crazy, fucked up path in the first place. I needed to focus on why I'm here. I was here to uncover who wanted to oust my mate. If I was successful, then everything could go back to normal.

Annalise's eyes flashed to mine. The look of pity evident in her gaze had me wishing the floor would open up and hide me from my humiliation. Turning abruptly to hide my reaction, I hustled toward my peeps with my head held high and a fake smile plastered on my face, pretending for all I was worth like the last five minutes didn't happen. If they wouldn't drop it, I could downplay and outright deny our interaction. I'd beg if it came down to it.

I tried to ignore the conflicting vibe I received from the group congregating around us as I approached my friends. Some regarded me as a pariah, but a few acted like I was the coming messiah. Not going to lie, it was a massive stroke to my ego, but the sensible side of me discarded their false adoration as part of the job. People's opinions shouldn't matter, but I found it hard to overlook when I considered most of those gathered would be my comrades during the next few days.

A loner at heart, partly due to my adoption, but mostly because of my ability, this new world was going to be hard to navigate. I was still open to adventure, but something told me this would be more like a crusade. The real game would be decoding who could be trusted and ensuring I stayed at least more than one step ahead of my opponents.

I was thankful non-verbal signals were universal when Beatress and Sher both clamped their mouths shut at my frazzled state when I stopped in front of them with my crazy smile and gave a slight shake of my head. I was in no mood to rehash my run-in with the sexy male while everyone was in earshot. Especially when they weren't even remotely trying to pretend like they weren't hanging on every word I said. Refusing to cry, I whispered past the lump in my throat, "Later. Ask me later, please."

The solidarity I felt when they both nodded their heads in agreement and stepped to either side of me was unexpected. Unspoken loyalty was a precious commodity, and I prayed I could prove I was worth the chance they were placing in me. Not to mention I hoped my trust in them didn't come back to bite me in the ass later. With both women at my side, I choked back all of the warring emotions churning within me and marched forward. Blocking out the obvious audience, I visualized my purpose and thought about my next steps.

One thing was for sure . . . I needed to stay away from Onyx. Avoiding a confrontation with her and her cronies should keep me off her radar. I wasn't sure what set her off the first time when I approached their group, but it would be easier for me to observe who she might be in cahoots with if I wasn't public enemy number one. To do that, it was vital to locate her so I could keep her in my periphery.

Not wanting to seem flighty or nervous, I searched the crowd periodically as we made our way to the palace. I was about to give up when I spotted her standing next to her despicable uncle, sporting the look of an innocent angel. I had no idea who she was trying to butter up, but her fake laugh made me want to gag. She was flirting shamelessly, and it made me feel sorry for the bastard on the other end. Knowing the culprit could be a possible suspect, I used my newfound height and stood on my tiptoes to see who she was talking to.

I couldn't help the growl that escaped when I found Kalen on the receiving end of her antics. Seconds away from storming over there, ripping her to shreds and publicly claiming my mate, I barely registered the claws Sher was digging into my arm to restrain me. The pain brought some clarity to my thought process seconds before she drew blood. In the back of my mind, I knew there would be no way to conceal myself if Kalen was able to smell my blood, which brought me up short. Looking over at her, I hoped my eyes portrayed my gratitude as I squeezed her hand in thanks. I was fairly sure she understood when she relaxed her grip and patted my arm with empathy before she released me as nothing had happened.

The distraction gave me a reason to pause as I assessed the situation instead of overreacting without a thought for the consequences. My eyes took in the scene as we approached them, and it didn't take me long to realize Kalen was only going through the motions as the lord and king of his people. His apparent disinterest only seemed to make Onyx try harder in her attempt to gain his favor.

Smart me would have kept my head down as I passed by them on my way through the palace doors. Smart me would have tried everything in her power to go unnoticed, but let's face it, I was not thinking with my brain when I opened my mouth and insulted the very person I was trying to avoid, "Poor girl must be desperate. She should learn to take a hint when someone's not interested."

I wished I could take it back the second the words were out of my mouth, but the resulting grin that flashed across Kalen's face before he had the sense to cover it was the highlight of my day. The high didn't last long, though, when my gaze took in the look of death Onyx was shooting my way. It made her outsides match the ugliness of her insides. The look didn't help me feel any better. It only solidified the sinking feeling in the pit of my soul that said she would stop at nothing to take me out of the picture.

Instead of laying low so I could suss out the bad guys from the good guys, my jealousy had made my situation worse than the last time I was here. On the verge of doing something even more regretful, like begging for her forgiveness, I panicked when I drew a blank on how I could fix the mess I had created for myself. Beatress must have been a saint in her previous life when she decided to be my friend. Without having any knowledge of why I said what I said, she somehow picked up on my mistake when she joined my offhand conversation, "Oh, I know. I think she finally got the hint when his boyfriend slinked up to him and gave him a welcome meant to be shared in private, if you know what I mean. It was absolutely scandalous."

Sher being a bit behind on what the hell had just happened, didn't disappoint the girl code when she nodded enthusiastically in response before adding, "Aren't the good ones always taken."

Not one to look a gift horse in the mouth, I smiled sheepishly at Kalen, Onyx, and Bastian and took the easy out. Averting my eyes to my friends, I gratefully played along, "You're telling me. Thankfully I've got a rather good gaydar. It's saved me from that same fate a couple of times."

It was pure hell not to let my eyes stray to the group one more time to see if any of them bought into Beatress' epic save. I'd owe her big time for sure if it worked. My shoulders deflated ever so slightly with guilt as I considered the ramifications of my actions when we passed through the palace doors. I couldn't believe I had almost sabotaged my whole reason for traveling back in time just because I was envious that some bitch was flirting with my man. It would be better if I could avoid seeing him because I had a feeling it would only get harder for me until this was all over.

Especially when I remembered as a virile male without a mate, he would have needs. Yeah, there was no way I'd be able to stand by and watch something like that. I couldn't draw attention to the connection between us, or I'd blow my cover. Time to stuff everything I was feeling into a box. No scratch that, cardboard wouldn't hold my shit back. What I needed was a safe, something like Fort Knox, with multiple layers of protection.

Straightening up, I stole a peek at my companions, and a piece of my heart thawed a little at the look of compassion and understanding they both wore as we came to a stop at the bottom of the stairs. Neither of them was pushing me to reveal why I thought it was an excellent idea to commit social suicide, but I could tell they would converge on me when we were alone. Grateful for the reprieve, I gave them a tight smile and hoped it conveyed I appreciated their silence.

Wishing I could veer us directly into the great room so I could hide in a corner for a minute was tempting, but the act would indicate I had something to be uncomfortable or guilty about.

Anxious to find out what and where the trials were, I wished I had a remote control that would allow me to skip to the good parts.

Trying to ignore Sher and Bea's concerned looks as they whispered back and forth from behind me, I sized up the competition and tried to guess what their gifts could be. I needed to find out when we'd have access to our powers because I was vulnerable without it. Kalen's concern for my safety had been sweet, but after learning how his mother died, I realized protecting myself sans my gift would be necessary for my survival.

I couldn't deny my curiosity. If I were lucky, someone around me would be able to read minds, and I could use it to explore Onyx's mind and find the smoking gun I needed to connect her to the crime. I had no idea what her gift was, but I highly doubted she'd be stupid enough to use it against Anolla. One could always hope. She behaved like she was hot shit, which could either mean she was flaunting her stuff or covering up for her lack of abilities.

As the foyer filled up with the other participants, I squared my shoulders and scanned the second-floor balcony for signs of Cenara. According to my calculations, she should be waltzing down the staircase at any moment. I didn't remember it taking this long the last time I was here. If I was honest with myself, it most likely had something to do with the fact I had been in shock. I was trying to absorb and assimilate all that was foreign and new around me.

If I didn't get control of the warring emotions swirling within me, I'd be a mess by the time we even started. Determined to not pass out from hyperventilating, I slowed my breathing and concentrated on what I needed out of this meet and greet. I needed to learn what kind of things we would be facing in the trials and choose who I would align myself with.

My imagination ran wild with the possibilities. Would we be subjected to a series of tests while judges graded us? That possibility seemed too easy. I conjured images of obstacle courses cholk-full of monsters and booby traps. With what little information I'd gathered, I was leaning towards something in the middle. I knew we could choose to work alone or together, but I was a little unclear on the challenges themselves. I threw up a silent prayer of thanks when Cenara descended the stairs and called our attention.

I never thought I'd be happy to be herded like cattle, but I was practically skipping after Cenara's announcement to gather in the great room. I'm sure my friends were questioning my mental stability. Having witnessed a full gamut of emotions in a matter of moments, they had to be asking themselves what they were getting involved in. I would be. I needed to do some damage control. Time to prove to them I wasn't crazy. Taking a deep breath, I took a gamble and tried for a bit of the truth, "Thanks for covering for me back there. I was feeling a little jealous and have no idea what came over me. I swear normally, I'm more in control of myself. Truly. I owe you guys."

Beatress cocked her head to the side, studying me before she responded, "Don't mention it. That's what friends are for. Trust me, Onyx isn't someone you want to be enemies with."

"You're from different planets. How do you know each other?"

"My aunt and her uncle are on the council. We've attended some of the same functions over the years. She's a spoiled brat but powerful. She always had a posse of disciples; for reasons I was never able to understand. I think it'd be best if we keep our distance from her," Beatress finished in a whisper as more trial participants entered the room.

My eyebrows shot up to the ceiling at Beatress's revelation. She had insider information, and although I didn't want to pester her overmuch, knowledge was power, and I needed the edge, "Did she ever reveal what her power was?"

"She's a strong terra-elemental. I believe her specialty is chalcedony."

Sher piped up, saving me from revealing I had no idea what she was talking about. "What's chal-see-donkey?"

Instead of looking down at Sher's ignorance, Beatress smiled fondly and simply stated the facts, somehow making it feel like she wasn't schooling us as she educated us. "It's a type of quartz made up of a microcrystalline structure, like jasper, agate, and onyx. She can make weapons, bridges, and walls of the stuff. Not someone we want to make an enemy of."

Sher whistled quietly and elbowed us, as the topic of our discussion entered the room with an entourage of disciples at her heels. I wanted to pester her for more information, but whatever I was thinking left my brain when I noticed Anolla among the group surrounding Onyx. They'd been at the same table the night she died, so it shouldn't have shocked me to see them together, but it did make me wonder what caused Onyx to take her out in the first place. Initially, I thought it might have been a random act, but the fact that they knew each other had me reevaluating motives.

Nudging Beatress, I nodded my head toward their group. I covered my mouth and quietly said under my breath, "Do you know the pixie?"

Beatress quickly scanned their group and hissed, "Yes. Her name is Anolla, and her Aunt Clary is a member of the council. Why do you ask?"

Not wanting to reveal my cards too soon, I threw out a lame excuse as I continued to study their group, "It's the first time I've seen someone with wings. Since you're the only one I know that has any connections, I figured it was worth a shot asking you."

"If you think wings are cool, you'd be even more impressed with Castice's gold and red display. He's a Phoenix Gryphon hybrid. His wings are a thing to behold." Dropping her head to hide the blush, coloring her cheeks, she added, "I mean for wings, they're pretty cool." Clearing her throat, she raised her head and said, "He's the only other person I knew before coming here. His Aunt Fansa is also on the council."

Looking over the two males in their group, I deduced the blond with the gold and red highlights was the male she referred to. I had a hard time imagining the bald hulk standing next to him with a full set of feathers. I might be stereotyping, but my money would be on the blond if I were a betting woman. As I processed this new information, I found it hard to believe it was a coincidence that both of the victims were close to Onyx. I just needed to find the connection. My mind was full of theories as I watched their interaction. I was zeroing in on a small spat between Onyx and Anolla that seemed to unfold before my very eyes. I hedged forward. I needed to hear what they were saying.

Nudging my way in their direction as inconspicuous as I could manage, my steps halted when I heard Onyx growl in annoyance, "I need to know what she's hiding. When did you grow a conscience?"

"Since the last time we were together, and my fairy dust mentally damaged that poor girl. I'm not ready to ruin another person's life. I'm here because I have a gift, and these people will help me hone it for the good. I don't care what you say. I'm not doing it. Grow up, Onyx. Until you become queen, you are not the boss of me." Anolla flitted away angrily as Cenara called order to the room, drowning out her last statement. But I could have sworn I heard her say, "Which I highly doubt will happen!"

Chapter Seventeen

Still reeling from the conversation I overheard, my mind went into overdrive as I tried to fill in the blanks. Assumptions were never anyone's best friend, but my instincts screamed they were talking about me. I highly doubted Onyx was aware of my time-travel, but if I valued my life, I shouldn't dismiss it either. Kalen's reaction to my presence was not something I could hide or take back. Our attraction to each other was on display for everyone to see. It might not have been as apparent as our first interaction, but it was enough to cause concern. When I looked at it from that point of view, it wasn't a far-fetched idea; she merely considered me as her competition. Considering the last time I was here she declared she was the king's mate, it made sense Onyx wanted to eliminate anybody she felt threatened by.

Cenara clapped her hands from the front of the room, pulling me from my thoughts before she addressed the room, "May I have your attention, please!" When it took another minute before the chatter died down, she was barely able to conceal her annoyance at having to corral a bunch of adults acting like children. Putting a fake smile on her face, she announced, "Listen up, everyone. I know some of you are itching to get started because you think you know all the rules but humor me for a minute. I'm positive you're going to want to hear the NEW things we have planned for the trials this year." Pausing for effect, as the room erupted into chatter, Cenara waited for everyone to quiet down before she continued, "I thought that might get your attention."

A few snickers could be heard in the crowd. With a wave of her hand Cenara levitated into the air. The act in itself was cool until I noticed the source of her power. She was using the air of her hecklers to fuel her wind supply. I was seconds away from interfering and ruining any chance I had at being successful when the people in question slumped to the floor, gasping for breath. Thank goodness they were alive. Cenara floated to the ground slowly, oblivious to gasps throughout the room. Her gaze raked the room in an open challenge. When it was apparent no one would oppose her, and she controlled the conversation, she continued, "That's better. Please hold ALL remarks, and sounds, for that matter, until I'm finished. I'll leave the floor open for questions I didn't already cover during my spiel. However, I want to make it perfectly clear, there is nothing you or I can do about reversing the changes made. So save yourself the trouble, work hard, and accept the hand you've been dealt."

When silence followed, she nodded once and continued, "A week ago, planets in our alliance launched a formal complaint. It seems they feel there are those of you who have an unfair advantage with our current system. To be more specific, since positions ride on placement in the trials, they claim anyone with past knowledge has a higher possibility of success. In particular, they refer to descendants or relatives of past trial participants; considering the trials have never been altered, they have a point. In addition, a second motion was also included in the complaint asking to bar all relatives of the current council from the competition."

Beatress gasped next to me but held her tongue as Anolla, Castice and Onyx raised their voices in outrage. Knowing the four near me were council relatives, I was surprised when a commotion to my right drew my attention to a fifth council relative. Beatress didn't mention knowing him. It made me wonder why not. Two men struggled to hold back a man with light brown wavy hair and golden highlights. One was holding his arms and the other covering his mouth. He stood a little over seven feet and looked like a golden god. His skin shimmered like it was covered in glitter, contradicting his snarling demeanor. Technically, his silent attempt wasn't breaking her request, but it didn't look like his friends were willing to find out.

Silently cursing myself for not taking the time to learn everything I could before jumping back in time, I studied the reactions of his companions. I contemplated their abilities as they struggled but maintained their hold on him. Outward appearances could be deceptive, and even though they weren't short by any means and were holding their own, Golden Boy had more than a foot on them. One of them looked deathly ill. His stark white hair and violet eyes stood out against his skintight black outfit. If I had seen him alone on the street, I would have bet money he had one foot in the grave. The fact that he was one of two holding back the golden boy made me wonder if it was all a disguise. If he was trying to look like the undead, his albino goth vibe went a long way in pulling it off.

The other guy sported electric blue hair and had skin so pale it was almost see-through. With everything visible, it was hard not to miss the metal skeletal structure running throughout his body. If I had to guess, I would say he was some kind of cyborg. I watched in fascination as his muscles contracted and retracted as he worked to hold back his companion. Shifting my gaze to Cenara, I waited for her reaction to the discord. I willed my heart to calm as I weighed the odds of what would happen next. Would she suck the life out of the four making a scene, which included my arch-nemesis? Did I want that to happen before I knew her real purpose? Fuck! Too many questions.

Cenara's voice cut through the montage circling my brain when she cried, "Enough!" I felt the word tremble throughout my body. When the cries and movement froze on the lips of Castice, Onyx, and Anolla, I began to appreciate our babysitter's abilities. Shifting my gaze to the fifth descendant, I was relieved to see him no worse for the wear. He shook off his companions and glowered at them, silently conveying he had control of himself while at the same time telling them to back the fuck off. He straightened to his full height, which must have been more than seven feet, and did an excellent job of acting like he could not care less that everyone in the room was ogling him. You could tell the attention happened often.

Clearing her throat Cenara said, "I trust we won't have to do that again." With one eyebrow raised in challenge, she looked about the room one more time before she continued, "Alright, moving on. As I said before, the motion was placed, but if you had let me continue, you would have heard me say we DID NOT accept. While it's not often, it isn't unusual for the council's descendants to end up as participants. What is uncommon, though, about this year's trials is that there are five. It's a well-known fact that most of them know each other and had ample opportunities to form bonds, putting us in a precarious situation. Although those on the council agreed with the council's notion, relatives might have an unfair advantage. They also realized we couldn't afford to exclude five powerful Sixers based solely on family ties. So, they altered the rules to give everyone a fair chance in a show of solidarity.

As you all know, positions are determined by how well you compete over the next three days. In the past, you were allowed to choose who or if you worked with anyone. Well, not anymore. Starting tomorrow, we will split into five groups based on your abilities, and those people will be your team for the duration of the trials. We tried to make them as even as possible, but considering what we had to work with, it was a little tricky. Each team can win regardless if they feel they are underpowered. You might have to get creative, but it's possible. As you know, it is in our best interest if you succeed, and for that reason, I promise we will do everything in our power to keep you safe.

Which brings me to the next topic of interest. We moved the location of the trials. Instead of using the obstacle courses in our controlled arena here on planet Strixton, the powers that be have decided to use real-world situations and environments to test you. We selected three planets based on the following criteria. They had to have breathable air, hazardous terrain, and many beasties to weed out the weak. In other words, you'll find monsters but shouldn't come across an intelligent species that could aid you in your endeavors. Daily, we'll drop the teams off at an equal distance from the finish line with nothing but the clothes on your back, a map, and the abilities of your teammates to get you to the extraction point by sundown the same day. Placement will not only be based on how quickly you get to the extraction points but also on how well you work together as a team. Your time will stop when the last member of your team reports in. Instructors will be watching and they'll make every effort to ensure your safety. However, we've never done this before, and nothing in life is guaranteed. Now that you've all been so gracious in not interrupting me, I'll open the floor for questions before I continue. Remember, I'm not here to listen to you bitch about your lot in life. No need to bring up the unchangeable."

Surprisingly enough, a timid girl close to the front was the bravest among us when she asked, "Why are there five teams?"

Cenara did little to hide her annoyance when she rolled her eyes and responded, "Seriously!" With a big sigh of defeat, she shook her head and said, "I would think that would be obvious, but let me spell it out. There are twenty-five contestants and five council descendants. To keep the five from working together, we split them up into five teams. Mathematically that means each team will have five members. Makes sense, right?" Without waiting for the girl who was now cherry red with embarrassment to reply, Cenara moved on, "Next question."

"What's stopping the new locations from being leaked?" A guy called out from behind me.

"The rules could have been leaked but seeing as each team has one council descendant, we figured it puts everyone on the same playing field. However, the council didn't choose the locations. We're fairly confident no one will have an edge over anyone else. Next question."

"What happens if we don't make it to the extraction point or if no one makes it?" Zoar asked with his tail tucked between his legs.

"With the power levels in this room, I'm fairly confident it will be a race to the finish. One I'm looking forward to watching, but as I mentioned earlier, we'll have guards posted for your safety. Someone will be on standby, if your team finds themselves in dire need of assistance. Next question."

"Wait. If someone rescues us, how does that play into our placement? Are you looking for our best two out of three?" Asked a stout man standing next to me with long black hair.

"In the real world, if you fuck up, you could get yourself and those around you killed. No second chances. No best two out of three. Just game over. So, let me ask you this: Do you think someone in need of rescuing deserves to be number one?"

As the guy next to me opened his mouth to answer, Cenara interrupted him and said, "If you're smart, you won't answer that question. We're looking for the best of the best to fill our top positions. Simply put, you're not the best if we have to rescue you. Everyone will have a spot based on how they perform. This is a test, treat it as such, and you'll do fine. Next question."

Before I could stop myself, I blurted out what I was sure everyone was dying to know, "When do we find out who's on our team?"

"Thank you. It's about time someone asked a valid question. You'll meet your teammates tomorrow morning on the dropship. That is also when you'll be able to access your gifts. Not much time to collaborate, but we want to see how you think on your toes. Any other questions?" When the room remained silent Cenara said, "Very well; next on the agenda is food, before we move on to sleeping quarters."

When Cenara's spiel turned to specifics of mealtimes and the like, my mind wandered back to my mission. The whole point of coming back in time was to get close enough to Onyx to figure out her end game and stop her before she had a chance to carry it out. That would be hard to accomplish if I were on another team or dead, for that matter? The thought of death made me regret my decision, even more when it occurred to me that I might never get the chance to hold my soulmate again. There was no way I was going to let that happen. People were counting on me. They might not know it, but they were. It was time to get serious and use my time wisely. Now more than ever, I missed my gift and would be counting down the seconds until I had it back. It made it that much harder to plan when I didn't know what I was working with.

Beatress bumped my shoulder, snapping me back to the present when she whispered, "I am so sorry. You can sleep in our room tonight if you want."

"Huh? What are you talking about?" I whispered back.

"Were you not paying attention just now? Cenara assigned roommates and you are the unlucky soul to be bunking with Onyx tonight!" Sher quietly replied as she looked over at me with pity shining through her fluorescent green eyes.

Chapter Eighteen

My eyes flew to the bitch in question, and I wasn't surprised to find her staring at me with hatred evident in her eyes. Shit! I wasn't sure if it were luck or lack thereof, but at least I'd have ample opportunity to figure out what Onyx was up to if we were sleeping in the same room every night. However, that would only work if I made it back each night and didn't get myself killed during the trials. Oh, and I also needed to make sure she didn't learn what I was up to at the same time. Speaking of which, I would need to find time to visit Adira and Natashia before bed. There was no way I could risk anything wearing off while sleeping. Not something I needed my enemy knowing. Damn, I wonder what else I missed while lost in my thoughts? I choked on my saliva when Beatress responded, "Depends on when you checked out. Did you miss the bit about the formal celebration dinner being held tonight in our honor?"

Sher pounded on my back as people filed out of the room. I waited until we were the last ones left before I held up my hand in surrender, cleared my throat, and whispered, "Thanks. I didn't realize I had said anything out loud. Um . . . did she say what we were doing between now and then?"

Beatress and Sher looked at me with their eyebrows raised before they each grabbed an arm and dragged me with them. Sher smiled sweetly at a passing servant before she finally answered me, "You want the short version or the long?"

Cringing at my stupidity, I gave myself a mental slap. There was no way I'd get out of this in one piece and save the day if my head was in the clouds. I swallowed past the lump in my throat and quietly replied, "I'll take the short version, please."

"You got it. First, we tour the palace and the surrounding grounds. Then lunch at the pavilion. Next, we get a physical and any necessary shots before we get our uniforms. I think we have an hour or so after that to get ready for dinner."

"Shots? Why the hell would we need shots?" I exclaimed with a gasp. I hated needles with every nerve ending in my body. I blinked when it hit me that I never once feared or got squeamish when I felt or even thought of Kalen's fangs. Even though technically they were just larger, shorter versions of my childhood fear. In fact, a ripple of awareness fluttered through my body when I recalled what he had done with them the last time we were together, which made me miss him even more.

"Why wouldn't we get shots? For one, I would refuse to step foot on a foreign planet without a few immunities to the beasties we encounter. I would hate to end up like my Uncle Reamus and his village," Beatress replied with a shudder.

I waited for her to continue, and when she remained silent, I elbowed her ribs and said, "You can't just end it like that! What happened to your uncle?"

"Oh, sorry, I was lost in a memory. My uncle contracted celluloplantaceous from a fern pixie while peeing. I guess you could say she wasn't too happy he used her home as a place to relieve himself," Beatress answered with an innocent shrug.

"What's celluloplantaceous?"

"It's a disease caused by the rydlynch fungi found in the saliva of the fern pixie. As the bite festers, it releases microscopic spores into the air that can infect others. Those unlucky enough to inhale the spores will face excruciating pain as their skin cells morph into fungus cells. The disease requires treatment within twenty-four hours, or it develops a root system. It will literally plant itself in the ground and consume its host. Leaving nothing but a beautiful purple spotted mushroom in its place. Sadly, we lost everyone from my uncle's village. My father and his men burned the village to the ground and poisoned the land. Their way of preventing it from spreading further. It's considered an infectious species. The area is still barren centuries later and is a constant reminder to my people to be humble. Even with all of our powers, we are not invincible and should take every precaution available to us."

"Fine, I need the shots. Doesn't mean I have to like them," I muttered with indifference.

"Wicked. I always knew there was a reason why I hated mushrooms. Why didn't someone go back in time and have your uncle aim in a different spot?" Sher asked in contemplation.

"Our elders forbid it. Fern pixies can be vindictive. No one was willing to risk another exposure and possible outbreak," Beatress whispered back as we caught up to our group.

"How did you know how he contracted it?" I asked as Cenara ushered everyone into a gymnasium or coliseum of some sort with large granite columns leading into an inner arena. Huge double arched doors guarded by uniformed trolls blocked our view. I may have stumbled a bit as my eyes did a double-take. In the past couple of days, I'd seen plenty, but somehow the presence of a couple of fairy tale trolls dressed in black fatigues had me questioning my mental stability. Luckily, my friends paid no attention to my strange behavior as they pushed me toward the outer stairwell.

"My cousin is an echoer," Beatress added matter-of-factly like that was all the information I would need. She must have seen the look of confusion on my face when she said, "He can replay events of the past, and sometimes if something is premeditated, events of the future. His gift uses the echo of time to reflect things back to him as if he's watching it from a mirror image. It comes in handy as a lawman when he can project those images or videos into the minds of those around him. He has a hundred percent success rate. It helps that he only takes on those he knows he can defend."

I was about to ask if she'd ever seen his gift in action when Cenara's next statement caught my attention. Our guide held up her finger as she grabbed onto the door handle. She waited for us to be quiet before she continued, "Normally, this area is off-limits to Sixers before their initiation, but seeing as we'll no longer be competing in this space, I thought it would be an interesting addition to our tour. This building serves as our training facilities the majority of the year and will be home to quite a few of you once you join our army. If I timed this right, we'd be able to witness some of our men and women in action. They scheduled a scrimmage this morning since the majority of our forces were here for the trials. Nothing like watching the young Sixers try and defeat the big guys. Rumor has it even the king plans on joining in on the fun."

My heart flipped with longing at the possibility of seeing my mate again. I pinched myself to bring myself back to reality as Cenara pulled the door to the stairwell open with a flourish. I couldn't afford to lose myself to the thought of his presence. I forced myself to move forward as we entered the stairwell one at a time. I jumped when she patted me on the shoulder with false encouragement as I passed. A shiver of warning worked its way up my spine when I heard the roar of a fired-up crowd cheering behind me. With trepidation, I entered the metal stairway and forced myself to climb. I wasn't sure I could control my reactions if Kalen were injured or hurt in front of me. I knew our group was passing through, and a small part of me hoped he was late to the party, but the piece of my soul connected to him knew he was already here.

Gasping for breath by the time we reached the top, I promised myself if I made it through the next several days, I would devote myself to a healthier lifestyle. Pushing myself to the front of the room needlessly as we crowded into an all-glass room had me thanking the stars I wasn't afraid of heights. The viewing room was suspended from the ceiling and gave us an unimpeded 360-degree view of the gruesome scene below. It was hard to justify the carnage when they were supposedly on the same team. As an outsider looking in, it appeared they were trying to kill each other.

A massive implosion in the center of the room drew my attention as I covered my ears protectively. It shouldn't have surprised me to find the man who starred in every wet dream I'd ever had to be at the center of the action. Rows of Sixers writhing on the ground in front of him were a testament to his power. The onslaught should have been a huge turn-off, but I found myself rubbing my legs back and forth to relieve the throbbing need between my legs. Eager to move on, I sidestepped the goth guy from earlier and tripped over my own two feet in my eagerness to escape the pull Kalen had on me.

Throwing my arms out to catch my fall, I squealed in surprise when warm hands jerked me to a stop, but not before I bit my lip in the process. The golden boy from earlier held me in place a moment longer than necessary before he deposited me on my feet and released me with reluctance. Swallowing thickly, he said, "Careful there, little one, I'd hate to see that silky skin marred in any way."

Oblivious to his physical response to me, I sucked on the injured lip and murmured, "A little bruise or scar, for that matter, only add character, in my opinion. Thanks for the save anyway." I pushed my way toward the blinking sign on the wall and prayed it was an exit. I sighed in relief when the door clicked closed behind me, leaving me to gather my unraveling thoughts—barely giving the desolate metal platform that overlooked the proceedings a second thought. I closed my eyes and took in a deep breath, only to cringe seconds later when the fighting below reached my ears. Counting the seconds until the tour moved on, I risked a glance over the edge and gasped. My mate was no longer in the center of the room. No, instead, he was headed right for me. Mindless in his approach, he shoved everyone out of the way and scaled the wall directly below the platform I was standing on.

Chapter Nineteen

Scrambling backward, I plastered myself to the wall. Why was Kalen headed my way. Until it hit me, I was bleeding. My hand flew to my split lip. Shit on a shingle, I was bleeding. Looking left, I contemplated if I'd have enough time to open the door and immerse myself within the group to buy myself some time but thought better of it when I heard and felt his possessive growl. No matter how much I wanted to move, his distress called to me. Frozen in place, I trembled with desire and a little bit of fear. Knowing full well I'd be in a load of trouble when my mate realized what I had been up to. Gah! If only I had access to my powers!

I drew in a trembling breath, sucking the injured lip into my mouth as Kalen vaulted the railing and landed in front of me with his head bowed and one knee bent. He reminded me of Superman or some kind of superhero. My ladybits flared to life as I looked at the specimen in front of me. Muscles bulging from tension, he stayed crouched, ready to pounce. He flipped around and assessed the area for my would-be attackers. When he was sure I was in no danger, he stood to his full height and inhaled deeply. A shudder pulsed through his body before he turned to assess me. I could tell the moment he recognized me from earlier as a look of confusion replaced the pure wonder stamped on his face moments before. I barely contained a squeal when he flashed to me, and his eyes searched my face for answers. I felt my resolve slipping and knew it wouldn't be long before I folded and begged him for forgiveness as my body and soul succumbed to the inevitableness of us.

My fight or flight instincts finally decided it was time to kick in as he leaned in to take a giant whiff. He must have noticed or anticipated my intention because before I could move a muscle, he pressed forward, caging me within his arms. Grinding his hips into my womanhood, he let me feel how excited he was to see me. Using my attraction to his advantage, he buried his face in my neck and inhaled deeply. He pulled away from my hair and snarled when the smell he was expecting to find didn't match my blood. I cringed at the look of frustration plastered on his face as I struggled to hold my breath. I knew the second I let it go; he'd find the evidence he was looking for. My eyes started to water, every cell in my body screaming for air. Looking up at the ceiling, I prayed for a miracle. I was no closer to finding out who was trying to kill us and take over the empire my mate had created. This couldn't be the end of my adventure.

Divine intervention couldn't have come at a better time as the door to my left slammed open. Kalen crouched as he turned to face the door. It shouldn't have surprised me when Golden Boy and his two friends stormed out onto the platform ready to defend me, but when Beatress and Sher pushed their way to the front, I slumped forward in defeat. A part of me appreciated the support these two girls willingly gave after only knowing me for a matter of hours. At the same time, the rational part of me feared for their safety as they butted their noses into something they didn't understand. They showed more loyalty than some of my closest allies. My family and close friends treated me worse for far more trivial matters, but there was no way they could know what they were stepping into. I'm sure they would rather be anywhere else if they realized they were getting between a Strix and his fated mate.

Kalen flipped around, ensuring he placed himself between the newcomers and me, and let loose a roar that rattled the metal platform we were standing on. If my friends were smart, they'd cower in his presence, but instead, Sher took a step forward, showing courage when she cut to the chase and demanded an explanation for his behavior. "Lord Kalen, unless you claim the woman behind you as your mate, I demand to know why you are scaring my friend with your brutish behavior."

If I weren't seconds from passing out, I would have hailed her bravery. Instead, I prayed she could see the gratitude in my eyes as unwanted tears invaded my vision and black spots threatened to pull me under. Not wanting my friends to pay the price of my rebellion, I reached out tentatively, my whole body shaking as I placed my hand on his back to get his attention. His already rigid form felt like it turned to stone in response. A far cry from our previous interactions, he peered over his shoulder at me with a look that said I meant nothing to him. I dropped my hand as if he burned me and cringed when he snarled, "I claim nothing! Cenara! These quarters are off-limits. Take our guests and leave this area immediately!"

"Of course, my lord," Cenara replied with a bow. Turning her attention to our group, she pointed to the door I'd come through and said, "You heard the king, everyone out!"

Even with all of my knowledge and the minuscule connection my soul was sure we still had, it was hard not to take his comment personally. Most of my brain was well aware when I finished this crazy mission, he would prove his love for me a billion times over, but the small, insecure and utterly human portion of my brain felt devastated by his declaration. My mouth dropped open to apologize and with it the breath I'd been holding. I realized my mistake the second Kalen inhaled sharply and released his breath on a shudder. Slapping a hand over my mouth, I peered at him through my lashes. I couldn't help the shiver that ran up and down my spine at the look of possession in his eyes. He closed the distance between us with a single step and grabbed both of my wrists. Yanking me into him, my hands landed on his chest before he flashed us away with my next breath.

The second we appeared in his bedroom, I pushed against him to put some distance between us. Only to groan out in frustration when he didn't move a millimeter. "Dammit, Kalen! Let me go!"

Something told me it was the familiarity in which I used his name, rather than the actual demand, that made him listen to me. So when he opened his arms wide, I stepped away quickly before he could change his mind. Unable to handle his scrutiny, I turned, pretending to assess the room. He watched my every move like a predator, ready to pounce if I tried to escape. Which was laughable if you thought about it, considering he could flash to my location whenever he wanted. Licking the wound on my lip, I cursed my luck before taking a deep breath and facing him. Wringing my hands together, I opened my mouth and closed it a few times as I tried to think of an explanation to justify my actions. In the end, I settled for ignorance and denial. "Why did you bring me here?"

"I needed a place to think," Kalen growled, shoving a hand through his black hair.

"That doesn't tell me why you brought me along for the ride," I snapped.

"You make me feel things that should not be possible," Kalen replied, cocking his head to the side in thought. He stalked forward and circled me like prey, mumbling to himself about his mental stability.

Aware of his animalistic nature, I didn't move an inch when he stepped up to my backside. Close enough for me to feel his heat, but far enough away that it made me want to eliminate the distance. I craved his touch. It left me aching and needy as anticipation coursed through my blood. I released a moan when I felt his breath on the back of my neck when he leaned down and pulled a strand of my blond hair to his nose. Growling out a curse, he released it just as quickly and stepped away. Taking his body heat with him. Moving to face me again, he searched my eyes before he admitted, "Either I'm going crazy, or fate is playing a joke on me. My soul screams 'you're mine', but my brain says 'you're not', because your smell is repulsive."

Gasping in disbelief, I couldn't stop myself from taking a whiff to verify I didn't smell foul before I responded, "Well, that was rude and uncalled for. You don't see me spouting off insults against you for kidnapping me! You big . . . big barbarian!"

"If that's your idea of an insult, you'll need to work on it some. Pretty pathetic if you ask me."

"Gah! Maybe I'm just smart because I know you're the king and can have me beheaded, for all I know, if I tell you how I feel about you! Take me back to my friends. I'm missing out on important information all because your brain has decided to play tricks on you."

"I believe you have a valid point," Kalen replied, tapping his finger against his chin in thought.

"Well, of course, I do!" I answered with a bit of skepticism in my voice. When he smiled at me wickedly, I shook my head in confusion and said, "Wait. Which of my points was valid?"

"The tricks part, of course. Something is definitely off here. Maybe it is you who is playing tricks on me, and until I figure that out, you're not going anywhere!"

"You can't do that! I have the trials to compete in . . . and . . . and I can't sleep in your room!" I sputtered out as I paced about the room and flailed my arms around for emphasis. I was lost in my thoughts and didn't notice Kalen go still from my comment.

The second I stopped to face him and demand he answer me, I froze at the look of murder in his eyes. Barely containing his rage, he seethed, "How did you know these were my chambers? Who do you work for?"

Refusing to let him intimidate me, even though I was practically shaking in his presence, I gestured to the gargantuan canopied bed in the corner and shrugged, "Um, calm down there, big guy. With the bed behind you fit for a king, I just assumed that was where we were at. Sorry, I didn't realize you were the type of man who took women to random rooms for hookups. Kind of gross if you ask me. I mean, how do you know if the sheets are clean? And to answer your other question, I think it's safe to say I'm unemployed."

"Before you answer this next question, female, you should know I don't like to be lied to. Why are you unemployed?" Kalen demanded.

When I continued to stare at him like he was crazy, he flashed to me, grabbed my chin gently, despite the anger swimming underneath the surface, and said, "Is your unemployment recent? Tell me, was it because you failed to snare my attention?"

"Ha! Are you serious right now?" When he maintained his glower at me, I continued, "Of course you are. Why wouldn't you be serious? My recent unemployment has nothing and everything to do with you!"

"You have five seconds to explain yourself before I have you thrown into the dungeon!"

"You'll regret it if you do!" I taunted. Which might not have been the best response considering he threw me over his shoulder and flashed us to the dungeon. Dropping me onto the cold stone floor, he sneered at me and said, "The only thing I regret is thinking you might be my mate!" Turning on his heel, he strode to the open door and slammed it shut behind him.

Scrambling to my feet, I called out after him, hoping he was just trying to give me a scare and wouldn't leave me here, "Wait.

I'm sorry. I'll answer the question! Come back!" When nothing but silence answered me, I screamed at the ceiling in frustration.

Chapter Twenty

When it was apparent I was alone, and he wasn't coming back any time soon, I stopped yelling, pressed my back against the door, and slumped to the floor. Besides a mattress that had seen better days in the corner and a shoddy wooden bucket, the room was empty. A single tiny rectangular window high up on the outside wall gave the only light, and by the looks of it, it wouldn't last long. I hoped they kept the hallway lit. The barred window in the thick wooden door would provide a modicum of light. It's not like I was scared of the dark or anything but being in a dungeon cell with who knew what kind of creepy crawlers in the pitch black didn't sound like my idea of fun.

Swearing out loud, I promised myself that if he left me there overnight, I'd make him regret it. Although if I thought about it, if that were to happen, I'd be the one begging for forgiveness. Considering the potion I took that morning lasted less than twenty-four hours, I probably had less than twelve hours before it wore off. If he waited until morning to collect me, he'd know without a doubt that I was his mate. And I had no doubt he'd make me pay for my deceit, regardless of how righteous I thought my plight was. Crap! Why couldn't I have answered his stupid question? I could have avoided incarceration. I was always a girl who believed everything happened for a reason, but I was having second thoughts when faced with a flawed reality.

Letting myself bask in the possibility this was anything less than desirable was an insult to my intelligence, especially considering my current accommodations. Kalen pampered me last time I was here. I had no doubt my second time on this planet was worse than my first time through. I mean, hands down, being treated like a queen beats a stint in the dungeons.

Pushing myself up off the floor, I took in the four black stone walls of my prison and shuddered. I tried to swallow the lump in my throat and choked. I was never any good with closed spaces. My mouth felt drier than the Sahara Desert. Forcing myself to dredge up enough spit to get my tongue off the roof of my mouth, I let out a sigh and began to pace. I couldn't afford to freak out. I needed to keep my cool so that I could figure out a way out of here. Considering it took three giant steps to cross the room, it didn't take long before I felt like I'd been spinning in a circle and got a bit dizzy.

Deciding to save my energy and the water left in my body, I approached the mattress with reluctance and nudged it with my foot.

I prepped myself to jump back at the first sign of any kind of life, be it critter or bug, as the room started to spin around me. When nothing made its presence known, I plopped myself down and instantly regretted it. I forgot about the things you couldn't see with the naked eye. I was coughing uncontrollably when a puff of yellow spores filtered up from below me. I scrambled off the mattress, knowing all too well it might be too late.

When my eyes started to close in irritation, and I felt a tickle in the back of my throat, I stuck my finger in my mouth until I gagged. Aware my very life might depend on it. I wanted to purge myself of the fungus already working its way inside me and prayed I wasn't too late. As my body expelled everything it was capable of, I waited patiently to see if I was overreacting. When nothing happened, I laughed nervously and backed myself into a corner, trying to stop myself from hyperventilating. Monitoring my body for anything abnormal, I eyed the bed with disdain. There was no way I was sleeping on that thing!

Besides feeling a bit faint from lack of water and my mouth tasting like the exactlies, Where you mouth tastes exactly like shit. I think I'm okay. Talk about torture. Damn, what I wouldn't give for some water. Maybe it was because I didn't know when my next drink was coming, but the more I thought about water, the thirstier I felt. Once my mind latched on to the idea that I would die of thirst, I could barely focus on anything else. I convinced myself I was losing it when I started hearing water dripping. Slamming my head back against the wall to stop the hallucinations, I cringed when I connected with the unforgiving black stone behind me. Cradling my head, I prodded the sore spot and sucked in a sharp breath when I encountered a golf ball-sized lump already forming. When my fingers came away wet, I expected to see red. Imagine my surprise when they were clear.

The sound of the water intensified. I glanced up at the ceiling, expecting to see drips forming above my head, only to find it dry. Pulling away from the wall, I looked over my shoulder and scowled at how dry it looked. Spinning around on my knees, I patted the wall like a maniac searching for any sign of moisture, only to come away empty. Muttering to myself, I dropped my head and probed the knot gingerly, "I'm not going crazy. This is a test. There is no water dripping. I'm hot. My head was merely wet from sweat. No need to give in to the insanity of this situation . . . Gah! I can't believe he left me here with nothing to drink!" Closing my eyes, I took a deep breath and blew it out forcefully. After a few more breathes in and out through my nose, I pushed myself to my feet and murmured, "The human body can go seven days before dying of thirst . . . I need to quit being a fucking baby, act like the queen I want to be, and start thinking of a way out of here!"

Grappling with the necklace, blocking me from my gift, I felt for some kind of button to turn it off. About to give up, I used my fingernail in place of my finger and almost squealed out loud when I detected three tiny buttons. I took a gamble and tried the first one. It didn't seem to press in, so I pushed it to the side with my fingernail and yelped when it delivered a shock strong enough to zap my fingers away. Sucking the wounded appendages into my mouth, I switched hands and tried my luck with the second button. Trying not to tense up, I closed my eyes before taking my fingers out of my mouth and made a fist. When I felt like my heart wasn't going to climb out of my chest, I opened my eyes. I was having trouble convincing myself a little bit of pain would be worth it even if said pain granted me access to my gift. Scrunching up my face with my finger hovering over the second button, I started counting down from three. As the word one was forming on my lips, a large drop of liquid hit my nose with enough momentum and volume that it splashed into my eyes. Not sure what was happening, I must have jumped five feet into the air.

Scrambling to put my back against the wall so whatever I faced would be head-on, I scrubbed my face frantically to clear my eyes. My gaze flew around the room with apprehension. I gasped when I spotted a drop of liquid collecting at the center of the room on the ceiling. It looked like an ever-expanding see-through balloon, capable of bursting at any moment. I laughed out loud at my luck. With no guarantee it wasn't teeming with microscopic bugs, I might have pounced on the chance to slake my thirst. I was thirsty but not thirsty enough to risk it . . . yet. Yet being the operative word. If they left me down here much longer, I might not have a choice. The water balloon was gaining size rapidly and soon had me wondering if drowning would be the cause of my death rather than dehydration. Oh, the irony. I sure hoped my mind wasn't playing tricks on me. Unable to resist getting a closer look, I approached the expanding liquid, hissing under my breath, "This better not be what they expect me to drink and bathe in!"

The water or liquid looked pristine and clear and was oh-so tempting looking. Studying it from every angle, I noticed I couldn't see my reflection. Wondering if it was a play on the light, I stepped closer and just as I was about to touch the surface when Levi's face appeared in the water like an apparition before he spoke, "Greetings dear one! I've come to save the day!"

Back peddling in surprise, I lost my footing and landed on my ass. Mouth wide open in shock, I swore I would never look at water the same way, as the liquid detached itself from the ceiling and morphed into the figure of a seven-foot giant before it touched the ground. At a loss for words, I watched in fascination as his body solidified into the man/creature Kalen had called forth the morning I went back in time. My brain practically tripped over itself as the magnitude of his presence caught up with me. How the hell did he know me? Realizing I was still staring, I closed my gaping mouth and looked away. Hating how inferior and small I felt, practically cowering on the floor, I pushed myself up off the floor. Taking a moment to gather my wits, I brushed myself off before I faced him, lifted my chin, and asked him flat out, "Save the day? How did you know I would be here? In fact, how do you know me at all? I went back in time, which means in the grand scheme of things, technically speaking, of course, you shouldn't be here yet or at all, for that matter, if I do my job right. I must be going insane!" The walls almost felt like they were closing in on me as I set about pacing from one side of the room to the other while waiting for his reply.

"Lass, you're not going insane. I have the gift of true sight," Levi offered, running his fingers through his hair. He looked uncomfortable with my distress and acted like his statement should answer all of my questions. Holding his arms up in placation, when he noticed my continued confusion, he added, "Time doesn't work the same on my species when we are actively using our true sight ability. I was in the middle of interrogating Selene when I felt you go back in time. As I watched everything rewind around me, I decided to stick around and find out what you were up to. Which it's a good thing I did. I'd bet my immortality you didn't anticipate you'd end up here." Sweeping his arms out dramatically as he made his point. When I giggled in response to his theatrics, he gave me a small smile and added, "Although I'd like nothing more than to find out what you hoped to accomplish with your unplanned time-travel, something tells me we should take this conversation somewhere else. Unless, of course, you'd like to wait for Kalen. I can feel him approaching, so we wouldn't have to wait long."

I froze at the mention of Kalen's name. I wanted to see him with every fiber of my being, but unless I intended to confess and give up any hope of being involved in solving this mystery, it would be best to leave before he returned. Levi must have noticed my apprehension and assumed it meant I was scared to face Kalen when he spoke up next, "You have no reason to be afraid of your mate. He'll never truly hurt you, no matter how much you anger him. Say the word, and I'll hide and let you two work it out." Levi finished moving into the corner. He cocked his head to the side as a door squeaked on its hinges in the distance. Raising an eyebrow, he opened his hand in invitation before he whispered, "The decision is yours. I'll still be around until I fulfill my assignment if you change your mind later. The doppelganger is a danger to everyone, and I won't stop until I uncover who hired it."

Knowing if I waited around until Kalen showed up, I'd lose my nerve to defy him. I sighed with longing before I made my way over to Levi. Stopping just short of his outstretched hand, I said, "You have it all wrong. I know Kalen would never purposefully hurt me. That's not the problem here. No, what I fear is the exact opposite. I'm afraid of his love. Once he finds out my life is in danger, he'll remove me from the fight even if he needs my powers. Our bond will blind him to the possibilities. He'll think he's protecting me from danger, but I know without me, he will fail. I'm selfish. I can't imagine a world without him now that I know of him. I'm willing to make this small sacrifice because, in the end, all this pain and heartache will go away. But man, do I crave the comfort his arms promise me. My heart and soul long for the connection our bond provides, but my mind knows that if I give into that desire and become complacent, lives are at stake. There will be time for Kalen and me to work things out at a later date. For now, he needs to stay in the dark."

Reaching out to grab Levi's hand, I glanced behind me with longing. The second our hands collided, I saw Kalen flash into the room. The look of surprise on his face was one thing, but when his gaze dropped to our clasped hands, my heart wept at the look of betrayal written all over his face. Trying to yank myself free of Levi's grip, I screamed in frustration when he pulled me close and wrapped himself around me. Blackness threatened to swallow me whole, but not before I felt Kalen wrap his arms around my middle and whisper in my ear, "Going somewhere, Jade?"

Chapter Twenty-One

Sandwiched between two men might be somebody's fantasy come to life, but I felt like taffy stretched between the two. I wasn't sure what Kalen or Levi were trying to accomplish, but each time we materialized somewhere different, they took turns pulling me back through the ether again. Like it was some kind of race, they hoped to be the victor, but considering we were touching each other, no one was in the lead. When we finally stopped, I felt like we had been at it for hours. Sick to my stomach and less than two seconds away from losing my guts, I shoved out with my arms and pushed out my ass. I was trying to give myself room to hurl. Taking deep breaths to calm my tumultuous tummy, I rested my hands on my knees and tried to focus on breathing. All while attempting to ignore the male posturing going on behind me. Once the nausea passed, I wiped the sweat from my forehead and stood up. Turning to face the music, I wished to fade into the background at the tormented look on Kalen's face.

"I should kill you for daring to steal my mate away from me, but something tells me Jade's just as much at fault as you are! You have five seconds to explain yourself before I squash you like caviar!" Kalen growled, sending shivers of awareness down my spine.

I wasn't sure if I was ready to explain myself or my actions to him, but it didn't look like I would have a choice. Especially when my would-be rescuer betrayed me with his next comment, "Considering you know less than I do Kalen, I'm going to ignore your last comment. Although when this is all over, if you would like to try and squash me, I would be up for the challenge. I haven't had a good spar in ages. As for an explanation, we'll need to ask your mate. You showed up before I got around to asking her what she hoped to accomplish by going back in time."

Caught like a bug in a spiderweb, I froze as both men turned their attention to me. My gaze bounced between their scowls, and for a brief moment in time, I considered dropping to the floor and faking some ailment or another so I could prolong the inevitable. When neither of them gave me any indication they would be lenient, I looked down in defeat, sighed, and said, "I doubt either of you will understand, but I'd hoped to uncover who was trying to kill me and sabotage your throne. It seems fate had something else in mind."

"You're damn right. I don't understand! How could I possibly begin to understand why my mate would choose to erase our mating bond!" Kalen roared.

With a gasp, my head whipped up to meet his gaze before I whispered, "I didn't erase it. It's still active on my side."

"How convenient for you," He growled. Pulling at his hair, he began to pace before adding, "You made me think I was losing my mind! Not to mention making me look like a fool in front of my people! What were you thinking!"

"Well, obviously, I thought I could save the day and prove I was worthy of being your queen!"

"Sometimes I forget how young you are." Shaking his head slowly, he pulled up short and turned to face me. "You speak of fate, but you know nothing of it! You had nothing to prove! Fate said you were mine! In fact, by going back, you basically told fate to fuck off! Tell me, where does that leave us?"

"What do you mean, 'where does that leave us?' There is no way you know the definition of fate if you have to ask me that question! Hypocrite much! Gah! Fate to me and the rest of the universe means we are destined! Regardless of how we get there! It means you and I belong to one another! My decision to use my gift doesn't change our fate; it just prolonged when we'd be together. Your decision to be an asshole before you have all the facts is another matter!"

"How dare you try and turn this around on me! I don't know all the facts because you high tailed it out of here! Leaving me feeling like I wasn't worthy or strong enough to protect you."

"Well, how do you think I felt when you proclaimed at the first sign of conflict that I should be ushered away to a safe room, hidden away like some damsel in distress. I am a powerful Sixer! When are you going to consider me an asset instead of a liability?" I screamed in frustration.

"You're not a liability!" Kalen countered with a roar. Cringing in remorse at his proclamation only made me feel worse. If I could do it all over, I'd start with an apology. I watched him war with himself as he tried to control his emotions and wished once again, I had never gone back in time. Breathing in deep, he let out a large sigh before he added in a defeated tone, "You are irreplaceable to me."

Without warning, he flashed away before I could respond. I wasn't sure how he thought it would be ok to just up and leave in the middle of our fight. Our eternity wouldn't be bliss if this was how he handled all of our disagreements! My growl of frustration turned to a squeak when I felt his presence behind me just milliseconds before his arm snaked around my waist. He pulled me into his chest roughly, moving my hair to the side with his other hand. Trailing soft kisses up my neck that sent shivers to every nerve ending in my body. The act lulled me into complacency as he nibbled on my ear seductively.

When I relaxed into his embrace, reveling in the connection, he whispered, "I should be considerate and allow you to tell me in your own time, but I'm having a hard time controlling my basic instincts. Especially since it seems your little stunt wasn't in your or my best interests."

Before I could answer, he sunk his fangs into my flesh and took a large pull. I couldn't help the gasp that turned into a moan at the erotic sensations his bite brought me. His answering groan was a balm to my insecurities. It told me I wasn't alone. My eyes fluttered closed in ecstasy as ripples of pleasure coursed through my body. A part of me knew I should be worried as he continued to drink. Not because I feared he would harm me. No, my soul knew he'd rather die than kill me. I was worried he'd never forgive me. I knew he wouldn't be happy with my decisions, but I could only hope he'd take my intentions and true devotion into consideration before he passed judgment. My heart was in the right place when I went back. That had to account for something.

As I felt myself slipping away into the darkness, I found myself letting go of my previous worries when Kalen's acceptance and forgiveness pulsed through our bond. The warmth radiating throughout my body gave me a false sense of protection, even as black spots dotted my vision. Using the last of my strength, I raised my hand slowly so I could caress his face. When he leaned into my touch, I barred my neck further in submission. Letting him know how much I trusted him. Levi's voice broke through my high, "I'm sure by now you've seen all you need to know, Kalen. Knocking her unconscious will only complicate matters between the two of you, and I don't want to have to step in. 'Cause, although I've known you longer, the lass deserves my loyalty."

In my languid state, I didn't feel Kalen retract his fangs. I only realized he was cradling me in his arms when he maneuvered my mouth to a trickle of blood coming from a nick he had made for me in his neck. He didn't answer Levi until he felt me latch on, but I could feel his barely contained rage the moment I swallowed my first mouthful of his essence. As flashes of our interactions assaulted my mind, I wanted to cry out with empathy. Witnessing the battle, his soul and brain engaged in each time we were near each other added another fracture to the already shaky foundation we had.

After watching his take on our interactions, it was easier to believe we could overcome anything in our path. Observing our bond from his perspective gave me hope. I watched our lives in the reflection of our could-be's and found myself wishing I could lose myself to the possibility of the us he envisioned. It felt like every time I blinked, we shared a different scenario, with a different outcome. At times the onslaught felt overwhelming, but a part of me knew it was the least I could do to atone for my decisions to leave him behind.

"Why are you still here? Jade and I have unfinished business," Kalen answered with a snarl breaking through the haze I found myself under as I watched our interactions through his eyes.

"I have no doubt that's true, but I'm here because you hired me, and I won't stop until I've fulfilled that duty. Plus, I just so happen to like your mate. Which brings me to the point that your little reunion will have to wait until we eliminate the threat against Jade."

"Get to the point. Jade's little excursion should have eliminated the threat against her . . . so even though I'm disappointed in the method she took, I'm pleased she's taken herself out of the line of fire," Kalen spit out harshly.

"Hate to be the bearer of bad news, but unfortunately, it might have only delayed their plans. I mean, in the end, they have no idea you sent Jade to the dungeons for a time out. No, instead, they saw a crazed Strix flashing away with a woman he's been sniffing around like a crazed male. Admit it, Kalen, would you expect anything other than a claiming if one of your men did the same. Regardless it doesn't matter, not with what I saw this afternoon," Levi stated bluntly.

"I feel like a broken record, and you are trying my patience. What did you see this afternoon that would make me change my mind?" Kalen countered with a growl of frustration.

"I spotted the doppelganger on the dock this afternoon and followed him to the palace. If that doesn't pique your interest, then maybe knowing he was meeting with a few of your councilmen would do the trick." Levi stated bluntly.

"Let me guess, one of them was councilman Bastian," Kalen said in a tone that sent shivers down my spine. Even though I knew he had access to my memories, it surprised me when he trusted my thought process concerning Bastian and Onyx. I knew I didn't have all the answers, but I appreciated his willingness to trust my theories.

I tried to pull away from Kalen's neck to add my two cents only to have him cradle the back of my head, locking me gently into place. He whispered words of encouragement until I resumed my suckling, although with less enthusiasm than the first time. I felt healed from my earlier consumption and wondered if he needed this more than I did. Stroking my hair softly, he made me want to forget everything and just feel, but Levi's next statement was hard to ignore. "Bastian was there, but so were Fansa and Clary."

"Well, that was unexpected," Kalen responded with a pensive air.

From my memory, I tried to recall why those two names would cause my mate fear until he pushed the faces of Anolla and Castice to the front of my mind. Pulling back, I couldn't help the gasp that escaped my lips. Pushing against his chest with a strength I wasn't aware I had, I sought Kalen's eyes, finding solace in the bewilderment that matched my own. I searched his eyes as I questioned my train of thought. Were Anolla and Castice killed to make Fansa and Clary cooperate with the coup? Were they victims in this scheme like the rest of us? Was I even the target? Damn, had

my insecurities and jealousy blinded my judgment? And if it had,

could I step in and be the bigger person if Onyx's life was in danger?

The bitch in me wanted to sit back and watch it all unfold, reveling

in the fact that Karma would have a chance to make her presence

known. The minuscule portion of me with a conscience, wanted to

give her a chance. I wasn't sure if I had it in me to find out.

Chapter Twenty-Two

As question after question bombarded my thoughts, it made me wish I had an emergency brake to end the onslaught. Whoever said knowledge is power obviously wasn't missing important information. Because partial knowledge that only brought about more questions should be considered dangerous. It was like trying to complete a puzzle with pieces missing; only you wouldn't know which ones were missing until the end. It felt overwhelming when I considered how much I didn't know until Kalen's voice broke through my thoughts, "Tell me, Levi, if I hired you to find the doppelganger, why in the world are you standing in front of me now?"

"You could say I got distracted. Jade's ridiculous disguise was driving you mad, which I can't deny piqued my interest even further and made me want to find out what she was up to. Imagine my surprise when I watched you throw her into the dungeon. I might not have a mate of my own, but even this recluse knows better than that," Levi declared with a devilish smirk.

I felt Kalen's body go rigid as he warred with himself on whether or not he should put me down so he could teach Levi a lesson. Taking the decision away from him, I twisted in his arms to face the giant shifter. "Ridiculous? Hardly! It worked on everyone else. Why not you?"

"I have the power of true sight, lass," he responded frankly.

"Is that your answer to everything?" I challenged with a snort.

"My gift allows me to see past any trickery, be it magic or potions. So even though I could see the skin you showed everyone else, I was also able to see the real you hiding underneath. Personally, I like you better as a brunette," Levi answered with a wink. Kalen's answering growl was the only warning I had before he flashed in front of me, dropped his fangs, and roared, "Jade is mine! If you value your life, you'll not speak of her that way ever again."

"It's been a long time since I've witnessed a newly bonded male. I forget how easy you are to provoke. I'll do my best to temper myself around you, but you're going to need to learn to check yourself in the future. I highly doubt others will give you the same courtesy," Levi warned before adding, "I'm sure you are well aware flying off the handle doesn't bode well for people in positions of power. Someone is always waiting on the sidelines to take advantage of your misstep."

Kalen seemed to sober with Levi's reminder, which gave me the courage to squeeze him from behind before moving to his side and changing the subject. "How did you make it so Kalen could see me? My potion shouldn't have worn off for another twelve hours by my estimate."

"The moment I touched you, your outer shell ceased to exist," Levi answered, followed by a shrug that spoke of his remorse.

I nodded Levi's way to let him know his guilt was unnecessary before it hit me; there might still be time to interfere with Anolla's death. There were so many variables to identify, but I couldn't let it overwhelm me if I wanted to make a difference. We just needed to digest each tidbit we were fed and make the best-educated guess possible. If only we knew how fast-acting the contagion was. Then we could determine what kind of a timeline we were working with, which would inevitably lead us to other people of interest.

Now that I couldn't be sure my supposed archenemy was guilty, it would be stupid of me to bury my head in the sand and ignore other possible suspects. I couldn't afford to be ignorant. If I wanted to stop future deaths, I needed to be willing to think outside of the box. Anything should be possible in a world where the impossible happens every day. Even if that anything . . . meant something I was uncomfortable with. We just needed to be in a place where we could interfere with our enemies' plans. "What time is it?"

"Do you have somewhere you need to be?" Kalen rumbled from beside me.

"Depends on what time it is," I teased, looking up at him flirtatiously. When he scowled down at me in response, I quickly added, "Sorry, I guess that was a bit too soon. I don't have anywhere to be per se . . . but as you'll recall from my memories, Anolla died at the dinner celebration, and I wanted to be there to see if my going back in time changed her fate."

"Still have a couple of hours until we eat. I know you believe Onyx is to blame, but I saw little proof in your memories to justify apprehending her. An accusation like that needs to be supported by ample evidence," Kalen chastised before turning his attention to Levi, "Now that we've sated your curiosity, I think it's high time for you to do what I summoned you here for. I want the doppelganger brought in alive so we can find out who hired him. The sooner, the better, in my opinion."

I expected Levi to argue, but with a nod, his body shimmered out to be replaced by his water form. I watched in fascination as he walked to the sink and poured himself down the drain. With his exit, I was even more aware of the pissed off Strix behind me. Wishing I could delay our confrontation for a moment now that we were alone, I examined our surroundings. While we weren't in the dungeon anymore, the room was simplistic, and besides the sink, it was empty. Which didn't give me a lot of time to search for the right words to make him understand why I did what I did. Perhaps now wasn't the time to present my case. I'd make him see it from my perspective when this was all over.

With a big sigh, I turned to face him and addressed one of the issues that took me back in time in the first place, "Could we at least grab Anolla and Castice and hold them until their time of death expires? If we remove them from the equation, it might just save one or both of their lives. Since their time of infection is unknown, it might help us narrow the timeline. Do we know when Castice died?"

"We can arrange that. I'll send Tanen to pick them up immediately," Kalen replied, staring at the wall above my head as he sent the mental command. When he finished, his eyes sought me out. For a second, he let me see the anguish my actions brought him before Kalen buried the look and gave me a version of himself that brokered no emotions. I knew he was hurt, but I had hoped he'd see how much he meant to me and would be able to forgive me. I searched his eyes a second longer and then dropped my eyes to the ground when it appeared he was shutting me out.

"As for your question . . . I have no memory of that time, except for what I could see in your memories. Don't worry, though, I'm highly aware of someone who might know. I think now would be a good time for us to visit her. Perhaps Natashia will also be able to explain to me how she thought sending you back in time would go unpunished," Kalen replied with a sneer.

My head snapped up at his comment. Pinning him with a death glare, I yelled, "Now wait just a damn minute! Natashia didn't send me anywhere. I sent myself, and you know it. I was the one that came up with the idea and practically manipulated her to help me. If you want someone to punish, you're looking at her!"

Kalen flashed to my location in an instant. With a squeak, I tried to step back, but he stopped me as he pulled me roughly into him and snarled, "Believe me, I plan on it."

I shivered with awareness as my body melted the moment our bodies made contact. It was easy to recall how good we felt together when we touched, and it made me furious that he would use that against me during a fight. How were we supposed to have a rational discussion when all my brain could think about was running my fingers and mouth over the male specimen I was attached to. My struggle only made the delicious, hard lines of his body more apparent. Especially when he swiveled his hips into me, reminding me of what I was missing. Unable to contain the moan that escaped without warning, I barely stopped myself from grinding against him. Panting and out of breath, I rested my forehead against his chest in defeat and said, "I'm begging you to leave Natashia out of it. If you feel she must learn a lesson, then make her watch you tan my hide. At least then, I'll be able to say I protected her, and I won't lose her friendship."

"And you were worried you wouldn't make a good queen. Only those truly meant to lead would martyr themselves to save those they are in charge of," Kalen whispered before he flashed us away.

Chapter Twenty-Three

I'm sure with a little more practice, I'll get used to flashing, but it takes a second for my brain to catch up with reality every damn time. It probably didn't help that the second we were on firm ground, Kalen released me to pace about the room like a caged lion. Thankful I didn't stumble and make a fool of myself. I gave myself a mental slap when his absence made me feel bereft and alone. I just had to remember our distance was temporary. My only consolation was I didn't feel the need to hurl after touch down. Hating the physical and emotional distance separating us, I glanced at our surroundings before I gave into my need for him and edged closer.

If I had to guess, we were probably in Natashia's quarters, but when it became evident we were alone, I tugged on Kalen's arm to get his attention. Frowning up at him, I was just about to ask him what we were doing in her quarters when Natashia walked out of the bathroom to the right of us. Dressed in a robe, fresh from a shower, she froze mid-step with her mouth wide open. At first, I thought it was due to the shock of finding us in her room but knew differently with Kalen's next statement.

"Natashia, I hope you understand my reservations around you for the moment. I'll unfreeze you when we can come to an agreement. I need your vow that you will refrain from using your power in any way that will make me lose my memories. If I let you go and you do it anyway AND I subsequently find out about it, I will consider it an act of war. If it comes to that, nothing my mate can say will stop me from punishing you. That is my vow. You may speak now, but considering our friendship's longevity, let me give you a final warning. You will face my full wrath if you cross me."

Natashia blinked once and closed her mouth, which was the only indication that she was alive and in complete control of her actions. She blew off his powers with a poise that belayed her predicament as she stood to her full height. Drawing in a deep breath, she answered him with an air of royalty I hoped one day to possess, "Your Highness, I can't say I'm surprised to find you here after your display this afternoon in the training room. Alright, that's a lie. I am surprised to find you in my quarters. You should know there was a part of me that considered skipping out on this conversation, but the larger part of me figured our friendship deserved better. While I refuse to apologize for helping your mate, I want you to know I felt like I had no other choice." She winced in my direction at her admission, but I didn't hold it against her. It was the truth, and he was more than aware of that fact. I mouthed the word *sorry,* and when she mouthed back, *ditto.* I knew no matter what happened; we'd have each other's back.

With a shy smile, she cleared her throat before she continued, "I know a part of you respects my loyalty to your mate, and with my next promise, I hope you know that trait also extends to you. "From this moment forward, I will not interfere with you and your mate unless your very lives require it. That's the best I can offer you, my liege, because even though my actions don't make sense to you now, I only did what I thought was best for you, her, and our people. We can't afford to lose you as our leader. Bastian would destroy everything we've ever built with his greed."

I released the breath I didn't even realize I was holding when Kalen conceded a cease-fire with a single nod before he said, "Very well. We have questions, of course. I'm hoping you can fill in the blanks concerning the death of poor Castice."

Natashia looked between Kalen and me before she nodded and said, "Of course. I'll tell you whatever I can. What details are you wanting?"

I had to give it to Kalen. He was a man of his word. I watched his demeanor switch from dictator to collaborator with her promise, "You arrived before we did. Were we given a precise time of death?"

"Not to the minute, but his roommate reported it shortly after four in the morning. He was apprehended as a suspect when he started demanding money for his troubles. I've kept my eye on him today, and for the life of me, I can't see how he might have poisoned the poor kid."

"Who was his roommate?" I demanded.

"I didn't catch his name, but he's Ranik's second cousin or something like that. I'm sure you noticed him out of all the recruits. He was the tallest and biggest tribute sent to us. If I'm honest, kinda hard to miss, with all his goldenness," Natashia finished, ducking her head to hide the blush threatening to take over her face.

"Golden Boy?" I blurted out and instantly wished I could take it back when Kalen stiffened and moved out from under my hand. Turning to face me, I could see the anger threatening to consume him before he spoke.

"His name is Kaspen, not Golden Boy!" Kalen roared.

"Are you serious! You're mad because I called him 'Golden Boy?' His fucking skin shimmers with gold. What else was I supposed to call him? The guy with gold skin? My lord, jealous much?" I spit out, folding my arms over my chest protectively.

"I'd prefer to be called Kalen, but Lord works just as well," Kalen answered with a smirk.

"Pompous jerk! You're not helping!" I screamed, feeling like a toddler as I resisted stomping my feet. Giving him my back, I turned to Natashia and tried to get our interrogation back on track, "Everything happened so fast when she collapsed. Do you remember if Castice was seated near Anolla during dinner?"

"Far from it, actually. Castice was late to dinner and was near the dining hall entrance when the poor pixie started having convulsions," Natashia answered.

"Damn. I was hoping we could make a connection between the two, besides the fact that they knew each other," I responded.

Chewing on my lower lip in concentration, I bit down on it with surprise when Kalen grabbed me from behind and whispered in my ear, "By the way, in my world, we don't call it jealousy."

Gah! The insufferable male was driving me insane! His proximity was wreaking havoc on my ability to function, but even I knew now wasn't the time to talk about our issues! Plus, it didn't matter what he called it; jealousy under a different name was still jealousy. I took a step forward and peered at him over my shoulder. I was sure the look plastered across my face was more than enough to clue him in on how I felt, but just in case, I added a bit more stink eye as I tapped my foot, waiting for him to continue.

An idiot should have clued in on my annoyance, but my mate must have decided to test me when he ignored all the signals I sent him and proceeded to march toward me. Flipping around to face him head-on, I couldn't help but take a step back as he crowded my space. Before I knew it, I was cornered and wished I could hide how turned on I was. I mentally groaned at how weak I was in his presence, when I practically panted like a dog in heat from his nearness.

"In my world, there is no such thing as jealousy. Instead, we prefer to call it territorial because make no mistake you are my property!"

I wanted to assure him I was just as much his as he was mine, but he never gave me a chance.

"Fate promised me someone I wouldn't have to be jealous of. When I found my mate, there would be no question in either of our hearts because my mate would want me as much as I want them. I know you want me. It's evident in your memories and the scent of your desire. The smell of the blood from your lip is driving me mad. It feeds my need to claim you again and ensure everyone knows you are mine as much as I am yours!" Kalen roared before seeming to fold in on himself. I could tell it took immense effort to control his next words, "Your deceit, no matter how well-intentioned, is hurtful and only makes me feel territorial—especially when I hear you speak of another man. Because if I had my way, you would have never seen him in the first place, which means you would have never formed that title. I hate that you developed a pet name for a male that isn't yours. If it were my choice, you would never give another male a nickname, unless that male was me or one of our offspring!"

Stunned at his revelations, I opened my mouth and then promptly closed it. Putting myself in his shoes, I had no doubt I'd feel the same way. Unable to handle the pain evident in his eyes, I dropped my gaze to his chin before I dared to answer, "I truly am sorry, and I realize my words will do nothing to ease your pain. I only meant to prove to you and your people that I was worthy of being your mate. No one knows better than I . . . without a doubt, I should have stayed here and worked with you. It was stupid of me to think I was capable of solving a mystery by myself. It was never my intention to hurt you, and I'll spend eternity making it up to you."

I jumped when Natashia cleared her throat and said, "Um, I've never wanted to be a third wheel, but you two are kind of giving me no choice! I shouldn't have to be the one to remind you, but you're wasting time getting to the root of the problem as you stand here bickering back and forth about what happened in the past! You guys are going to have to shelve your issues until a later date. Our people can't afford for either of you to wallow on what happened . . . we need to focus on what we're going to do next. I need you two to get off your pity party train and be rational for a moment. Once we've dealt with the issues that affect our people, you'll have time to address your petty love quarrel."

I had to hand it to Natashia . . . she stood up to my mate, and the look on his face was priceless, but when I felt the room charge with his unneeded temper, I scrambled to hold him back. Thankfully I didn't have to put too much effort into it when Levi stormed into the room dragging a pissed-off Natashia look-alike behind him. Kalen ushered me behind as he threw his arms out, freezing the room before he snarled, "Levi, please tell me the being in your grasp is our doppelganger!"

Chapter Twenty-Four

I had to admit Kalen's alpha protective side was definitely hot, but it only made me miss my powers even more. Now probably wasn't the time to bring it up, but there was no way in hell I was leaving the room until someone made sure I had them back. Reaching up to finger the offensive but useful device, I was both thankful and astonished my mate left me out of the gravity hold he had on everyone and everything in front of us. I poked my head out from behind him to get a peak and marveled at the enormity of his gift. My eyes swept the room and cataloged what we were facing.

A glass of water Natashia must have knocked over as she backpedaled was frozen midspill, and the individual droplets sparkled with tiny rainbows as the light from the window hit them just right. Dust particles seemed to stand out as they hung in the air eerily. I dragged my gaze to our intruders. It was hard not to gawk at the doppelganger. Levi must have been in the process of flinging the poseur into the room when Kalen froze everything. The Natashia wannabe was suspended midair and resembled a ragdoll, bent in impossible ways. Besides the unnatural pose, the resemblance to my friend was startling.

My gaze bounced between the two replicates as Levi ground out, "Aye, tis' the imposter." Surprised by the hatred in Levi's tone, my eyes flew in his direction. His Scottish brogue was more apparent, but the object of his attention was not. I expected him to be angry at the being in his hands, only to smile when it appeared he had his eyes on the real Natashia like she was an enigma he was more than willing to solve. I chuckled to myself when I saw the same expression reflected on my friend's face for several seconds before she shivered and closed her eyes on a sigh. I wasn't a gambling woman, but I'd bet money those two would be perfect together. I had no doubt I'd be prodding her about that look next time we were alone.

Kalen's growl of impatience interrupted my thought process. The fury evident in his response threatened retribution by tone alone, "Levi . . . I hope you have a good explanation for why you brought an assassin into our midst. For your sake, you'd better because I refuse to think you'd put my mate in danger without reason. I happen to know you were aware I wanted him brought to the dungeons!" Straightening slightly from his protective crouch, he raised his eyebrows with annoyance.

Preparing myself to intervene if things got out of hand, I sighed with relief when Levi answered.

"Had to make sure it left her alive," Levi grunted as he struggled to break free of the gravity keeping him in place. Never once taking his eyes off Natashia. I watched the veins on his forehead extrude to the point that I thought he was going to have an aneurysm. So it didn't faze me when he let loose a feral roar, "Release me!"

My mate made no move to acquiesce, and before I could second guess my actions, I wrapped my hand around Kalen's bicep and gave it a little tug to get his attention. When he peered down at me, I cleared my throat and said, "Darling, I'd like to pow-wow with our friends so we can narrow down when Councilwoman Natashia, our dear friend, might have been copied. Considering the lengths you'll go to protect me, I think we should give Levi a break, don't you?"

I wasn't sure how Kalen would react to my interference, but it felt like I was setting a precedent on how we would rule together. I didn't want to be a wallflower, but I also didn't want to appear like I was threatening his rule. It's not like I wanted his job, but I also wasn't going to stay quiet when I thought he was going too far. I gave him a demure smile and prayed I hadn't overstepped some imaginary line or something. The look of shock was enough to tell me he hadn't picked up on the way Levi and Natashia were reacting to each other. Typical male. I flicked my eyes towards our friends before I waggled my eyebrows jokingly. He returned it with a wink and tucked me into his side.

I felt the pressure in the room drop the moment Kalen released our friends and jumped when the glass Natashia had knocked over crashed to the ground. The squawk coming from my friend was unexpected, drawing my eye. Her backward momentum had her tripping over her own two feet. I watched Levi dissolve into a man-shaped liquid a millisecond before he collapsed to the floor in a puddle—only to solidify as a solid man next to her less than a second later. He caught Natashia before she hit the floor and held her there. Like they were in the middle of ballroom dancing, and he dipped her at the end. Natashia cleared her throat and tapped Levi on the shoulder when it appeared he had no intention of moving.

Blushing shamelessly, she hissed, "Let me up, you big oaf!"

Levi blinked at her barb, and even though he didn't show it, I could tell her comment wounded him. His look of wonder turned to a frown as he righted Natashia and took a small step back from her.

He faced my mate with a look of brotherhood before he nodded once and said, "I find myself in unusual waters. I've never failed to finish a job, but it appears my priorities have changed. If you find someone to transport that piece of shit and relieve me of my promise, I'll return your last payment with interest."

"I'll take that deal as long as you promise not to take off until after we've had a chance to tie up all of our loose ends." Kalen answered quickly. Taking in a deep breath, he kissed my forehead, lingering a second before he leaned down and purred in my ear, "There are no lengths I won't take to ensure your safety. You'll find me more amicable if you don't fight me every step of the way."

"I'll be more harmonious when I don't feel so defenseless," I mumbled under my breath, dropping my eyes to the floor.

Kalen used a finger to raise my chin gently, forcing me to look at him before he responded, "Why would you feel defenseless?"

I sighed, pointed to the power-blocking necklace, and said, "Don't get me wrong. It's a great translator, but…" I stuttered mid-sentence when Kalen flipped me around, moved my hair to the side, and released the hold the necklace had over me. I shuddered in delight as my gift flared to life. I couldn't help the sigh that left my lips, feeling complete for the first time since I went back in time. With a smile, I backed into Kalen, cleared my throat and said, "I was going to ask if you wouldn't mind demonstrating to our prisoner just what he's messing with, but I have a better idea."

Tapping into my gift, I borrowed Kalen's gravity to bring the doppelganger to us. Kalen growled but didn't stop me. When it was eye level, I used my hands to pull its limbs taught, making sure it knew who was in control before I addressed it, "I've never been one to endorse torture, but I've also never been in a position where something so barbaric might be necessary. So, do everyone here a favor and start talking. Because even though I might not be able to stomach it, the guy standing behind me will have no qualms in doling it out."

"You offer me nothing to make me talk besides death. To my kind, that's an insult. I'd rather die than divulge information just to save my skin," the doppelganger replied without an ounce of fear in its eyes.

I cackled like a witch before I said, "Who said anything about death? I know I didn't mention it. Nope, I'm positive I said torture. And when you're begging us to end you, I'll heal you, so we can do it all over again."

If I hadn't been watching, I might have missed the flash of fear in his eyes before he schooled his features and hissed, "What are you?"

"Enough!" Kalen growled, tucking me back under his arm again as a couple of guards carrying heavy silver chains between them flashed into the room. Kalen pushed the doppelganger towards the newcomers and said, "Bind and escort our prisoner to Cell-block II for questioning. Tanen is already there with his packages and will assist with preparations until I can get there."

"Until YOU get there?" I hissed, two seconds from telling him what an asshole he was as his men left the room just as quickly as they had arrived.

Kalen rolled his eyes but corrected himself with reluctance, "I meant we. Until WE get there." Pointing at everyone left in the room. "But first, I wanted to give Natashia a chance to talk to us about what she remembers."

I glared at Kalen for a moment before I turned my attention to Natashia and said, "Are you okay?"

Natashia glanced at the brute glued to her backside briefly before she answered, "As well as can be expected after the recent revelations. And before you ask, I do not know about an attack or when that thing might have possibly had the chance to copy me."

She shuddered as she looked around her room before she added, "I

mean, the only time I don't have complete knowledge of my

whereabouts is when I'm asleep." She shrugged and continued,

"Although the thought gives me the creeps, it's the only time I can

think of that I might have been vulnerable."

Levi growled and stepped a bit closer to Natashia before he

rasped out, "Unless you took a nap or woke up extremely late today,

I don't see how that is possible. I witnessed the doppelganger's

arrival this afternoon on the docks, and besides the last few hours, I

was tailing him. I can guarantee I would have known if he crossed

paths with you."

Natashia pulled her towel closer, closed her eyes, palmed her

forehead for a second before she pushed her hand through her hair.

She glanced at Kalen for a moment before she sighed heavily, took a

deep breath, and answered, "I couldn't sleep after Jade went back in

time and I passed out for a couple of hours after morning report.

That's why you caught me indisposed. I took a shower after my nap.

I was trying to wake up."

Levi huffed and said, "You should get dressed. I mean, so

you can be ready to accompany us to the dungeons."

Natashia scowled at Levi over her shoulder but started toward her wardrobe before she stated. "I didn't realize you were so appalled by my skin."

"Only appalled that others can see it as well," Levi scoffed before adding, "Make sure to dress for cold temperatures, something that covers more of your skin. Ask Jade, the dungeons are cold, and if we have to spend any amount of time down there, you'll want something warm."

I looked at Levi like he'd lost his mind, and he only shrugged his shoulders when he caught me staring. His eyes, for the most part, followed Natashia around the room as she gathered her belongings. When he moved to follow her into the bathroom, she slammed the door in his face. I couldn't help but laugh as he staggered backward and landed on his ass.

Hopping up as if nothing happened, he glared my way and swore under his breath, "Will ye wheesht!"

I couldn't help but snicker at how flustered he was, but as a friend, I gave him pity and tried to change the subject, "Hey Levi, how old are you?"

He looked at me in confusion. Probably trying to figure out where I was going with my questions. Shaking his head slowly, he began, "Um . . . is old an answer?"

"Not even close. Do you have a guesstimate?" I encouraged, happy with how easy it was to distract him.

Levi seemed to consider the question for a moment before he sighed, shook his head, and admitted, "Time ceased to mean anything to me after my kind died out and I became the last Leviathan. To be completely honest, I have no idea how old I am."

To say his admission wasn't heartbreaking would have been a lie. What I'd meant as a distraction turned into something deep and painful and made me wish I could take it back. I was in the middle of concocting something else to say when Natashia opened the bathroom door abruptly and saved me from making a fool of myself again. Dressed in her tight black fatigues, she said, "You guys should go on without me. I've told you everything I know. If I think of anything else, I know how to get a hold of you."

Levi looked frantic and only relaxed when Kalen insisted we needed her. "While I have no doubt you'd contact me with anything of importance, I insist you come with us. As someone I trust, I need your help controlling the outcome if it comes down to it."

Natashia's gaze bounced between Kalen and Levi before she nodded and said with a sigh, "As you wish, but I want your promise that if I determine the only way to control the situation is to go back in time, you won't hold it against me."

Kalen bristled slightly before he took a deep breath and replied, "I promise I won't pass judgment as long as you ensure my mate is kept safe at all costs AND you keep me informed of everything."

"I accept those terms. Should I assume we are following you to the dungeons?" Natashia replied stoically.

"We'll meet you there. I'm sure you know the way. Don't keep us waiting," Kalen replied before wrapping me in his arms and flashing us to the hallway outside Cell-block II.

Proud the transport hadn't left me in disarray; I spun around like a schoolgirl only to come to a halt when I saw what was behind us. Even though I knew Tanen was collecting them, seeing Anolla and Castice detained behind glass walls as a precaution was a wake-up call. Not only was this real, but if we didn't get it right, more lives besides the two behind me might be at stake.

Chapter Twenty-Five

I jumped back when Castice rushed the glass. Throwing my arms up to block the incoming glass, I closed my eyes tight and held my breath, bracing for impact. When nothing happened, I lowered an arm and peaked over the top, only to jump back a bit when Rom and Kiso flashed in front of me, slightly blocking my view. I huffed at my lack of bravery when I found Castice on the floor, palming his head in pain. I hadn't heard a thing. The walls didn't look thick, but they appeared impenetrable and soundproof. Anolla looked determined yet disturbed as she paced her cage, ignoring everything around her while talking to herself.

I was just about to say hello to my old guards but stopped myself when I remembered they wouldn't remember me. Turning to Kalen, I raised an eyebrow and said, "I realize I was the one to suggest we detain them, but is all this necessary?" Sweeping my arm at their elaborate prison for emphasis. When he continued to study me without replying, I added on a shrug, "Seems a bit overkill to me. Surely we don't need to treat them as prisoners? After all, they're victims in the grand scheme of things."

Kalen nodded like he agreed with me, only to throw me for a loop with the next thing out of his mouth, "Even though you have a lot to learn, I appreciate your council. But in this instance, I think we should exude caution. We don't know enough about the infectious agent at this exact moment. Your friends might already be infected. Until we do, we shouldn't take anything for granted. If Anolla doesn't portray any of the symptoms shortly before or after her historical death, then we will revisit their accommodations."

Grateful he didn't make me feel like a fool, I gave him a playful smirk before I asked, "Can we at least talk to them?"

I had no idea what I would say to them, but if history repeated itself, I'd never forgive myself if I didn't, at least, tell them why we brought them here. I felt like I owed it to them. The questions I kept tossing around were, *if it were me . . . would I want to know? Would I be grateful for the time? Would I use that time to make peace with my demise, or would the anticipation of my looming death be like an early death sentence?* In the end, I decided if it were me, I would want to know so that I could make peace with myself. With my decision made, I hoped like hell Anolla and Castice would agree with me. Crossing every body part possible, I used my eyes to convey how much I needed him to side with me.

With a sigh, he heard my silent request and agreed, "I don't see the harm in it." Grabbing my shoulders, he squeezed them before he turned me around and molded my body to his. Almost like he was reminding me of what I was missing. I shivered with awareness with how right it felt as waves of desire coursed through my body. When he took his time sucking and kissing my neck, I knew I'd never be able to deny him anything. I was panting with need by the time he whispered in my ear, "Do me a favor, please don't try to be a hero." Tapping my necklace reverently, he added, "I'm trusting you won't make me regret turning this off."

I scoffed at his remark but didn't want to give him any reason to change his mind. Turning to look at him over my shoulder, my gaze bounced between his eyes before I replied, "I won't let you down, but as for promises . . . I only have one to give. From this day forward, I promise to spend eternity ensuring you have no reason to doubt me."

Kalen gave me a small smile that didn't touch his eyes before he answered, "I look forward to it. I'm sure you remember Rom and Kiso. They'll be here as well as Tanen while you talk to your friends. I'll be assisting Zarina as she interrogates the doppelganger." Kalen replied. Pushing me toward Tanen while he addressed his second in command, "Guard this woman with your life because if she dies, I won't hesitate to follow her."

I stumbled forward ungracefully but managed to stop myself before I made a complete fool of myself. I should have been thinking of what I would say or ask the victims in front of me, but I couldn't get over what Kalen said. He was talking about suicide if something were to happen to me. Heck, I'd be lying if I didn't admit that I was more than feeling territorial when Kalen mentioned working with a female that wasn't me! Flipping around, I opened my mouth to ask him what he meant, only to find he had already flashed away.

Ten minutes earlier and I wouldn't have been able to do anything about his abrupt departure, but I wasn't a poor defenseless female now. Reaching out with my gift, I contemplated which power would suit my needs best. Not wanting to chance flashing too far into the room or not far enough, I opted on using someone's ability to phase through anything except water instead. Marching forward, I passed through the soundproof wall undetected and stopped behind my mate. Tapping my foot in annoyance, I ignored the snarls coming from the doppelganger and waited until my mate turned around to face me before I blurted out how I was feeling. "Although I would prefer you live forever regardless of what happens to me, I accept your Thelma and Louise offer. Where you go, I go. Starting now."

I smiled sweetly, squealing in surprise when Kalen swept me into his arms. He erected a bubble around us and growled, "I have no idea what you mean by your Thelma and Louise reference, but I can only assume it means where you go, I follow. And if indeed that's what it means, then I accept."

I giggled in response, finding it hard to be serious in his presence. I felt nothing but love and acceptance emanating from our bond. I wasn't sure how he expected me to respond to his query.

"You are making it extremely hard for me to contain my animalistic nature. I want a mate that can rule beside me, but I also want to hide you away from anything and everything that could hurt you. It is a dichotomy I doubt I'll ever master, but I'll make an effort to try. Let's start with finding out why you are mad. I thought you wanted to question Anolla and Castice?"

When he responded so rationally, it made me feel like a child throwing a temper tantrum. I needed to remember why I'd come in here in the first place and use my damn words. If there was any chance of us having a happily-ever-after, he needed my honesty first and foremost. Taking a deep breath, I ripped off the band-aid we'd managed to place on our mangled entanglement and admitted on a sigh, "I did . . . I do. I mean, it's just that . . . Gah! Fine, you want to know what's wrong?" I paused for a moment while I searched his eyes, trying to gauge if he was interested in the truth.

When his gaze showed nothing but concern and curiosity, I dropped my head along with my pride and laid it all out on the line, "I thought we'd do all of this together. Talk to the victims, torture the prisoner or prisoners if need be, whatever it was . . . I envisioned us doing it together as a team. I didn't anticipate feeling jealous of a female named Zarina, who would be working beside you. I didn't foresee hating her before I even had the chance of meeting her."

Kalen lifted my chin with his finger and wiped away a tear I didn't realize had escaped before he replied with a sweet smile, "You'll never know how much your confession soothes my soul. I only thought we would divide and conquer. You know the saying, kill two birds with one stone. You question your fellow trial participants while I secure the doppelganger during Zarina's interrogations."

I raised my eyebrow at how accommodating he was, and with a snicker, he reluctantly admitted, "Alright, the time constraint wasn't my first concern. I wanted to keep you as far away from the assassin as possible but didn't want to feel like a neanderthal.

245

However, even you must feel the clock ticking. Anolla's original time of death last time around is less than half an hour from now."

Feeling cocky, I smirked, "Time is irrelevant when you can wield it. Instead, I'd like you to introduce me to Zarina. Perhaps you can explain to me what this interrogation will entail. I'd like to know where I could be of help. Afterward, if we are short on time, I'll make more."

"Are you sure you have that power? It doesn't look like Natashia and Levi followed us here," Kalen asked with a frown.

"I'm sure. They might not be here, but Natashia is still close enough. Regardless she's not the only one with the power," I replied, wondering where we were in retrospect to everyone else. If I had to guess, I'd say somewhere in the middle because I'd never felt so many different and unique gifts at my fingertips. It was almost overwhelming. There were plenty of people who had some version of time manipulation that I could rely on my power to use the most convenient and reliable one to get the job done.

"Interesting," Kalen replied as he rubbed his lower lip in thought.

"Not to sound clueless…but why is that interesting?" I asked in confusion.

"Time-travelers are required to declare themselves. Natashia is one of two in our army, and Takhor is on a mission off-planet," Kalen answered with an expression of worry.

Scrunching my forehead, I tilted my head from side to side as I tried to come to terms with Kalen's admission. I wasn't one to rat people out, but I knew there were at least a dozen different Sixers with the capability of manipulating time in some way.

Licking my lips, I took a deep breath before I continued, "Don't get me wrong, not everyone has the same power as Natashia, but she's not the only one able to control time in some way or another. For instance, there is an elemental that can travel at the speed of light. Also, you should know there is someone made of light," I answered reluctantly.

Kalen looked at me like I'd lost it before he replied, "The elemental you're referring to would be Parthyn. He's a councilman with the ability to control electricity. One of the perks of his gift would be his ability to travel at the speed of light. In contrast, the being of light you might be referencing is Zarina. The woman you wanted to meet. She's a Sulnitian from the planet Sulnix in the One Galaxy. Regardless of their identities, though, I don't see how their gifts have anything to do with time-travel."

I cocked my head and thought about it as my power poked and prodded at the intricacies of each gift. At the surface, Parthyn's ability to manipulate electrical energy made it appear he could do nothing besides wield electricity. Still, I knew without a doubt he was capable of so much more. I could almost see the abilities like levels in a video game. The Sixer couldn't access their next ability until they'd mastered their current level, but my gift was like having the ultimate cheat code. I knew all the secrets and had access to every aspect of the gift without playing the game. I'd known announcing my prowess was somewhat of a death sentence, but if I wanted to be a queen, I needed to act like it.

Taking a second to dissect Parthyn's gift, I smiled, disabled Kalen's gravity bubble around us, and said, "If that were the case, I wouldn't be able to do this." Pulling on the elemental's ability, I sucked in a deep breath when my body started glowing. At first, it was subtle until it wasn't, and my body shuttered as it transformed into a being of electrical energy. Not giving myself a chance to second guess myself, I opened a wormhole from one point in time to another and jumped through. I dropped the light-being persona as soon as I appeared beside my past self. I was beaming with pride, having timed it perfectly. My prior self had just finished saying the words, *watch this,* before she turned into a walking lightbulb and blinked away less than a second later, in essence catching up to the me who just arrived. If Kalen hadn't been watching, he would have missed seeing two of me at once. As it was, the look of despair and then amazement on his face was priceless.

Looking at me with caution, he scanned the room a few times before he said, "How did you do that?"

"I accessed his gift of electricity and opened a wormhole between two points in time," I answered with a frown. Not understanding the fuss, I asked, "What's the big deal?"

"I've known Parthyn for thousands of years and traveling at the speed of light is a fairly recent discovery. If I'm correct, that only happened within the last one hundred years. Are you telling me you have more control over his power than him?"

"I don't know about control or stamina, but I have complete confidence in the fact that I know every nuance of his gift— anybody's gift, for that matter. Comes with the territory, I guess," I explained with a shrug.

Kalen opened his mouth like he wanted to say more but was interrupted by a female voice.

"My lord, I don't mean to interrupt, but I feel like I need to remind you of my presence. Normally I'm hard to ignore, seeing how bright I shine, but you seem a bit occupied. Would you like me to come back later?"

Turning around to face Zarina, I had to slam my eyes shut as a defensive measure. Calling her bright was an understatement and had me wondering how I didn't notice her sooner. Throwing a hand up to block her brilliance, I looked over my shoulder, waiting for my mate to introduce us or, at a minimum, respond. When he continued to just stare at me, I cleared my throat and whispered, "Kalen . . . the nice lady is asking you a question."

Kalen continued to look at me with awe before he shook his head and finally answered, "No, that's ok, Zarina. We're on a tight schedule. I'd like to get started right away with the interrogation, but before we do. Have you had a chance to meet my mate, Jade?"

"Can't say I've had the pleasure," Zarina replied with a bow of her head.

Using my hand as a shield, I faced her with a smile plastered on my face and said, "I'd say the pleasure is all mine, but to be honest, I need a welder's mask to stand in your presence. Seriously do you have a dimmer switch?"

The brightness in the room dropped immediately. Dropping my arm, I gave Zarina a lopsided grin and said, "Thanks."

"No reason to thank me. I should have done it as soon as you turned around. I love it when people dare to ask for what they want. I must say I'm looking forward to watching you put this Strix in his place. When needed, of course . . . Will anyone else be joining us, or should we get started?"

Kalen scoffed, cleared his throat, and answered, "Natashia and company are running late, but I see no reason why we should delay. Where do you want me?"

"Wherever you feel comfortable, to be honest. I know you know the drill, but here's my standard spiel. Think of it as a precaution. I can't guarantee the prisoner's safety if they are allowed to move a single muscle. My leeches become aggressive if they feel threatened."

Kalen nodded, braced his feet, and said, "I'm ready when you are. He won't move a muscle."

I looked between the Sixers and couldn't help but ask, "What exactly will you be doing? I mean, don't take this the wrong way, but the gift I can sense from you has nothing to do with torturing the truth out of this imposter."

With a chuckle, Kalen leaned down and rasped, "I love your ability to read people's powers and capabilities, but Zarina is a package deal. As a being of light, she has a symbiotic relationship with a colony of mind-leeches. They'll extract the information we need, and she'll project the memories they obtain onto the wall behind us for all to see like a movie."

At that revelation, the doppelganger started changing his outer appearance while screaming in protest, "No! Offer me money. Offer me prestige. Offer me anything. At this point, I'm not picky! Let me keep my dignity!"

Chapter Twenty-Six

With every step Zarina took, the doppelganger changed the face he was wearing like he was hoping one of his impersonations would grant him leniency. The first was an old man, "You wouldn't harm a defenseless blind man, would ya?" When that didn't stop Zarina's progression, the doppelganger morphed into a small, malnourished girl with dirty brown hair that begged, "Please. I'm innocent. Don't hurt me. I'm scared! I want my mommy!"

It was hard to watch the trickery, but when she continued without faltering, my respect for her grew. She paid no attention to the child's pleading as she continued to march forward. If I needed to deal out torture or, for that matter, order it, then the least I could do was stomach the ordeal in front of me. Trying to ignore the punishment about to commence, I tried to focus on Zarina, but a familiar voice caught my attention, "Jade help me. I know you don't know me and that I come off as a grade-A bitch, but if you'd lived even a fraction of my life, you'd understand why. I've had to harden myself against the world. Please stop this. I beg you!"

No matter how much I wanted to ignore her pleas, I found myself enraptured by the fiery siren strapped to a bed in the center of the room. She looked identical to the redhead with an attitude from my transport ship. Nudging Kalen, I whispered, "That's Cynosis from Acelex. We arrived here together, but besides that, we had no connection. Why would it have her face?"

"I have no idea, but we are about to find out. I'll send Tanen to fetch the siren and bring her back here. I have no doubt she'll be easy to recognize. Not many people I know have her coloring," Kalen replied while pointing towards the doppelganger for reference.

I assumed Kalen's silence meant he was communicating his order to his second via telepathy. My guess was confirmed when Tanen flashed away seconds later.

Zarina approached cautiously, nibbling on her bottom lip as the doppelganger continued to beg for mercy. It was fascinating to watch him flip through different faces as the doppel tried to work our sensitivities. Kalen brushed past me, cutting off any further complaints or face changes from the imposter with a flick of his hands. I could tell Zarina was still nervous as she stopped next to the doppelganger, who had taken on the appearance of a twenty-something man with Down Syndrome before Kalen cranked up the gravity surrounding him. I almost wished Kalen had waited for a second longer so I wouldn't have to stare at the innocent face he was wearing. The young man's look of acceptance and empathy was close to my undoing.

Averting my eyes as a last-ditch effort, I watched Zarina glance back at my mate one more time before she nodded and said, "We only need about a minute, maybe two, depending on how old he is."

"He's not going anywhere and won't move a muscle. Take your time and be thorough. I don't want to miss anything important besides the obvious of who hired him. I want to know why they hired him and the reason why they went after my mate," Kalen growled.

Without knowing what to expect from Zarina's gift or her pet mind-leeches, I almost choked on my saliva when she held her hands out, and glowing slug-like things dripped from her fingers. It was almost like watching someone making pasta with a Cuisinart. Cutting off pieces of dough as it squeezed through the machine. In total, six leeches dropped onto his chest—each one roughly the size of my pinky finger.

I heard Kalen swear as the doppelganger's last disguise melted away to reveal what I could only assume was his true self. A grey face that resembled modeling clay with glowing, yellow eyes stared back at us. The look of terror on his face as they inched their way up to his head would haunt my nightmares.

"My lord? Do you have him?" Zarina pressed with a look of concern on her face.

"If I try any harder, he'll implode. I have no idea how he's moving!" Kalen hissed.

I could see sweat gathering on his forehead and wanting to help; I borrowed the first gift that could assist us. It had to be something useful and foolproof in ensuring the doppel stayed still. Kalen, no doubt, wouldn't like my next move, but seeing as I needed to be close to use my newly gained power, he'd have to get over it. Closing my hand into a fist, I approached the doppel's head, and when I was close enough, I opened my hand in front of his face and blew. As expected, a cloud of fine dust covered his face. He'd have no choice but to follow my direction. When his face went blank and he ceased struggling, I told him not to move anything. When he stopped breathing, I realized I might have taken the command a bit too far.

I was about ready to amend my command but stopped as I watched the first leech dissolve into his eye, followed closely by the rest. I'm not going to lie; I have a phobia of things touching my eyes.

The act made me shudder and had me taking a step back before I spoke up, "Um, not to put any pressure on you, Zarina, but . . . um . . . could you speed this up?"

"I'll try, but no promises. My friends are working as fast as the speed of light. Think of a mind like a map with vast distances between memories. Even though they travel at the speed of light, it still takes time to reach their destination. Why do you ask?" Zarina replied, cocking her head to the side.

"Well, probably 'cause I accidentally commanded him not to move anything. I didn't realize it would cause him to stop all bodily functions. Guess I didn't realize how powerful the pixie dust would be," I answered in a higher voice than usual as I tried to play off my fuck up like it was no big deal.

"Jade?" Kalen growled from behind me.

I cringed and turned on my heel. Taking a deep breath for courage, I lifted my gaze to meet Kalen's and immediately wished I hadn't. His look of uncertainty made me nervous. I didn't want him to lock me away or, worse, lock my ability away again. Swallowing the lump in my throat, I croaked, "Kalen?"

"Come here," he rumbled, fisting his hands at his sides. He looked like he was ready to explode and was barely holding himself back.

Standing a bit taller, I cleared my throat and replied, "I'm not so sure that would be a good idea right now. I mean, I have no idea how long my command will last. I should be close in case I need to do it again." My eyes flicked towards the doppelganger before they moved back to the man who set me on fire with just his voice.

"Do you mean to tell me Clara's gift is the only one nearby you can use to control his mind?" Kalen challenged as he edged closer to me.

"Clara?" I questioned.

"I believe Clara is the pixie you are referring to. She's a member of the council and Anolla's aunt. You met her briefly at the council meeting before you haphazardly went back in time. Regardless, her dust can make her victims do what she wants, but she's never been able to bypass one's will to survive," Kalen explained with a look of admiration on his face once again. He took another step closer to me like a predator not wanting to spook his prey. Which almost made me laugh, considering he could flash to me in an instant. But he probably didn't want to chance losing control over the doppelganger.

In the back of my mind, I knew it was only a matter of moments before he wrapped me in his arms, but I couldn't find it in myself to step away or make a break for it. Instead, I found myself nodding my head slowly before answering, "I see." However, I didn't see and felt out of sorts. Trying to decipher what he was implying, I continued nodding my head like a fool. Only to be saved from having to address what he was implying when Zarina yelled, "They've got what they need and are on their way out. Give us five more seconds!"

I flicked my eyes in Zarina's direction, trying to determine if the doppel was still alive. His lips were already grey, so it was hard to tell if he was turning blue from lack of oxygen like a human would. I moved to get closer and squealed when Kalen dragged me backward, pulling me into his chest as he growled into my ear, "You're trying my patience, Jade. I want you to use your power. Your gift is amazing and something to be proud of, but the need to keep you safe overwhelms that want. I'm unable to control this creature on my own completely; I don't trust you near him."

I could tell it took a lot for him to admit what he perceived as a failure, but I needed him to know that where his gift left off, mine would take over. True partners would fill the gaps in each other's lives, making us an abominable opponent as a whole. We'd fail if he didn't start trusting me. We needed to learn to lean on each other if we expected to make it out of this mess on top. Wrapping my arms around his arms, I replied, "You don't have to trust him. You just need to trust me."

Kalen nuzzled my neck, breathing me in before he rasped, "Trust goes both ways, mate." At the same time, Zarina announced, "Done!"

With her hand extended to the doppel's face, she caught the last mind-leech as it seeped from his eye. I watched in awe as it dissolved into her skin. "Where would you like to view his memories, sir?" She looked over at us with a raised eyebrow before she added, "Not like it's any of my business, but if you intend to let him live, now would be a good time to reverse your command."

"We'll meet you in the council room," Kalen answered, ignoring her last statement. I looked up at Kalen and could see he could care less if the doppel lived or died. It was also apparent he wasn't letting me anywhere near him. With a sigh, I tried changing my command. Maybe the pixie dust was still viable? "You may move everything again."

When his body arched off the bed, I scrambled backward as his mouth opened in a silent scream. Kalen tightened his hold on me and called for assistance. Five Sixers flashed into the room as the doppelganger dropped back onto the bed immobile. His eyes stared off into nothing. He was dead. I couldn't stop the tears as I wailed, "Oh my god, I killed him!"

Chapter Twenty-Seven

Kalen murmured reassurances in my ear as I went limp in his arms, "It might not have been you, and even if it was . . . he was a horrible being and, in my opinion, deserved what he got. Don't beat yourself up about it. You can't change what happened and accepting it will only make it easier in the end."

"But I can change it. I could heal him or reverse time so that I didn't command him to cease living. He might not have been a good person, but it shouldn't be up to me to be his judge and juror," I choked out on a sob.

"Please don't cry; it's killing me," Kalen whispered in my ear.

Not wanting to hurt my mate or make a fool of myself any more than I already had, I swallowed my cry and watched without emotion as a couple of Sixers cautiously approached the still doppelganger. I was having a hard time reconciling my gift was capable of taking a life. He should have been fine, damn it! Zarina's bugs had been in and out in less than a minute. Most humans should be able to go without fresh oxygen for two minutes or more before injury or death . . . Shit! He wasn't fucking human. I should have taken into consideration that his species might be different. Damn, what was I thinking?

Averting my eyes from the lifeless doppel, I studied the Sixers Kalen had summoned to help. I didn't recognize most of them, but it gave me hope when I spotted Dr. Annalise Triste. She was the first to reach his side and didn't waste any time as she began sweeping her hands over the doppelganger's body. I started to worry when a frown marred her face, and she dropped her hands in defeat seconds later. Looking at me, she said, "I'm sorry. He's passed over the line, my power can't reach him. If he's still needed, we could request a necromancer to reanimate him."

Struggling to free myself from Kalen's hold, I swore, "Damn it! The threat is dead. Either come with me or let me go!"

Kalen released me but crowded my backside as I rushed forward to see for myself he was indeed dead. Ignoring those around me, I reached for Annalise's gift and placed my hands over his core. Pumping her healing juju into his chest, I visualized compressing his heart, trying to mimic the motion of CPR. I wouldn't take no for an answer. I'd will him to live, even if I needed to turn him into a zombie. At least then he'd be something other than dead.

Feeling drained, I directed the last of my energy into his resurrection and would have pushed more if Kalen hadn't interfered by flashing us to the hallway outside of the doppelganger's cell. I whimpered when I felt the doppel's lifeline flicker and wished I was close enough to help. A part of me knew I was pushing my limits. I could tell my energy reserves were close to being depleted, but I knew his life was salvageable. I just needed to be close enough to make a difference, or did I? As I let my gift guide me, I realized if I left my physical being, I'd be able to finish what I started.

The moment I felt myself disconnecting from my body, something shoved me back in with force. At the same time, I heard a mysterious voice in my head, "What are you an overachiever? You've got nothing left in your tank. Let me handle it!"

Shaking my head, I looked down at my hands and wondered why I'd push myself so far. It felt like I was seconds away from trading my life for the doppelgangers. If the mystery man hadn't stopped me when he did, I very well could have. Chancing a peek at my mate, I recoiled when he pinned me with a glare. I could feel the rage rolling off him in waves. I knew better than to ask him why he'd flashed us away. I was lucky he hadn't taken me to my own prison to keep me from injuring myself further.

"I'm still considering it," Kalen growled low.

I gasped and turned to face him. Knowing I hadn't spoken out loud, I questioned him, "Considering what exactly?"

"Don't play coy. I'm still considering locking you away for your own good!" Kalen seethed.

"How did you know I was even thinking about that?" I asked with a frown.

"Tanen's been keeping track of your thoughts for me," Kalen replied with a shrug.

My mouth dropped open at his revelation. I promptly snapped it closed and spun around in search of the Sixer who'd been spying on me. I spotted Tanen leaning against one of the glass enclosures. When he noticed my glare, he held his hands up in the air and said, "Sorry Jade. It was an order, but after listening in on your suicide mission, I'm glad he pushed it. I don't think my best friend would be consolable if he had to mourn the death of a mate he just found. I'd ask what you were thinking, but I was in there, and you weren't thinking about anything except saving that thing even if it was at the cost of your own life."

I was speechless. Tanen was right. I hadn't been thinking, and it scared me. With tears in my eyes, I faced Kalen again and whispered, "Sorry. I promise I don't have a death wish. I just didn't want to be the cause of someone's death."

Kalen's anger melted away at my disclosure before he flashed the short distance to me and gathered me in his arms. I fisted his shirt and buried my face in his chest. His strength was a balm to my frayed nerves. How would I live with myself if the mystery man wasn't able to save the doppelganger?

"What mystery man?" Kalen asked, lifting my chin with a finger until he could see my eyes.

"I didn't get a look at him, just heard his voice. He pushed me back into my body and told me I was an overachiever . . . among other things," muttering the last bit under my breath. As I thought about the interaction, it made me curious how the stranger had known I was about to attempt something of that nature in the first place. Just another unknown in a long list of questions I wasn't sure I had the energy to find answers to. Pulling away from Kalen, I peered around him and said, "He said he'd handle bringing the doppel back." The room the doppel occupied was a flurry of activity, and I couldn't tell what was going on. When Kalen remained silent, I turned my attention back to him and said, "Was he successful?"

Kalen was staring at Tanen like I'd lost my mind, and he was looking for guidance on how to handle me. My gaze bounced between the two Sixers, and when I couldn't take the silence any longer, I probed again, "Was the mystery man able to save the doppelganger?"

My mate looked down at me and cupped my cheek before he replied, "I don't know about your mystery man. We thought you were responsible. No one outside of those already in this room has been around, but to answer your question . . . technically the doppelganger is alive."

"What do you mean by that? Technically? Is he brain-dead?" I pushed, choosing to ignore his other statement. The one that implicated I saw things.

"No, his brain is functioning," Kalen answered uncomfortably.

"Then what's the issue?" I demanded.

"He's been wiped clean. He has no memories," Tanen responded.

I whirled around to face Tanen and said, "Wiped? How's that possible? Nothing I did should have wiped him. Could the mind-leeches have done it?"

"Not their usual modus operandi. If the leeches become flustered during their work, they'll attack the brain from the inside and will take more than just memories. No, this was something else. Something outside of your control as well, so don't beat yourself up about it," Kalen replied before adding, "Speaking of memories. Zarina is waiting for us in the council room. Did you want to talk to your friends before we leave?"

Talk to my friends? Damn, in all the craziness, I'd completely forgotten about Anolla and Castice. I took a deep breath, turned to face them, and noticed that Cynosis had joined them in a cell of her own. I expected her to be pissed off, but instead she looked like a lost puppy as she stared at Tanen in wonder. Tilting my head to the side, I raised an eyebrow and said, "How do I talk to them? I thought the glass was soundproof."

"It's one-way glass. They can hear you, but we can't hear them," Tanen answered as he studied Cynosis with interest.

"Great, I'll hold a one-way conversation with them. Seriously, I know you guys are aware that's not conducive to an interrogation. How can I hear what they have to say to my questions?" I shot back with a nervous chuckle. I hated being caught off guard by that knowledge.

Kalen threw Tanen a dirty look as he approached Anolla's cell. He placed his hands on the glass, and before long the enclosing glass sunk into the floor, revealing an electrical force field surrounding them instead. I moved to intervene when he kept his hands in place, afraid he was being electrocuted until he removed his hands in surrender with a chuckle and addressed my fellow trial participants, "It's safe on this side of the enclosure, but not yours. I wouldn't recommend touching the walls from your side unless you'd like to find out what two million volts of electricity feel like."

Turning to me, he smirked at the look of surprise on my face before he said, "You should be able to hear them now."

I expected our captives to start voicing their concerns, but all of them looked at me with apprehension. They were waiting for me to explain why we imprisoned them against their will. Swallowing the lump in my throat, I cleared my throat a couple of times before I found my voice. Thankful when it came out strong, "My name is Jade, and I had you brought here for your protection."

"No offense, but I don't know who you are and if your true intentions were to protect us, why are we in the dungeons?" Anolla demanded with an air of indifference despite her circumstances.

Castice chose not to engage but observed me while he paced his quarters. Cynosis didn't even bother to acknowledge my existence as she continued to stare at Tanen. I did not doubt that if she had a chance, she'd make him pay. I could practically see flames burning in her eyes at her kidnapper. I wrapped my hair around my finger while I contemplated how I would answer. I could use my gift to remind them of who I was or ignore it for the most part while I addressed the real issue . . . their deaths.

In the end, I went for honesty, "You should all know me as the tall blond who was supposed to be participating in the trials with you tomorrow." When they started to protest, I held up my hand and added, "To be fair, this isn't the first time we've met . . . the person you saw today was a facade. I wanted to hide my true self so I could go undercover to solve a mystery when I went back in time."

While I let that thought sit, I eyed each of them before I addressed why we had them incarcerated. "Not to be the bearer of bad news, but I feel it's only fair; you should know why you are here. Anolla and Castice . . . we brought you here because both of you died within hours of each other . . . by the same thing."

Anolla gasped in response and slapped her hands over her mouth, shaking her head back and forth in denial before she screamed, "No! It's not possible. You're lying!" At the same time, Castice stammered out, "What did we die of?"

Anolla's head snapped to Castice in surprise. You could tell she wanted to reprimand him for his betrayal, but after opening and closing her mouth a few times like a fish out of water, she shut her mouth firmly and looked at me with disgust. Choosing silence instead of admission, she crossed her arms over her chest in defiance. Ignoring her wrongly placed attitude, I addressed Castice instead, "We're not sure. No one has been able to narrow down the causative agent. It's one of the reasons why I asked them to bring you here. Besides my prior knowledge of what and when something happened in the past, we're flying blind. Unless, of course, one of you might be able to tell me who might be out to kill both of you. Any kind of lead is better than nothing."

"That's not what I meant!" Castice roared.

Kalen growled next to me, directing our reluctant captive's attention to my mate. Castice licked his lips and directed his gaze to Anolla instead of the real threat in the room. Curious. I couldn't help but watch their interaction. Not bothering to hide her disdain, Anolla glared at Castice before she shook her head and said, "Defiance, deceit, death."

Castice's face fell in response before he turned to Kalen and answered in a flat tone, "I meant no offense. It's just that I think it would help us narrow our focus in the right area if we knew."

I opened my mouth to tell him how they died when Cynosis chose to speak up, "Why am I here? I mean, you said Anolla and Castice died in this alternate time, but why am I here? Are these cells on their own air system? I mean, if it's contagious, I don't want to catch something from them."

Turning my attention to Cynosis, I replied, raising my hands in the air, "It doesn't appear to be airborne, so although I have no idea what type of ventilation system they've got going on in here . . . .you and everyone else should be fine." Dropping my hands in defeat, I added, "To answer your question, though, you're here because an assassin recently copied you, and we need to question your loyalties. Determine if you are with us or against us."

Cynosis cocked her head to the side, a frown crossing her face before she answered, "Loyalties? I'm as loyal as they come, and what do you mean copied? By what?"

"A doppelganger," Castice uttered with a wild look in his eye.

Flipping my attention back to Castice, I wanted to ask him how he knew that information, but then I remembered they had a front-row seat to the doppelganger's torture session. Heck, they might have even seen him turn into Cynosis. Clearing my throat to address Cynosis, I jumped when I heard Anolla scream out in pain. Instinctively I knew what was happening, but a part of me hoped as I turned toward her that history wouldn't repeat itself. Natashia had said she'd tried multiple times to save the girl with no success, and it seemed my attempt was no different.

Chapter Twenty-Eight

Anolla dropped to the floor and clawed at her neck, frantic for breath. The look of horror on her face as she crawled across the ground towards me would give me nightmares for years to come. I stood frozen as I watched her murder for a second time. Even though I knew what was next, watching her bend in half on a silent scream as black blood seeped from all of her orifices would never be easy. Both Castice and Cynosis backed as far away as their cells would allow while they cowered in fear. I closed my eyes and wished I could hide from the reality of the situation. When her cries cut off, I dared to open my eyes and immediately averted them when I realized it wasn't over. Kalen had dropped the glass wall around her cell so we wouldn't have to hear her screams.

The gesture was appreciated and would have been a perfect resolution if Cynosis and Castices' cries didn't remind me of the situation. As it was, I could hear Cynosis whimpering while Castice kept repeating, "It can't be. It's a mirage. Anolla didn't break the pact in any way. It can't be . . . It can't be."

Talk of a pact drew my attention, and although I didn't want to attack him when he was already having a hard time dealing with his friend's death, I'd be neglecting my duty as future Queen if I didn't question him further. Going off instinct, I approached his cell and waited until I had his attention. I pointed in the direction of Anolla and said, "Does that answer your question?" I waited until he looked at Anolla before I continued, "I didn't want her to die. I was hoping by whisking you guys here, I would prevent the infection from happening. Unfortunately, it was a gamble that didn't pay off for your friend without knowing the incubation period. Now that you know what you both died of, do you have information that would lead us to who might be responsible?"

"In the past, how . . . how many hours elapsed between our deaths?" Castice asked with a quiver in his voice, nodding to Anolla with tears in his eyes.

"We don't have the exact time of your death, but Anolla died in the evening at our banquet dinner, and your death was in the middle of the night. We're guessing anywhere between eight to ten hours apart. Which leads us to believe you were infected at different times. I can tell you're hiding something. Help us help you and tell us who you think might be responsible for your demise."

Castice shook his head a moment before he looked up at me void of all emotion and said, "I don't know what you're talking about."

His response surprised me. I was confident once he faced his killer, he'd spill everything. Was my prejudice once again warping my reality? Taking a deep breath, I tried to tame my temper before I questioned him again, "Are you telling me you've never seen anything like this before?"

Castice averted his eyes before he answered, "I've never seen anyone die such a horrific death."

To say I was frustrated with his lack of cooperation was an understatement. Not wanting him to know how disappointed I was with his answers, I tipped my head and replied, "Very well. I'm sure you'll understand our need to keep you here under surveillance."

"For how long?!" Castice demanded.

I spared him a glance as I stalked past his cell to stand in front of Cynosis before I bothered to answer him. Keeping my eyes on the redhead whose only crime was being in the wrong place at the wrong time, I replied, "If you're not dead within the next twelve hours, I think it will be safe to assume you weren't affected."

"So if I'm still alive at the end of your timeline, you'll let me go?" Castice asked, pushing off the wall with unsure steps.

"No. That's not what I said," I answered with a smirk, looking back at him with pity.

"You said we were here for our protection," Castice complained with a look of confusion on his face.

Nodding my head in agreement, I gave him a sinister smile before I answered him, "There's truth in that statement. There's also truth in the statement that we brought you here to protect everyone from being infected by an unknown agent. Although, I must admit the largest contributing factor to why I'm keeping you incarcerated is because I suspect you know something about what killed Anolla. You should know that I don't like being lied to. Call it a pet peeve, but I have every intention of keeping you here until you tell me what you're hiding from us or die . . . whichever comes first." Giving him my most innocent look, I purred, "Are you sure you don't want to change your mind?"

Castice's gaze flicked between Anolla's corpse, Kalen, and me a couple of times before he dropped his gaze in defeat, took a deep breath and said on a sigh, "I have nothing to tell you."

"I have a hard time believing that," I replied sarcastically as I approached his cell before I added, "In fact, I'd be willing to make a wager."

Castice raised his head, pinning me with his gaze. I knew he had no idea what my gift was, but I could practically see him calculating his odds as he studied my face. Confident in himself, he finally answered, "I have no secrets, so I have nothing to lose. What kind of wager do you propose?"

"My wager is if you're lying, I get to choose your job after the trials. If you're not, then you'll choose mine," I replied with a grin.

"How would you know I'm lying?" Castice stammered as he struggled to look me in the eye.

I laughed until tears ran from my eyes. I wiped them away and said, "You have no idea what I'm capable of, do you?"

Castice looked at me with apprehension before he replied, "I'm beginning to think you're about to educate me."

"Would you like to change your answer?" I countered with a raised eyebrow.

"My life is forfeited the second I reveal my secrets. I doubt anything you could offer would make me change my story. I'm sorry. I wish I could help you, but my path was decided a long time ago," Castice replied in defeat.

"What if I was the one to reveal your secrets? Would your life still be at risk?" I prodded. I watched for any signs my words were on target.

A hint of interest flashed through his eyes, which gave me hope that if I used my gift to pry the information from his memories, he be unharmed. Trusting in myself, I released my breath slowly as I closed my eyes and grabbed ahold of Tanen's mind-reading gift. It took me a moment to drown out the voices that were thinking of me, but once I figured out how to block them, I focused on individual thoughts.

Thankfully, a person's thoughts resembled their actual voices. I isolated Castice in my head. I expected to find his mind going in a million different directions, but instead, he was focused and kept repeating the phrase, *Nothing to see here*, over and over again. His resourcefulness had me smiling. If all I could see were his thoughts, his smoke and mirror trick might have worked, but my gift revealed a back door to his inner mind and provided me the lockpick to open it.

Visualizing myself cracking a safe, I flung open the door to his mind and stopped abruptly when I found myself in a giant circular colosseum with nothing in it but thousands of doors. I looked around and groaned. Shit! I don't have time to investigate each one. I wasn't here to see his first steps or be a voyeur on one of his wet dreams. As I looked around me, it felt like I was at some kind of crossroads, and time was not on my side. I needed to consider all of my options. I could waste valuable time opening every door until I found what I was looking for, or I could walk away and focus my energy and time on other possibilities.

Castice wasn't the only one with answers to our questions. We still needed to see what Zarina and her mind-leeches were able to extract, and the only way we'd be able to do that was meet her in the council room. Hopefully, they'll have the smoking gun we're looking for, but if not, it would be a good idea to listen to her anyway—that way, when and if Castice finally cracked, we'd be able to compare notes.

In the end, I gave up and backed out the same way I had come. Opening my eyes, I looked at my mate's best friend and trusted bodyguard and said, "Gah! I don't know how you do it, Tanen! I mean, how do you narrow down which memory to open? Castice had thousands for me to sift through, and he's only twenty-five years old! I can't imagine what it'd be like to face an immortal. Not like it'd be easy to count, but I'm sure their memories could easily top a billion. You'll have to let me in on your secret someday."

Tanen frowned in response and looked at my mate with concern. After what I could only assume was a silent conversation between them, he finally gave Kalen a slight nod, plastered a half-smile on his face, and addressed me, "What do you mean by memories? My gift allows me to hear the thoughts of people thinking of me specifically. Although recently, if I concentrate, I can hear the thoughts of those around me, whether they are thinking of me or not. It's harder to catch and takes focus, but I'm twelve thousand years old."

Biting my lip, I barely stopped myself from blurting out, *Holy shit Dorothy, you're not in Kansas anymore!* As it was, I had to remember my thoughts were like an open book if I didn't start protecting them. With a smirk, I thanked Castice and began singing, *Hokey Pokey*, on repeat in my mind just in case . . . before I threw my shoulders back, squared my feet, and replied sarcastically, "Um . . . let's see . . . you just asked me to explain to you what a memory was? Are you serious right now? Or are you being sarcastic?"

When he looked at me in confusion, I opened my arms wide and explained, "A memory is stored information and has a prewritten storyline, whether real or planted. Which, as you know, differs greatly from a person's thoughts. Those are fair game to easy

281

manipulation and are usually in the present tense unless, of course, they're reminiscing."

Kalen placed a hand on my shoulder, drawing my attention. I dropped my arms in defeat, looked over my shoulder and stared at his hand until he removed it. With a smirk, I gave him my attention and tried not to lose myself in his gaze. He studied my eyes for a minute before he took a deep breath and said, "Tanen isn't able to see people's memories, Jade. Only their thoughts. I know I've said it before, but this just proves it. Your power is something to behold. Something beyond average. It scares me, to be honest." Kalen finished on a whisper.

"Why? You just admitted I'm capable of kicking ass," I exclaimed with a silly grin.

Turning me to face him, he crushed me to his chest and uttered, "There are people out there that would love to have control or access to your ability, and if they weren't able to secure your services willingly, they'd make sure no one else had access to them either."

Chapter Twenty-Nine

I'd never considered myself better than anyone else, and it felt weird to have it pointed out to me. Something I took for granted as normal was anything but, and it had me questioning my place in this new world I found myself in. It made me consider I might be worthy of being Kalen's mate after all. Sometimes life tended to be a rude wake-up call to your expectations, and I was its newest student. Placing my hands on Kalen's chest, I pushed with all my might and only managed a small gap between us. It was enough for me to see his eyes before I practically growled, "I can't change who I am, nor do I plan on hiding my abilities. What are you suggesting?"

I'd never seen Kalen more uncomfortable than he was trying to come up with an answer to my question. I decided to give him a pass since he was new to this whole relationship business when I answered for him, "Just like I wouldn't expect you to shy away from adversity. I would hope you would grant me the same courtesy. I'll be the first to admit I have no formal training and promise I won't openly engage in warfare until I feel like I can hold my own. There is just one thing . . . I'll never be okay with being left out, or worse, kept like a dirty secret."

Kalen looked like he'd been slapped in the face by my statement and took a moment to collect himself before he answered me, "First off, you are not a dirty secret. I couldn't be prouder to have you as my mate. If it were up to me, I'd advertise our union across the cosmos, but in doing so, I'd be putting an even bigger target on your back. Every enemy or potential enemy will try and use you against me. If I were the one hunted for my gift, what would you do?"

"We don't have proof someone's after me at the moment," I replied, holding up my hand to silence my mate when he opened his mouth to argue with me. I waited until he closed it with reluctance before I continued. "Thank you for letting me finish. I think you are overreacting a bit, but hypothetically speaking, I would listen to what you have to say, and then I'd probably never leave your side," I replied with a shrug.

Rom barely covered his laugh behind a cough at my admission. I smiled at him over my shoulder before I returned my gaze to Kalen. "I get you have primitive instincts screaming at you to lock me away for my protection," using air quotes to emphasize the word protection, "but I need your promise you'll control yourself from doing something that will drive a wedge between us. I deserve to be at your side. Please give us a chance."

Kalen searched my eyes for what felt like minutes. I could practically see the moment he gave in to my request when he released a deep sigh and told me the words I wanted to hear. "I promise to keep you by my side. No matter what happens. We'll do it together. Word of warning, though, I'm taking your suggestion to heart. I plan on being glued to your side for the foreseeable future."

My mouth dropped open in surprise at his proclamation. His words didn't match the severe scowl he had plastered across his face, but I decided to take his words at face value. I cleared my throat a couple of times before I dared to answer him. "That's all I'm asking. A chance to prove to you that we're stronger when we work together. I promise not to disappoint you or make you regret your decision. Shall we see what Zarina has for us while we let our friends stew on their life choices?" Nodding their way with my head.

"Hey now, wait just a minute! What do you mean stew on my life choices? I'm not a part of these guys' inner posse. The only thing I'm guilty of is competing and winning my planet's version of the trials to secure my spot as their representative in this year's All

Gathering. I have no idea why or when some kind of mimic might have copied me. You can't just leave me here!" Cynosis cried out.

I was almost ashamed I lumped her in with Onyx and her gang but gave myself a little bit of wiggle room when I considered how much stress I was under. Turning to face her, I nodded my head in understanding and waited until she finished before I answered her, "I'm sorry. I didn't mean to insinuate your involvement either way. To be honest, I'm a little overwhelmed and figured you'd speak up for yourself if you had anything to tell us that would either confirm or deny our suspicions. Since you're just as clueless as we are, I hope you understand our need to keep you here while reviewing the doppelganger's memories of the events leading up to your duplication. I promise we'll release you after everything is over."

"What do you mean release? Are we talking about being released to the general public, or are we referring to my freedom?" When I stayed silent, she turned her attention to Tanen and asked in a broken voice, "Will I still be allowed to compete in the trials?"

Her pain was obvious even without listening into her thoughts, but even I was startled when Tanen rallied for her further involvement in the trials with murder evident in his voice. "When she's proven innocent, there should be no reason why we'd deny it.

This is something she worked her whole life for," Tanen replied with a snarl.

His tone made me think he was angry on the siren's behalf, but the look of anguish on Tanen's face as he stared at Cynosis with longing was a contradiction in and of itself. His reaction made me want to know more, and it would be so easy to eavesdrop on their thoughts. But just because I had the power to do it didn't make it right. I needed to consider their privacy and remember I wouldn't want someone peeking in on my thoughts.

The moment I made up my mind Tanen looked at me over his shoulder and said, "Thank you, Jade. I wish I could offer you the same courtesy. There are times I wish I didn't know what people were thinking about me, but it's saved my life and those of my friends just as many times."

Cynosis let out a little gasp drawing our attention back to her. I could tell the second she realized he knew exactly what she was thinking when her face morphed from fascinated to horrified to pissed in the blink of an eye. If I had to guess, I'd bet her thoughts were anything but pure when it came to the mind-reading Sixer in front of her. Of course, Tanen was following her reaction and laughed out loud at something she must have been thinking.

Touching the cell in front of her, he dropped the glass enclosure silencing the retort she might have had when he said, "It will be my pleasure to prove you wrong when we return, Firecracker."

Turning on his heel, he faced us with a lopsided grin and said, "I believe you said Zarina was waiting for us in the council room. I know she's highly sought after; we shouldn't keep her waiting."

A part of me felt terrible as I watched Cynosis have a breakdown on the other side of the glass. Still, the piece of me that knew what we were up against, something bigger than her dreams, locked up the empathy I felt toward her, allowing me to reply, "With any luck, she'll have something concrete we can focus on. I hate feeling like we're a step or two behind, especially when we're not sure how many players are in the game."

"We'll follow you," Tanen replied, pointing to Rom and Kiso in reference before a slight grimace crossed his face.

I could only imagine the names Cyn was calling him as I grabbed onto Kalen and braced myself for transport. I imagined flashing would get more comfortable with practice, but it still took me a second to get my bearings after we popped out in the council room before I trusted myself to walk a straight line. I dropped into my seat with the grace of a robot and decided to own my goofiness. If they couldn't accept me at my worst, they didn't deserve my best. Chuckling at myself, I said, "I keep telling myself flashing will get easier. If I'm wrong, I'd rather not know. Because they say the definition of insanity is repeating the same action over and over again and expecting a different outcome and sometimes ignorance, or a good imagination, is bliss."

Kalen stood behind me, squeezed my shoulder and murmured, "You handle it better than most recruits. Don't worry, love, it gets better over time." Looking about the room, he nodded at the few people in attendance before he faced Zarina and said, "Sorry to keep you waiting, Zarina. What do you and your friends have to show us?"

"While we were waiting, I skimmed his early memories for anything of importance. Normally I wouldn't pay any attention to a target's younger years, but this one had an interesting upbringing. The Mengh demolished his home planet, and raised him in a mining camp in the outer reaches. It was unclear how he escaped, my friends were in a rush, but they were able to identify who hired the doppelganger to wage an internal coup. One designed to stack the odds in their favor," Zarina answered with disgust as she shook her head.

"What do you mean stack the odds? Was he hired to take out more than one person?" Kalen asked with a frown.

"Oh, it's more than that. It's a very elaborate scheme of domination. Don't take my word for it, though. Let me show you instead," Zarina replied with a smirk.

Chapter Thirty

Without knowing what to expect, my mouth dropped open in surprise when Zarina blinked a couple of times, and images began streaming from her eyes like a movie projector. I was just about to say I wish we could hear what was being said but choked on the words as she opened her mouth and sound poured out like a surround sound system.

On a long exhale, I whispered, "That's cool as fuck."

Kalen squeezed my shoulder again, either in agreement or as a warning to be quiet, but he had nothing to worry about. I was so engrossed in the memories of the doppelganger, whose real name was Skorn, that I was barely breathing. Zarina selected specific scenes to show us, so it was a bit choppy, like bloopers at the end of a movie, but in the end, it shaped the assassin and gave us a clue on who and what we were dealing with.

I had no idea if she gave us his background on my account, seeing as I did not know the supernatural world, but I appreciated it. His species are known hermaphrodites and usually don't choose a gender or a name until they've taken a mate. Skorn didn't get that choice. They forced him to be male during his captivity in the mining camps. My guess was the Mengh must have been looking for a more aggressive assassin. Regardless of the reason, the decision shaped the doppel we had in our custody. Even his chosen name made sense; to scorn something means to reject or hold in contempt. I didn't want to victimize the guy, but it was hard not to feel a little empathy towards him when you had access to some of the torment he endured.

Kalen's deep voice brought me back to reality when he said, "Enough. Show us this elaborate scheme you referenced earlier."

Zarina blinked a couple more times, and a new set of memories played out for us. I started sweating as I watched Skorn meet with Bastian several times. At least one of the meetings looked to be on his home planet. Secretly I was hoping Onyx would appear in one of them, so I could say I told you so, but the last meeting squashed those hopes.

In the first couple of encounters, it was apparent Bastian hired Skorn to help his family take over the council. He mentioned in their second meeting that one of their planet's most prized prophetesses foretold my arrival. Although at the time, it wasn't evident who it would be, just that the future queen would be a part of this year's trials. Skorn's first objective was to identify Kalen's mate and take her out if she wasn't their pick. Kalen's death was the last resort and would only be necessary if their main plan failed. When I recalled my first encounter with Onyx, she mentioned something about a seer foretelling she would be the king's mate. At the time, I thought she was lying, but perhaps she was being led to believe she was the one in the prophecy. Or was she in on it the whole time?

"Oh, hell no!" I spit out as I listened to their sinister plan to trap Kalen into mating with a puppet of their choice by killing me off and giving Kalen a love potion of some sort to make him think he'd found his mate. If that didn't work, Skorn was supposed to kill off Kalen and assume his position until they could transfer power somewhere else.

At the mention of my death, Kalen started growling, and when the final meeting, the one that included Bastian, Fansa, and Clary, concluded, he scooped me out of my seat and addressed the room, "I want someone following those three. Have Colton mark them with one of his pets. I'll be in touch."

"Wait!" Tanen called out.

Kalen leveled him with a glare and replied with a growl, "What?"

Tanen swallowed loudly but stood up straight before he answered, "What should I do with Cynosis? It wasn't completely apparent, but it looked like he was copying people at random in hopes he would get lucky and find your mate. He's strong. I've never known one able to copy a person by a simple touch, but it explains how he was able to steal so many people's identity without their knowledge."

"I'll leave her release to you," Kalen responded with a chuckle. "Oh, and by the way, I want to double the number of guards in the infirmary with instructions that they should keep their distance. I don't want any frivolous testing either. He either lives or he doesn't. If he makes it, we'll see if he's had a change of heart and would like a chance at true vengeance."

"How are you going to keep his incarceration a secret?" Natashia asked from behind us.

At hearing her voice, Kalen turned and bit out, "You're late."

Rolling my eyes at his brusque approach, I slapped his arm and said, "We need to work on your manners, dear. Put me down."

"No," he snarled, tightening his hold on me in defiance, completely ignoring my other comment.

His embrace was soothing, so I didn't push the issue. Let him think he had the upper hand. I'd save my fucks for a different battle. I smiled at my friend with a shrug. She returned my smile briefly before she stepped forward, only to be stopped by Levi's large hand on her shoulder. She looked up at him with annoyance and hissed under her breath, "I'm not going anywhere. I made a promise. Your mistrust is uncalled for."

When he dropped his hand reluctantly, she faced us again and continued, "We'll lose the element of surprise once they know we're holding him. As it is, they might already know and could be scrambling. What if this time around they decide just to eliminate everyone? I think we should either bring in Fansa preemptively, force her to tell us what we're dealing with or have Jade do it. Fansa should be capable of seeing something of this magnitude in one of her visions."

Kalen's whole frame stiffened at the mention of my possible demise. I half expected him to flash us away to the safe room. He surprised me when he dropped his head to mine and breathed me in. I felt him relax before he pulled back a bit and said, "Feel like being a fortune-teller?"

At one time in my short life, I thought the only things I was afraid of were needles and spiders, but the thought of seeing the future was terrifying. With a trembling voice, I said, "What if I don't like what happens. I have no doubt I'd drive myself nuts dreading the inevitable."

"Knowledge of the future is a powerful tool, but only if you use that information to your advantage. Trust me. We won't squander the gift of foresight," Kalen replied, cupping my cheek in his hand before he brushed his lips across mine in reverence. I melted in his arms and wished we were alone. His answering groan made me smile against his lips before I answered, "I'm willing to give it a go. IF you put me down."

His chuckle was music to my ears. He lowered me to the floor, letting me feel his rock-hard erection on the way down. A week ago, my answering moan would have embarrassed me, but there was no hiding what the man did to me. I bit my lower lip as I recalled how perfect he felt inside me and practically pouted when he flipped me around and engaged me in his arms. He leaned down and purred, "Be careful Jade, if you continue down that line of thought, I'll claim you right here in front of everyone."

I can't say the idea didn't hold a certain amount of intrigue. In fact, in all honesty, the thought was a complete turn on, but there is no way I'd be able to face these people again if they saw my "O" face. Now, if they were strangers and we were incognito . . . that might be something we needed to explore down the road. Clearing my throat, I tried to bring myself back to reality to respond with my brain and not my libido, but I was finding it hard to concentrate. It probably didn't help that I could still feel the outline of his cock nestled in my crack. When he swiveled his hips, I bit my lip to stop myself from moaning. The pain and subsequent drop of blood was a sobering moment, especially when Kalen flashed us to his quarters and threw me onto his bed.

He didn't waste time as he flashed out of his clothes and slowly began climbing up my body, making sure to drop kisses along the way that lit a slow-burning fire inside of me—driving me crazy with desire. I knew I should be demanding he take us back; I had a job to do, but the higher he climbed, the less I cared about anything but us. His hands pushed on my knees, and I parted them willingly. Eager for him to join me. He was having none of that. Taking his time, he pushed my silky green dress up an inch at a time until he rested his big hands on my waist and lifted me with his power. Using his gift to support my weight he blew softly. I shuddered in ecstasy just from his breath. When he buried his face in my pussy, I knew we were beyond the point of no return, and screamed, "Fast now, slow later!"

Kalen chuckled as he lowered me to the bed and pushed up onto his haunches. He gave me a devilish grin before he ripped the thong I was wearing from my body and growled, "I want no complaints. I'll finish when you do!" When he moved to insert a finger or two, I bucked him off and said, "Trust me, I'm more than ready for you."

With a sparkle in his eye, he leaned over and grabbed a knife, and nicked his neck before I had a chance to protest his action. When my eyes latched onto the trickle of blood, he lined himself up at my entrance and drove into the hilt. Lifting me, so I straddled his kneeling body, he directed me to his wound as he cradled me in his arms. When I latched on, he shuddered and whispered, "Blood of you, blood of me. Forever mine, forever yours. For all eternity." My orgasm took me by surprise the moment he sank his fangs into my flesh and sealed our bond for a second time. As I rode the high, I knew I'd never make that mistake again, especially if one could expect a life-shattering orgasm like this one on the daily.

I tore my mouth away, needing to say the words. My breathing was fast, but I managed to murmur, "Blood of you, blood of me. Forever mine, forever yours. For all eternity." Returning to his wound, I licked it clean and treasured the spasms running through my body as Kalen lifted his head and roared to the ceiling before he emptied himself into me.

Stroking his back, I closed my eyes and memorized our quick but intimate experience. It wouldn't beat any time records, but our need was off the charts. To be fair, this had been building since our run-in on the tarmac that morning. Little by little, the part of my brain not fascinated with the gorgeous male specimen in front of me started coming online. At first, it was just a nagging feeling that I forgot something, but it didn't take long before my senses returned, and I gasped, "Shit! We have to get back!"

Dropping my head into my hands, I mumbled, "Shit. They're going to know what we just did, aren't they?"

"That's what you're worried about. Everyone has sex. I think I have more reason to be concerned than you do, though," Kalen replied with a chuckle.

"Oh. Why's that?" I teased.

"The guys are going to give me hell for coming too fast. I swear if anyone mentions you might be happier with them because they are known to last longer, I won't be held responsible for my actions."

Snorting in response, I held up my hands and said, "You're right. That is worse. Delaying our return for your reputation would be something I might consider if we didn't have to worry about exposure, but we don't have time to indulge our egos. Get dressed, mister, and take us back to the council room. Shit, I need new underwear. You ruined mine."

Kalen flashed away and called out from his closet, "You'll have to wear a pair of mine."

"What do you mean? My closet was full of clothes the last time I was here. I'll just wear something from there," I replied as I scooted off the bed and sauntered toward our adjoining bathroom. Kalen snaked his arms around me from behind and whispered, "Last time I had all day to plan for your arrival. You played hard to get this time around. Which means the only thing in that closet is the jewels I've been collecting for you since I was a young man. Either wear something of mine or wear nothing at all."

Looking down at my dress, I pulled it away from myself and tried to ascertain if it was see-through. Stepping out of Kalen's arms, I turned in a circle, giving him a look-see before I asked, "Are my girly bits showing?"

"No. If they were, I'd be the first to tell you. I don't share well with others," Kalen growled.

"What was all that about earlier when you said you'd bend me over and take me right there in front of everyone!" I asked, shaking my head, trying hard to hide the smile wanting to come out.

"I wanted you just as wound up as I was, so I could have an excuse to claim you, yet blame my animalistic side," Kalen responded with a wink.

"Gah. If I didn't want you to do it to me again, I might have an issue with how you manipulated me with sex," I replied with a smile before I held out my arms and said, "Let's not keep them waiting any longer."

Kalen closed the distance and wrapped me in his arms before he whisked us away once again.

Chapter Thirty-One

I'm sure my face was bright red when everyone in the council room turned to look at us upon our arrival. Stepping out of Kalen's arms, I shrugged in embarrassment and said, "Sorry for making you wait. I'll get started right away, so we don't waste any more of your time."

"Sorry for the intrusion, but if my presence is no longer needed, may I be excused? My friends and I need to recharge while the suns are still up," Zarina asked, looking duller than usual.

"Of course. As usual, your service was impeccable. Please make sure and thank your friends for us," Kalen replied, pulling out the chair in front of me while motioning me to sit.

"They said it's a pleasure to be of assistance," Zarina replied with a smile before she turned to face me and said, "You might want to close your eyes, Jade. I'll be turning on my light. It's the fastest way for me to travel. Unless, of course, someone wants to give me a ride outside?"

"Sorry, Z. Need all hands on deck," Kalen answered at the same time I said, "I can close my eyes."

"Very well, my lord, lady. A and if you don't mind me saying, I hope you make them pay for their disloyalty. Alright, I'm lighting up. In case you didn't know, that means it's time to close your eyes," Zarina replied as she waited for me to comply. I closed my eyes and then ended up covering them with my hands on reflex when her presence felt like it was burning through my eyelids. Having the ability to travel at the speed of light would be fun, but I don't think my brain could live with the overwhelming brightness. At least if I borrowed her ability, I wouldn't have to worry about sharing my body with the mind-leeches.

Kalen tapped my shoulder when she left the room, "It's safe to look now."

I dropped my hands and opened my eyes, blinking a few times to clear the spots blocking my view. Natashia was the first to speak, "I hate to nag, but I think it's best if we follow your original line of thinking. That way, if you come up blank, we might still have time to capture Fansa and see if she has better luck."

"Luck shouldn't have anything to do with it. Why would I draw a blank if the gift I'm borrowing is one that tells the future? Do you doubt my abilities as a borrower?" I pressed as I pushed myself to stand and leaned against the council table. I wasn't trying to be intimidating, but I thought I had more than demonstrated I could handle using the gifts around me with ease. Her comment made me feel like I was inferior.

"Telling the future can be tricky is all she was trying to convey, lass. Even the oldest seers can draw blanks or get it wrong from time to time. 'Grandfather Time likes to keep us guessing,' is what my ma' used to say. The future holds many variables. No one expects your prediction to be perfect, more like a guide to what could happen," Levi explained gently.

I'm sure the look on my face was one of confusion with a hint of determination. I imagined I looked thoughtful, but knowing my luck, I probably looked like I was taking a shit or something. Not able to help the frown marring my face, I answered, "Thanks for the clarification. I guess we won't know what I can do until I try."

"That's the spirit, lass," Levi encouraged.

I could feel Kalen's annoyance that I had Levi's attention, but he wasn't the only one that looked uncomfortable with the praise. Not wanting to dwell on the tension, I piped up, "One prophecy of the future coming up."

Taking a deep breath, I blocked out the commotion around me and used my power to scan for the best seer. Once I was reasonably confident I knew the gift's intricacies, I let my body enter deep meditation. I emptied my mind and didn't have to wait long for a string of images to flash across the back of my closed eyes. At first, it was hard to make sense of what I was seeing. Until I held up my hands in my mind, and the images came to a screeching halt. As soon as I realized they were backward and upside down, I flipped them around and started the pictures from the beginning.

I felt like I was catching only a portion of what we needed to know and not the significant bits. In one image, I was in captivity, in a padded white room. Surrounded by an army of undead bigfoots in another vision, but it almost looked like they were protecting me. Another looked like a warzone, with casualties on both sides, but the last image scared me the most. Held between two green men, that could only be the infamous Mengh. I could hear Kalen's anguish as he watched my beheading and then proceeded to use his gift to crush everyone around him until his men eventually took him down so they could save those that were left.

I had no idea what happened to make that possibility a reality, but the vision was part of why I was hesitant to look at what the future had in store for us in the first place. Why couldn't I have seen a happy ending? Hearts and flowers would have been a nice turn of events, instead of doom and gloom. Another round of images inundated my mind the second I broadcasted my need for a happy ending. Since it wasn't my first rodeo, I quickly stopped their progression and put them to rights to see them in sequential order.

As I watched my happily ever after playing out before my eyes, I found myself wondering which version of events would come to pass. How could there be such a difference between the outcomes? I mean, I've always believed in the theory that if I projected my dreams to the universe, they would come back to me. Could this possibly be a version of that? Deciding to test out my theory, I focused on insecurity and failure before welcoming another round of images.

Surprisingly enough, the images were similar to the first round, except for a few more details I hadn't noticed at first. Nothing helpful. Frustrated with how fickle the future was, I tried to hone the vision into something beneficial to identifying choices we could make. I needed the events that led up to the outcomes I saw, something that would lead us down the road of happiness instead of devastation. It would also be advantageous to our cause to know when the events would take place. It's not like I could use our aging faces to indicate that our happily ever after followed my capture. Plus, it was in my best interest to keep my head.

I braced myself for a new set of images based on my intent and was pleasantly surprised to see they were already right side up and in the proper order as they played out in front of me. It made me feel like the gift was coming to heel instead of me being at its bidding. No longer would I be forced to live with the bits and pieces it was willing to give, without knowing the context behind the motives. It reminded me of presidential ad campaigns back home. In my opinion, it forced the seer to guess with only minimal facts to guide them. It wasn't like the full story wasn't available. My gift knew it was possible to see it all, but as I was finding out, my intent and focus played a larger role than I initially thought.

I almost lost my concentration when the first scene to enter my mind was something relatively recent. Swallowing my outcry, I thought, *Now this is something I could work with!* In the vision, I left the council room with instructions to immerse myself back into the fold of my peers. The consensus wanted me to glean more information about what kind of part Onyx had to play in the whole mess.

We still didn't know what killed Anolla and Castice the first time around. Adira had been adamant it wasn't a known poison or chemical. At the time, I hadn't questioned her abilities. Looking back at it, maybe I should have checked for myself before I leaped back in time. Although dwelling on the past would do me no good. Unless, of course, I planned on jumping back again to correct the mistakes I'd made during my trip. I could see it becoming an infinite loop, where each journey from the future to right the wrongs of the past would generate new mistakes in the process.

Shaking the thoughts from my mind that took my focus away from where it needed to be, I concentrated on learning why I needed to go undercover in the first place. What would I learn from sharing a room with Onyx, and what outcome did this particular detail belong to? Unless I could prove to Kalen spying would lead to the proof we were looking for, he would never go for something that meant our separation.

I wanted to believe stepping into the lion's den would lead to a future of happiness. One where Kalen and I were holding our grandchildren as we watched our son's royal coronation. If my theory of intent was to be believed, spying on Onyx shouldn't lead to my gruesome death. The question was: Was I willing to take a chance on that possibility? Was I ready to bet my gift was so incredible I was able to do what no other seer could do? If I was a betting girl, I might have gone with the odds, but after already making one big mistake, I was gun shy about committing another. Maybe I should skim the files per se of each outcome and ascertain the highlights. The answers were close. I just needed to seize enough of them to make an educated guess.

Gathering everything I wanted to ask in my final query, I sent it out in a Hail Mary and gasped out loud when image after image assaulted my brain. The transfer was too fast for me to see, but I knew if I took the time, I'd be able to see every detail leading up to every possible outcome of my infinite life. Excited to finally have something useful to help our cause, I accessed the roommate file and hit play. I could hear a buzzing noise in the background. At first, I thought it was a bad recording, but I could make out Kalen's concerned voice when I hit pause.

"Don't get lost in there, my love. Please come back to me."

Checking back into reality to make sure I wasn't hearing things, I opened my eyes and looked at Kalen before I said, "How does one get lost in their head?"

Kalen gleamed at me and replied, "You'd be surprised by how many people get lost in their thoughts and never to make it back out again. It's alright if you didn't see anything. You wouldn't be the first to come up empty."

"Empty? Oh, I didn't come up empty at all. Far from it," I answered with a smile.

Chapter Thirty-Two

"Whatever you have to tell us will need to wait. We have incoming, my lord," Rom warned with a growl.

Tanen shot me a look before he flashed away just as Kalen started issuing commands, "Kiso, lock it down. I'd rather deal with the aftermath of them making assumptions rather than come up with something on the spot for our gathering. Natashia, be prepared to freeze time if anyone makes it inside." He turned to me, gave me a half shrug and said, "Not that I want to put you on the spot, but we don't have a lot of time. What did you see?"

"That's a loaded question. I saw a vision of us happy as well as one of our demise. When you guys indicated the future was tricky to predict, you weren't kidding. If I had more time to study the possibilities of our future, I'd have something more concrete for us. Considering I was just getting to the details of the visions the gift showed me, I'd only be postulating," I explained, wringing my hands in front of me nervously.

"Cut to the chase, woman! Do you or don't you know what's going to happen? We don't have time for your theatrics!" Kiso exclaimed, holding his arms out like he was physically pushing those approaching away.

Kalen's answering growl pierced the room. With a snarl, he tucked me into the crook of his arm before he spoke, "This will be your only warning. You will speak to the woman next to me with the highest respect given to our people. Otherwise, you'll find yourself without a tongue!"

My mouth dropped open at his exclamation, but there was no way I was going to reprimand him for sticking up for me, regardless of how barbaric he sounded. At least he was my barbarian! Reaching up, I placed my hand over Kalen's heart. When he looked down at me, I smiled and whispered, "Thank you. No one's ever stood up for me before."

He returned my smile and gazed at me with longing before he replied, "There's nothing I wouldn't do for you. Blood of you, blood of me. Forever mine, forever yours. For all eternity."

I blushed as I recalled what we were doing both times he recited those words in the past. It made me squirm as my pussy quivered at the memory. Everything around us faded away until he was the only thing I could see and feel. I would have happily stayed that way forever, but Natashia cleared her throat loudly, breaking the bubble I'd mentally erected around us. I couldn't help the scowl I sent her way before I addressed Kiso.

"I don't have the answers yet. I'd be lying if I told you I did. I saw war. I saw my death." Before I could continue, Kalen interrupted me with a growl, "Death! How do you die?" His grip on me tightening at the same time.

"How I died doesn't matter," I answered with a hiss.

"Like hell, it doesn't matter!" Kalen roared to the ceiling.

I knew standing up to him in front of his people wouldn't go over well, but there was no way I was going to let him speak to me that way. Twisting in his arms, I poked his chest with my index finger until he gazed down at me with a puzzled look. Then I let him have it, "Knowing the way wouldn't help us in this situation, but knowing the who might."

Kalen grasped my upper arms and gave me a slight shake before he spoke with a deep voice that sent shivers down my spine, "I'm not going to ask you again. How do you die, and who was responsible?"

"Fine. Make me recite how I died out loud. It wasn't like the memory wasn't going to haunt my nightmares in the first place, you bastard! I was just trying to save you the same fate. The Mengh sliced off my head while you watched. Happy now?" I screamed, trying to slow my breathing before I started to hyperventilate. His look of fury turned to defeat when he dropped his head and said on a sigh, "No. I'm far from happy about what you just revealed. How did they capture you?"

"That's what I've been trying to tell you. I'm not sure. I was just figuring things out in there when I heard you call for me. It appears my intent guides the visions. On my last query, I focused on the outcome where we all get to keep our lives, and it showed me returning to my quarters so I could spy on Onyx," I barely finished saying her name when he roared, "Absolutely not! You're not leaving my side!"

Cocking my head to the side, I glared at him and said as calmly as possible, "If you would have let me finish. You would have heard me say that I couldn't be certain if that pathway would lead to my death or our happily ever after. You would have also heard me say I needed more time. I'm not stupid, and I don't have a death wish."

"Are you sure about that? Wouldn't be the first time today you've put yourself at risk," Kalen growled.

I took a step back and gasped. It should have been an indication to quit while he was ahead, but Kalen continued. "I have half a mind…" He didn't get the chance to complete his statement before I cut him off with a warning, "You better not finish that sentence." Taking a couple more steps back, I placed my hands on my hips and stared him down. I was watching his every move, ready to defend myself if necessary. When Rom spoke up, I kept my attention on the Strix in front of me, wondering how he would decide to move forward.

"My lord. Please excuse the interruption, but our unwanted visitors have evacuated the area. If you wanted to get out of here, now would be the time to do so," Rom cautioned nervously.

Kalen appeared to be relieved with the interruption. He stared at me for a few more seconds before he sighed and turned to answer my guards. "Thank you, Rom. I'd like you and your brother to head to the infirmary. The longer we're able to hide the fact that we know about their little assassin, the better."

"And if they're already aware?" Kiso asked.

"Notify me immediately, and we'll rendezvous in my office," Kalen replied before addressing Natashia next. "Would it be possible for you two to stay behind and make sure everyone gets out without being seen or caught? If it was a clean getaway, meet us in my office. If it's not, transport them to the dungeons."

Levi held up his hand, cleared his throat, and said, "Just a second. I have a question before we all scatter." He turned to me and continued, "Jade, have you used your gift to see if one of the Sixers around here can produce the toxin or poison we're looking for? Seems to me identifying our killer should be our number one priority."

I scoffed at myself when I realized I never thought of looking. "No, I didn't even try. I should have, though, especially after Adira was adamant it wasn't a toxin or poison produced in nature. At least not one she knew about. Do I have enough time to take a quick look?"

"I can't guarantee we have the time," Rom replied with a frown.

"Don't worry about it. Let's just go with the original plan and split up. Jade can look after we leave here successfully, and if anything needs investigating, I'll let you know. Everyone clear on their assignments?" Kalen asked, giving a nod in acknowledgment when they answered yes.

When the brothers flashed out of the room, I turned to face my mate. Now wasn't the time to lock me away, and I would do everything in my power to make him understand I wouldn't go down without a fight. As he stalked toward me, I held up my hands, and using his power against him; I pushed him back. When he looked at me like I'd lost my mind, I said, "I meant what I said. I won't be locked up while everyone else puts their lives in danger. You wouldn't do it. You shouldn't expect me to."

I opened my mouth to ask for a truce and swallowed the words when Kalen disappeared. It didn't surprise me at all when he reappeared behind me and encircled me in his arms. His breath on my neck sent tingles of awareness throughout my body. He took his time kissing my neck on the way to my ear before he whispered, "Seems we have a misunderstanding. Perhaps I should demonstrate what I had in mind before you rudely cut me off and accused me of atrocities I hadn't yet considered."

My answering shudder was all the answer he needed before he flashed us away to his quarters. I pushed away and spun to face him. "I thought you said we were rendezvousing with the others in your office."

"I think we have a few minutes before that needs to happen. I'd rather continue our conversation," Kalen replied with a mischievous look, taking a step toward me.

"Are you trying to tell me you weren't going to say you had half a mind to lock me away for my own good?" I seethed, taking a step back.

"No," Kalen answered as he took another step.

I waited for him to explain himself as I continued to back away slowly. Frustrated with myself for how turned on I was with his alpha tendencies. He matched my every step without saying another word. I knew without looking I was about to run out of space. Not wanting to feel caged or vulnerable, with no escape, I stopped, held up my hands, and said, "Well then, enlighten me. What did you intend to say?"

"It'd be more fun to show you, but seeing as we are short on time, I'll humor you with an answer. As you pointed out earlier, patience is something we both lack. If you had let me continue, I'm positive you would have liked what I had to say because I can think of nothing else. I can't deny that I crave it. All I see is a vision of you bent over as I take you from behind, reminding you of where you belong. It doesn't escape my intelligence that we face many barriers. Our past and present are just the beginning of our story. I know that everything would be different if either of us had been patient, but I'm not interested in the past. Only the future. And in that future, I envision us working together. Notice I said the word 'together,' and that's because I mean it. There is no future where I will ever let you out of my sight again. We'll investigate everything side by side, just like you wanted. Regardless of what you envisioned, I'll never agree with you going undercover. I will not put your life in danger, especially when I'm not there to defend you. Please don't ask that of me."

When he started talking about us doing things together, I couldn't help the smile spreading across my face. It proved to me he'd been listening when I'd mentioned something similar while we were in the dungeons. It made me feel like there was hope for us yet. We just needed to stay alive long enough to experience it, and if I wanted that future, I had work to do. Dropping my hands, I released a big sigh and said, "Thank fuck. That's what I needed to hear."

"Truce?" Kalen asked, holding his hand out to me, waiting for me to come to him.

"Truce," I replied, eliminating the distance between us.

I placed my hand in his. He took advantage and pulled me into his chest. Wrapping me in his arms. He kissed the top of my head and groaned, "I want to be selfish and hide away from everyone and everything."

"I can't deny that it's tempting, but one of us has to be the adult here, and I don't want to fail," I answered, pushing back so I could see his response.

"Fail in what exactly? There are no expectations on you," Kalen answered quietly, stroking my cheek softly.

"I beg to differ. 'Jade, what did you see? Jade, did you use your gift to find out if a Sixer is responsible for producing that toxin?'" I mimicked with sarcasm, using air quotes for emphasis before tacking on, "I'm not used to falling short. First, I couldn't predict the future with accuracy, and then I completely missed scanning those around me for that deadly ability. Not to mention my brain is more interested in shagging my mate than solving the latest crime!"

Kalen captured my cheeks in his hands and smashed his lips into mine, cutting off my words. I responded in kind. Kissing him for all I was worth. He pulled back slowly when I was entirely under his magic. Nibbling on my bottom lip before he responded in a husky voice, "You're too hard on yourself. You didn't fail as a sightseer. I've never met anyone that could see what they wanted when they wanted. Most are at the mercy of the gift and try to make sense of a single scene. Like you referred to earlier, I believe those people end up guessing to fill in the blanks they didn't see. As for scanning everyone, nothing is stopping you from doing it now."

"What if I find something?" I stammered.

"Then we move on them with the full force of the Sixer army!" Kalen replied fiercely.

I wanted to point out if I identified someone, it would just be another fail on my part, but whining about it wouldn't do me, or anyone else any good. Nodding my head once, I closed my eyes and probed the powers at my disposal. Searching for an unknown substance that could kill a person from the inside out seemed like an impossible feat. There were multiple Sixers capable of creating deadly toxins and poisons, but none produced the black gelatinous goo. I tried to reach Adira's gift to validate her claim, but I couldn't locate her anywhere. She must have been too far away from me. Frustrated and relieved at the same time that I hadn't found the culprit, I opened my eyes and said, "We have a lot of dangerous Sixers around here, but no one that warrants being brought in for questioning. How far away are we from the main compound?"

"Less than a mile. Why do you ask?"

"I wasn't able to reach Adira's gift," I answered with a frown on my face.

"She's probably in her lab, which would be beyond your reach from here. We can visit her, but it will have to wait a bit. Tanen is insisting we return to the dungeons. Something about 'we need to see it for ourselves to believe it,'" Kalen replied with a scowl.

Chapter Thirty-Three

My gaze swept the room the second we materialized in the dungeon, scanning for anything out of the ordinary. Not wanting to add more fuel for my nightmares, I skipped over Anolla's cell and noticed that only Castice, cowering in the corner, remained captive. I did a double take as I scoured Cynosis's empty chamber. I would never have pegged her as an enemy. My mind started spiraling as I tried to establish her role in the plot against us. Swinging my attention to Tanen, I was surprised to find him calm, cool, and collected. His demeanor only had me second-guessing the reason behind her absence. Opening my mouth to voice my concerns, he stopped me with a finger in the air and a shake of his head. Without saying another word, he pointed behind us with enthusiasm.

I turned slowly, bracing myself for the worst, but couldn't stop myself from jumping back in fright. Nothing could have prepared me for the scene playing out in front of me. Blinking in hopes that something else might appear, I forced myself to acknowledge the grotesque-looking starfish sucking face with the glass wall of Anolla's cell. Covered in hundreds of needle-like spikes of varying lengths, some as long as my arm, it appeared to double in size as the barrier between us started disintegrating before my eyes.

My hand flew to my chest as I took a step back and stammered, "What the hell is that thing?"

Tanen answered, "Never seen one before, but I have a hunch Castice has." He tilted his head toward Castice, who at the mention of his name, stood up and rushed the glass wall in front of me. By the surprised look on his face when he touched the glass enclosure and flew three feet back from the jolt of electricity, he must have forgotten Kalen's warning. He landed on his ass several feet back and shook his head as he stared up at us. He regained his footing quickly when the creature let out a high-pitched squeal.

Keeping his hands in the air, he spoke quickly as he approached us again, desperation evident in his voice, "You have to get me out of here."

"And why would we do that?" Kalen responded with a growl.

"I thought you brought me here to save my life! Or was that just a lie?" Castice retorted.

"We did originally, but your silence made me change my mind. As far as I'm concerned, if you are not with us, you are against us. Furthermore, harboring secrets that could harm the Allegiance could be considered treason. Should I go on?" Kalen answered.

"But you can't just leave me here! That thing eats organic matter and continues to grow until death! Your enclosure is nothing but a snack," Castice cried out.

"What else can you tell us about it?" I ventured.

"Are you serious right now?" Castice shot back.

"Deadly," I replied with a smirk. Daring him to question me with a raise of my eyebrow. Little did he know I had every confidence Kalen or I could squash that thing like a bug.

After a short pause, he dropped his shoulders and replied, "Fine, but I'm going to need protection from . . ."

"From what?" I prompted when he stopped abruptly. When he continued to stare at me like a lost boy, I looked over my shoulder at Kalen and shrugged in question. He nodded his head toward Castice in response.

Seeming to come out of it, he shuttered and said, "I guess there are some things I can't say no matter how much I know my life depends on it. It's as if the memories are gone until I stop trying, and then they all come flooding back.

"Well, what can you tell us?" I demanded.

"It's a diabolitum," Castice quickly answered.

"Where did it come from?" I asked.

Castice opened his mouth to tell us, and when nothing came out, he shook his head and said with frustration evident in his voice, "Guess I can't tell you that."

"Alright, let's try another approach. Um. How about. Uh. What is it?" I hedged.

Castice let out a sigh of relief and answered, "A silicate-based lifeform."

"Seeing as you can't tell me where it comes from, I doubt you'd be able to confirm who sent it?" I asked half-jokingly.

He slowly shook his head no and lowered it. I looked at Tanen and tilted my head to the side. Tanen's attention was directed at Castice with such intensity and focus that the veins in his face and neck were bulging. When he heard my thoughts, he turned to me in defeat and said, "I can't get into his mind no matter how hard I try. I've got nothing."

I nodded and said, "I got in before. I'll try again."

I closed my eyes and used Tanen's gift, accessing Castice's mind with ease. I found myself in the same room as last time, but this time his thoughts were blank. Opening my eyes to look at Castice, I asked, "What are you thinking about right now?"

"I'm thinking about who's responsible and all the shit I can't seem to say. Why?" Castice answered, approaching the glass wall with caution.

"Huh. Try thinking about something else," I prompted as I breached Castice's thoughts again to hear him say, *She must be crazy! A diabolitum is feet away from us, and she's acting like we have all the time in the world for a quid pro quo session. Gods, I need to get out of here before . . .* His thoughts went blank again as his mind entered a no-go zone I couldn't see or hear. Someone or something must have put a mental block on him.

"What do you want me to think about? How quickly death will come for me?" Castice asked angrily.

Not paying him any attention, I turned to Kalen and Tanen and said, "He's got some kind of mental block on him. I can hear his thoughts easily until he starts thinking about the person or people responsible for the thing." Hooking a finger over my shoulder at the diabolitum in question.

I turned when the creature made another one of its high-pitched squeals and watched it latch onto the glass wall separating the cells and attack the barrier voraciously. Castice cried out in fear, drawing my attention. He plastered himself against the opposite wall and looked beyond terrified. It made me feel bad for torturing him needlessly. Taking pity on the half-phoenix half-gryphon, I used Kalen's gift to envelope the diabolitum in a bubble. I maneuvered the creature into the center of its cell and returned my gaze to Castice before I said, "As you can see, that thing is no longer a threat to you. One final question, and we'll relocate you. Did that thing come from a Sixer?" His inability to respond was all the answer I needed.

Returning my attention to the squirming starfish, I found myself thankful I couldn't hear its screams as I compressed the field around him. I felt a slight resistance like the being was somehow capable of pushing back. Doubling my efforts, I startled when Kalen shoved me behind him, breaking my concentration as General Jaleal flashed into the room carrying Adira, who bellowed, "Stop! What are you doing? I need that thing to identify the causative agent and possibly develop a cure for it."

"How did you know about the creature, Adira?" Kalen growled maliciously.

Placing my hand on his back, I peeked around my growly mate to see Tanen take a step forward before he said, "I advised Jaleal of the creature the moment I arrived here. Upon my return, I suggested grabbing Adira to help us identify it."

"Return? Why did you leave in the first place? Better yet, why wasn't I the first person notified?" Kalen barked.

Tanen stood tall as he addressed Kalen, "I meant no disrespect, just trying to be efficient. I was literally gone and back in a flash. I shouldn't have to explain to you why I needed a moment. You of all people should understand my need to keep Cynosis safe."

"I see," Kalen replied, steepling his fingers as he turned to address Adira. "As an alchemist, how do you think you would help this investigation? We already know what it is, a silicate-based lifeform, not a toxin or poison."

Adira swallowed loudly before she replied, "It might not be a poison or a toxin, but it could produce one. Maybe I could isolate it and make some kind of antidote."

I felt Kalen tense under my fingertips before he stalked forward and placed his hand on Castice's cell wall. Both the glass wall and metal bars slid into the floor. Kalen captured Castice with his power and brought him forward. When they were eye-to-eye, my mate removed the field around Castice and let him drop to the floor before he said, "Is an antidote possible?"

Castice raised his head and replied, "Not that I'm aware of, but I highly doubt you'll be able to get close enough to study it. I doubt you have anything that can contain it. It eats organic matter."

"I know fire kills it. You could contain it that way," I interjected.

"Perfect, my assistant's sister is a fire-elemental. I'll have her meet us there. I know there has to be something I can do. Maybe it paralyzes its victims, and I can develop a serum to prevent that from happening. Please. Help me bring it to my lab so we can at least study its dynamics," pushed Adira, clasping her hands in front of her in desperation.

I couldn't understand why she was so insistent about studying it. It gave me the creeps and reminded me of the movie *Alien*, where the AI unit took an interest in the killer xenophobes. If she started spouting off shit about how fascinating and precious it was, I don't think I'd be able to trust her. Kalen must not have felt the same way when he nodded in approval and barked out orders, "Tanen, take Castice to my bunker. He'll be safe there until this is over." He was about to say something else when Castice interrupted him, "That's not a good idea. My gift is telling me you shouldn't keep it. Destroy the damn thing before something bad happens!"

Castice's outburst surprised me. I was just about ready to tap into his power to make sense of his ramblings when Rom flashed into the room and announced, "Bastion and his men have found the doppelganger. He's mounting an insurgence on the infirmary. My brother needs back-up immediately."

I looked up at Kalen and wondered how he appeared so at ease when I felt anything but calm. My nerves were a bundle of tangled firecrackers, where at any minute I might give up and just light the whole wad. Kalen pulled me forward and tucked me into his side before he said, "Jaleal, gather your squadron and attack them from east. I'll transport the girls to the lab so that Adira can begin her research. Tanen, after you drop off the kid, grab Paine and Parthyn, meet us in the lab and we'll attack from the west." Looking down at me, he held my gaze for a second before he spoke, "You can't let the flash disrupt your control. Do you think you can do that Jade?"

I nodded once and said a little silent prayer that I could deliver on that declaration as Kalen approached the diabolitum's cell to disengage the metal bars. I brought it as close to us as I dared before I grabbed onto Kalen's offered hand. He held out his other hand at the alchemist and barked, "Adira, hurry; we have no time to waste."

I crossed my fingers and took a deep breath focusing all of my power on controlling the force field around the monster behind me. Kalen squeezed my hand as the only warning before he flashed us away.

Chapter Thirty-Four

When I detected our arrival, I flipped around to make sure the diabolitum was still in my control and let out a deep sigh to find it precisely where it was supposed to be. I assumed the two girls approaching were Adira's assistant and her sister. I don't remember seeing either of them the last time I was in here, but I was ready to release the monster in my grasp the second the blond fire-elemental gave me the green light. She erected a cage weaved with fire around the diabolitum and gave me a thumbs up. The second I released my control, I heard a loud thud behind me and turned just as Kalen dropped to the floor, convulsing in pain.

I rushed to his side and reached for his gift of flashing, only to find my power unavailable. Raising my head to ask Adira what was going on, I found myself face to face with my nemesis, Onyx. "You! What did you do to him?" I screamed, scrambling to my feet.

"Me," Onyx replied, placing a hand over her chest innocently. "I didn't stab the king with a neurotoxin that paralyzes and acts as a memory eraser. No, that was our local alchemist's job. Along with bringing me the blond! With that statement, she faced Adira and demanded, "I thought I told you to bring me Jade!"

When I laughed out loud at her statement, she spun on her heel and said, "You won't be laughing for long once I hand you over to the Mengh! I'm sure they wouldn't mind the extra snack for their long journey. I won't even charge them." Turning back to Adira with her hands on her hips, she said, "Well! Where is she?"

Adira pointed at me and said, "That's Jade. I brought her here like you asked."

"Are you sure?" Onyx questioned, raising an eyebrow in question.

"Yes, I'm sure. Kalen called her Jade by name. Now give me back my sister."

"I'm afraid that won't be possible, my dear. You see, your sister is already aboard their ship. Unless, of course, you wish to trade your life for hers," Onyx said in a higher than thou voice, pausing for a brief moment. When Adira's eyes filled with tears, she continued, "I didn't think so. Pity you *might* have had a chance at being recruited in their army with your expertise. I doubt your sister, who's only ability is contortionism, will stand a chance of surviving."

Adira deflated as her tears spilled over onto her cheeks. "Bu .

. . but you promised me," she stammered, wiping her nose with the

back of her hand.

"Well, I lied!" Onyx snapped, showing her true colors before

she straightened her outfit and did a Dr. Jekyl and Mr. Hyde switch

before my eyes. Her whole demeanor changed as she turned to face

Adira head-on. When she finally spoke, it was in that sickly sweet

tone I despised, "Is this going to be a problem between us in the

future? Because when I'm queen, I won't hesitate to end your life if I

feel for a second that you've betrayed my family or me!"

Adira made eye contact with me for a brief moment before

she averted her eyes to the floor in a sign of submission and said,

"No problem, my Queen. M..may I be excused? I'm not feeling very

well at the moment."

"I don't think so. In fact, I think you should be present to

witness my triumphant moment. After all, this wouldn't have been

possible without your help," Onyx replied, cackling like a witch

when Adira paled in response.

Onyx flipped around, whipping her long braid dramatically

over her shoulder as she faced me once again. She stroked her hair as

she eyed me up and down before she finally spoke, "I don't see what all the fuss is about, but apparently, you are a very wanted Sixer. You're going to make me a wealthy woman. Tell me, do you have a magic vagina or something? Is that how you deceived my mate into having sex with you?"

The woman was delusional. I couldn't help the smirk that crossed my face. I needed to stall so our reinforcements could arrive in time to assist us. At the minimum, I needed to figure out why my powers were inaccessible. My only hope revolved around antagonizing the bitch enough that she'd confess her sins without even realizing it. Giving her my best evil eye, I finally answered her haughtily, "My pussy is so magical Kalen couldn't keep his hands off me. Although, in my defense, he wasn't wearing a ring and didn't tell me he was attached. I thought he was fair game. My mistake." I shrugged innocently and gave her a small, demure smile before I added, "Will you ever forgive me?"

I bit my cheek to keep myself from laughing uncontrollably when her mouth dropped open in response for a moment before she composed herself and said in a low voice, "You're lying!"

I shrugged again but didn't offer her another answer.

"What is your gift?" Onyx demanded in a voice I think she believed authoritative, but in truth only made her sound like a whiny bitch.

"I'm surprised you don't know. Makes sense, though," I said casually, looking down at my nails like I didn't have a care in the world. Taking the time to take a quick peek at Kalen to ensure he lived. He no longer looked like he was in pain, but his eyes implored me to quit while I was ahead. They begged me to save myself. I gave him a defiant but barely perceptible shake of my head and went back to inspecting my cuticles.

"What makes sense?" Onyx snarled. Although I could tell the statement had her second-guessing her position in the grand scheme of things.

"Your lack of knowledge, of course. If you don't know, it means you're disposable," I replied flippantly.

"Why, you little bitch!" Onyx roared, turning her arm into an onyx blade as she took a step in my direction.

I glanced around the room for something I could use as a weapon and came up short. I doubt I'd have enough time to grab anything before Onyx started getting stabby anyway. Why did I have to antagonize her when I was powerless? My brain was the only tool

I had left. Standing as tall as I could, I used her greed against her and prayed it bought me more time. "Being a wanted Sixer and all, do you only get half price if you deliver me dead or injured?"

My statement stopped her dead in her tracks. Her blade arm dropped to her side and morphed back into her regular hand while she struggled for a moment to pull herself together. It gave me the impression Onyx wasn't used to curbing her anger. She tried to play it off by laughing like she found my statement funny. She flattened her dress methodically before she answered, "It doesn't matter what you can do. I mean, it's not like you can use it now. In your time of need."

"I admit you have me at a disadvantage. How'd you do it?" I queried, crossing my fingers behind my back that it was something I could reverse.

"I could be a bitch and just say fate, but I'm rather proud of this win. Since your departure from this planet is mere minutes away, I can't see how it will hurt to let you in on my secret. I've known since childhood; Lord Kalen would be mine. A prophetess from our village foretold the most powerful female Sixer to attend the Gathering this year would be Kalen's mate.

Over the years, I made sure I knew every nuance my power was capable of and honed it into a lethal weapon. I have no doubt I can beat any opponent I face, but I needed to admit my plan had holes. I realized if I wanted to be all-powerful, I couldn't rely on my gift alone. I began collecting artifacts and unique Sixers. Of course, I found troubled individuals easier to manipulate. Nothing was off-limits if I thought it would help me secure my position as Kalen's Queen," Onyx explained, waving her right ring finger back and forth before she continued, "This was the first addition to my collection. Do you like it?"

I studied the black ring on her finger that resembled a crown of thorns and shrugged before I answered, "A little dark for my taste. I didn't take you for a goth girl, but to each their own, in my opinion. Were you rebelling against your parents, princess? Shit, do you have tattoos too?"

Onyx ignored my teasing and continued like she hadn't heard me, "Do you know what I like best about it?"

"No, but I have a feeling you're about to tell me," I muttered, rolling my eyes in annoyance.

I could tell my insolence pissed her off when Onyx brought the ring up in front of her face, like it was the most interesting thing in the world, examining it closely before she replied, "This thing allows me invisibility."

Containing myself proved harder, the longer Onyx spoke. If I only had minutes left on this planet, I needed to hurry this conversation along. "I think you got swindled; that or our definition of invisibility is different," I replied with a shrug before adding, "But you do you, and I'll do me, is what I always say. Although I am curious to know what's blocking my gift?"

"I'll get to that, but first, I think I should elaborate. It doesn't make me invisible, just my powers," Onyx replied with a smirk.

"When you say it that way, it leads me to believe you're hiding something? Which begs the question. What could a chalcedony user have to hide?" I answered, thanking Beatress for that tidbit of knowledge.

"How did you know that was my specialty?" Onyx questioned with a whine.

"I picked up on it when we flashed into the room," I lied with ease.

"Impossible! Besides my cloaking ring, Kema here is a suppressor. It's one of the reasons I collected her. Her ability to suppress a Sixer's gift is a game-changer, in my opinion," Onyx challenged.

"I admit my power is missing now, but I had access to detect a few gifts in the room for a brief moment upon our arrival. Your ring must not work against me," I answered, hoping she'd take the bait and ask me to elaborate.

"What are you?" Onyx asked with a frown.

"I'm a compendium," I replied with a curtsy, "My ability allows me to identify the powers of other Sixers."

Onyx scoffed at my admission and said, "It has to be more than that; otherwise, why would the Mengh want you?"

"Probably because I can see everything a Sixer is capable of doing. Or it could be because I can provide them with instructions on how to access that ability if they haven't yet mastered it," I responded with a straight face. I couldn't help but grin when Onyx stomped her feet in a fit.

I half expected her to throw a full-blown tantrum, but she shook her head instead and said, "No." Pausing for a moment she raised her head and studied me for a minute before she spoke, "I admit you weave a fascinating tale, but did you really think I would fall for it? Granted, I practically handed you the idea when I told you

I made it my mission in life to master my gift. The chance to prove I have nothing left to learn is a nice carrot to dangle in front of my eyes, but for what purpose is my question."

"You seem like a smart businesswoman. I'm gambling on the fact that you'll realize my worth and what I could bring to your army. Surely you must see handing over such a precious commodity is detrimental to your end game. Especially when your enemy will use it to strengthen their army," I countered.

Onyx stroked her braid while contemplating before she spoke, "I can't deny I'm curious, but you have one thing wrong. The Mengh are not my enemy. We've come to an understanding. If I deliver you, they've agreed to sign a peace treaty. Ending this millennia-old war when I take my place alongside my mate. Even you should see the beauty of your sacrifice."

"Gutsy decision, in my opinion. I don't know whether I should applaud you for your bravery or ridicule you for believing the Mengh would stop. Their need for my services should be proof enough they aren't looking for peace," I opposed, throwing my hands in the air for emphasis.

"You could be lying about your powers just to make me second guess my decision," Onyx added, cocking her head to the side.

"True, but you could always test me. Choose anyone in this room, and I'll tell you every little thing there is to know about their special abilities," I replied, pointing to the other Sixers present.

Onyx shook her head and said, "No. If you're going to read anyone in this room. It will be me."

Holding my arms open wide, I looked over at the Sixer suppressing my powers and said, "I'll need you to call off your lackey if you want me to work my magic."

"Kema," Onyx barked, giving an imperceptible nod when the petite blond with a messy bun spared a glance her way. Kema's ocean blue eyes held a hint of rebellion when she answered, "I don't think that's a good idea, Your Highness. What if she overpowers us with her gift?"

"I didn't ask you for your opinion, but you do have a point. Jade will have five seconds to start talking. If she's wrong or hesitates, simply suppress her gift again," Onyx snapped, crossing her arms as she dared the Sixer to argue with her again.

343

Kema withered under Onyx's glare, losing some of her spirit. Dropping her shoulders, she sighed and said, "As you wish, Master."

Chapter Thirty-Five

The way Onyx treated Kema and Adira gave me hope that when shit hit the fan, her allies would prove less loyal than mine. My nemesis' ridiculous timeframe left me scrambling to deliver results without being able to explore my options beforehand. The stakes were too high for me to make a mistake. I needed to stall. I needed to take matters into my own hands by feeding Onyx small bits I already knew about her gift, so I'd have more time to study the available powers within my reach. If I'd learned anything in the last few days, it was that my tendency to jump into things without a plan tended to backfire. I knew it was a gamble to assume my gift could see past Onyx's 'invisibility' ring, but something told me to have faith.

I wanted a foolproof plan, but to do that I needed to prepare for the worst, which included being ready to retreat with Kalen in tow if need be. At least I had the element of surprise on my side, but I couldn't afford to let my guard down. Overconfidence could lead to my subsequent failure. If it were just my life on the line, it would be one thing, but the thought of my mate's death brought me to a place of darkness. One I didn't know I was capable of. It made me realize I'd do anything to save the Strix at my feet, including killing the other people in the room with us. Without question! Of course, I'd prefer a solution that didn't include death on either side, but if it came down to them or us, I had no doubt I'd be able to protect us.

Knowing my luck, I'd only have one shot. If I intended to make it a powerful one, I couldn't take any chances. I braced myself to cut off Kema's gift the moment her power over me receded if Onyx's ring actually worked. I breathed a sigh of relief when I felt my gift return in its entirety and barely stopped myself from fist-pumping the air when my bluff paid off, and I could see her chalcedony power in its entirety. I blurted out the first thing Beatress told me as I mapped out our escape, "As a chalcedony user, you use your power to make weapons from the cryptocrystalline structure."

"Is this a joke? You already knew I could make weapons. Again, I showed you that talent. If that's all you've got, you're wasting my time," Onyx sneered.

She looked past me to Kema but before she could say anything, I spit out the next thing she was capable of, "Your gift allows you to erect large structures, such as walls, bridges, and buildings. I imagine an Onyx temple would be something to behold." Her silence gave me permission to continue, "Your gift can also produce chromium, which is lethal in large doses."

When Onyx started nodding her head in agreement, I felt compelled to find something she didn't know she could do. No matter how small it was. "Were you aware that if you produce enough hexavalent chromium, you can remove the oxygen from the air and suffocate everyone in the process? I highly recommend having a fail-safe, like an oxygen tank, when you try that one out. I'm positive even YOU can't survive without it."

Onyx paused for a moment in thought, which I used to my advantage. Switching gears, I dissected Kema's power and skimmed over the cliff notes my gift provided me. I was surprised to discover her talent didn't just suppress a Sixer's gift. In fact, she was capable of stopping all six senses within a ten-yard radius. If push came to shove, I could take away everyone's sight and sound as we made our escape.

"Interesting. I always felt like there was more I could do with it. Continue," Onyx finally replied with a hint of excitement.

Stalling for time again so I could jump back to her portfolio, I asked, "You did? I've always wondered if the person could tell they were missing out. Did you have a sense of unfulfillment? I mean, how did you know?"

Onyx cocked her head at me in curiosity. No doubt, trying to assess my sincerity. I kept her gaze as she studied me and prayed she'd buy my bravado and attentiveness as earnestness. I used the time to look at the next significant ability she possessed and shuttered with uneasiness. I started second-guessing my delay tactics. Maybe it wasn't a good idea to teach my enemy how to kill me in a multitude of different ways. I opened my mouth to redirect the conversation when Onyx interrupted me with an unladylike snort, wrinkled her nose, and said, "No. Don't be absurd. It just felt like the element had more potential. I got sidetracked perfecting something else but have faith I'll begin experimenting with chromium immediately. What else can you tell me?"

I blinked a couple of times in shock before I gained my composure. This battle was no longer about just my survival, not after that statement. I wouldn't be able to live with myself if I let Onyx escape knowing she planned to torture people with the knowledge I provided her. It was my responsibility to ensure she would never have the chance to harm anyone else ever again. There was no way I'd let myself be an accomplice in any way. "Uh . . . um. Let's see," I stammered before I cleared my throat and said, "Your ability to create a bloodstone is the stuff of nightmares."

"What do you mean? Besides using it to focus my thoughts. I found the stone useless," Onyx stated as she produced one in her outstretched hand and studied it.

"The iron oxide in the gemstone can pull the hemoglobin from an opponent without even touching them, essentially draining them of their life source, like a bloodsucker. The gem stores the blood of your victims, which you can use later if you need to heal yourself," I answered with reluctance as I started to see all the different ways she could kill a person.

"How do I do it?" Onyx asked as she looked at the stone in her hand with newfound reverence.

"I'm afraid that would take more time than we have. Would you like me to continue, or have I said enough to prove I wasn't lying," I stated like I didn't have a care in the world when in actuality, I'd never been more frightened in my life. Gah! I know they say there's a first for everything. I just wish my test didn't have to be during a life-or-death situation. Even though I could read every gift within a one-mile radius, I'd never used more than one at a time. Of course, if I thought about it, technically, I used more than one every time I borrowed someone else's gift. There shouldn't be any reason why I couldn't add more to the mix. At least that's what I was hoping for.

"Time isn't a factor," Onyx argued, taking a step in my direction.

"Oh? I was under the impression you were handing me over to the Mengh after our little chat," I protested at the same time Adira spoke up, "I hate to intrude, but Lord Kalen's potion will only last another fifteen minutes at the most."

"Fine. What else can my power do? You've yet to list my favorite one," Onyx conceded with a taunt.

I contemplated ignoring her request when I came across an ability that acted as a mirror. One that would allow me to redirect Kema's power back on her like a deflector shield. Virtually canceling out her ability as well as anything Onyx tried to send my way. Unfortunately, her jab had me questioning what else the sadistic bitch might be capable of.

"Your favorite? Huh. Let me see if I can guess what it is out of what's left," I hedged, carefully surrounding myself with the mirroring ability before I probed her gift one more time. I skipped past anything non-lethal and almost lost my composure when I realized what she might be referring to. Cocking my head to the side, I began with, "Do I get anything if I am right?"

"Depends. Your release to the Mengh is not up for discussion, but anything else is fair game," Onyx responded easily.

"I don't want Kalen anywhere near the Mengh. Promise me he'll be far away when you make the transfer. I wouldn't put it past the monsters to try and hurt him when he's vulnerable," I declared with passion. Even though I knew we'd be long gone before anything like that could happen, I found myself promising myself I'd make sure she paid for her treachery.

"Granted," She replied quickly with a chuckle.

When I looked at her in confusion, she said, "Your appearance in his life made me question my destiny. But your admission points out you have a weakness. Ordinarily, I'd exploit that flaw and use it to my advantage, but seeing as his safety was never an issue, I think you'd have been better off picking something else to bargain with. Can I be honest with you?" Onyx asked, adopting a sweet demeanor.

"Does that mean you've been dishonest with me the rest of the time?" I replied with a frown.

"A smart woman never believes the words of a stranger, an enemy, or someone they screwed over," Onyx answered, counting the reasons on her fingers one at a time. "Considering I fit all three of those categories, you shouldn't trust a thing I say." Chuckling to herself, she continued, "Of course, that statement could also be a lie, so I'll leave you to decide for yourself what you choose to believe."

Shaking my head slowly, I scoffed before I said, "Good advice, I think. What did you want to be honest with me about?"

My hackles rose when Onyx looked down at my mate on the floor with tenderness before she answered, "He's handsome and all, and having his offspring will be no hardship, but I always thought I'd feel different when I met my mate. Probably a byproduct of all the fairytales they told us as little girls. You know, the ones where they fill your head with fantasies that your special someone would somehow miraculously complete you. That statement always made me feel like they were telling me I was broken. Which, as you can imagine, didn't go over very well. So really, in the end, I have those tales to thank for who I am today."

Her look of tenderness faded as a frown marred her face. Raising her gaze to mine, she said, "For such a brief affair, you seem mighty attached to him. I mean, you act like you actually care for him? Does it make you sad to know you'll never have him again?"

"I'm feeling anything but sad right now," I replied with barely concealed rage. I gave Onyx my most sinister look and added, "No. The only thing I'm feeling is disgust and pity. Does it make you feel happy to know Anolla suffered immensely as your little creation ate her from the inside out?" Pointing at the squirming diabolitum in its cage of fire.

"Ahh, you figured it out. Fascinating creatures aren't they," Onyx answered as she waltzed toward the fiery cage with a faraway look in her eye.

"I wouldn't consider calling a silicate-based lifeform that consumes all organic matter in its path fascinating. It might just be me, but I think it's creepy," I seethed.

Onyx ignored my reply as she stared down at her gruesome creature with admiration. "I discovered the wicked talent when I was young, six to be exact, when my nanny found my secret stash of stolen gold and gems. I panicked when she said she'd tell my father. Everything happened so fast. I just remember feeling threatened when I made a diabolitum the first time. My nanny being the unintended victim. My uncle found me in tears and helped me cover it up. It wasn't until I was older that I discovered my body uses them in self-defense. Of course, I can also produce them at will now, but it's nice to know I always have someone watching my back."

"Like I said, creepy. I like being able to converse with the people that have my back," I replied haughtily, making sure my deflector shield was in place.

Onyx snickered before she turned to me and said, "You really are naive. Let me give you a bit of advice before I send you on your way. Your destination won't be teeming with loyal allies. If I were you, I wouldn't trust anybody but yourself. I mean, you're welcome to try, but don't say I didn't warn you."

I nodded my head slowly as I did my best to look defeated. Onyx strode to the other side of the room, putting distance between her and Kema before she turned around and said, "Well, even though our visit hasn't been fun, I can honestly say it was educational. Thank you. Pity I already made a deal to get rid of you. Kema, be a dear and make yourself useful."

My pulse picked up at her statement. It was now or never. Steeling myself for action, I turned my body so I could see everyone in the room and smiled in relief when I sensed Tanen, Paine, and Parthyn approaching. Our back-up had finally arrived. Knowing he would hear any thoughts directed at him specifically, I told him what they were about to walk into before I put on a malevolent smile and said, "Has anyone ever told you Karma is a bitch?"

"Of course, they have. I just don't believe in it. I make my own fate," Onyx sneered.

"Well. You should; considering you're just about to meet her," I snapped back.

"Meet her? You really are crazy. Karma is not a person, my dear. It's merely the idea that you reap what you sow," Onyx answered with a fake laugh. Turning to Kema, she hissed, "Kema, do your job and shut this bitch up!"

It was my turn to laugh, and I took joy in making it maniacal. "I assure you I'm not crazy. It's just that I imagine if Karma had a face, it'd be that of a woman you pissed off. Like me, Anolla or even the nanny you killed years ago. I'll let you pick. Oh, and by the way, I'm sure if Kema could answer you, she'd let you know she already tried silencing me, but it sorta backfired."

Onyx snarled like a cornered animal. "You'll pay for this. I'm sure the Mengh will understand why I couldn't make good on my promise once they find out how untrustworthy you are! I hope you choke on your own blood."

"Uh . . . You might want to reconsider that line of thought. I mean, it should come as no surprise to you that I lied about my gift. In my defense, it was a lie of omission, but a lie nonetheless. I wasn't lying about the fact I can see every nuance of a Sixer's ability. I just neglected to mention I could also use those gifts like they were my own. I'm what you call a borrower. In fact, you can call me the Borrower Queen, seeing as my mate happens to be a king."

Chapter Thirty-Six

The look of astonishment on her face was priceless, but I didn't get to savor it for long. It melted into a look of alarm when Tanen and company flashed into the room at the same time five identical little grey men made their appearance. Wearing silver one-piece suits, they looked like something out of a B-rated movie. Flanking Onyx, they stepped toward me in unison, raised their right hands like they were a bunch of synchronized swimmers, and froze the occupants of the room before they spoke without opening their tiny mouths. "It's so nice to meet you, Jade. We've been searching for you since the date of your parent's death, but courtesy of your father, were never able to pinpoint your origins."

"What are you talking about? Are you saying m..m..my parents were Sixers?" I stuttered, taking an instinctive step back.

They cocked their heads as one, watching my movement with a look of wonder. "We didn't know your father, but your mother was one of our top agents. Unfortunately, we lost contact with her when she met your father. She made contact with us shortly after you were born, scared for her life as well as yours. Your dad wasn't too keen about your existence once he discovered her secret. Before she could tell us her coordinates, we lost communication with her. It was only later we learned of their murder-suicide. We worried you perished along with them."

"You're lying. A drunk driver killed my parents in a car accident. I saw the pictures myself. Aunt Kathryn left them out one night after an argument she had with Uncle Peter on whether they should divulge how my parents died. I'd been bugging them for weeks to tell me. In the end, I stopped asking about it because I had my answer, and they never brought it up again," I explained with tears in my eyes.

"It matters not if you believe us. It is time for you to take your place on our side. To fill the role your mother once held," They replied in unison.

"Well, I hate to disappoint you, but that's not going to happen," I scoffed, squaring my shoulders. I couldn't let their mental tactics deter me from my prime objective.

I gathered from the looks on their faces that that wasn't the answer they were expecting. They looked between themselves before they took another step towards me and repeated themselves, "It matters not if you believe us. It is time for you to take your place on our side. To fill the role your…"

"My mother once held," I finished for them. "Yeah, you said that. Uh . . . I mean thought that whatever you guys call it. Repeating yourselves isn't going to change my mind. I'm not going anywhere with you! I've found my place and it's not with you!"

When four of the quintuplets nodded in agreement with me, the fifth pushed to the front of their arrow formation, and the others immediately stopped. The act was strange and had me looking at what kind of gifts they could use against me. It appeared they had some type of symbiotic relationship, where they could amplify the power of one if they directed it by standing in the 'V' formation. The guy standing at the apex appeared to be a magic warder. He had no defensive moves, but his ability would make it hard to use offensive magic against them.

I studied the Mengh he had replaced and wasn't surprised to find he had the gift of persuasion. It almost made me laugh that they thought they'd teleport in here, say some words, and I'd follow after them like a pied piper rat. Obviously, they had no idea what they were dealing with. I considered the gifts of the other three. One could heal. Another was a time-warder, which was probably how they teleported in here. The last was telekinetic.

When none of them spoke, I borrowed Tanen's mind reading ability to listen in on their private mental conversation, only to find them in the middle of an argument about how to handle me. From outward appearances, the five Mengh had no gender specific traits, but I was sure the two females, the healer and time-warder, wanted to retreat from listening to their internal exchange. Meanwhile, the males were adamant, my capture was just what they needed for a promotion. My suspicions were confirmed when the time-warder stepped toward her sister and said, *Brothers, I understand your need to climb the ranks, but Myra and I only agreed to come with you on this adventure because you promised it was foolproof. The Marni cannot be trusted. Let us retreat.* She looked at Onyx with disgust.

The magic warder stepped toward his sisters as he spoke up. *She failed. You'll hear no argument from me concerning that, Lyra. But you should reconsider her usefulness to us in the future. In case we have no choice but to leave without our prize.*

Lyra looked at Myra for direction and answered when her sister nodded in agreement. *Fine, Kyro, but one of you will be responsible for her.* The persuader volunteered before she continued, *Thank you, Nyro. We can kidnap her during her upcoming trials. And if that doesn't work, we'll come back with reinforcements. The discovery of Kishala's daughter will still be ours and will have to be enough. I am not willing to risk our lives for the sake of your ambition. Tyro, you're welcome to try and bring her with us, but if it doesn't work, Myra and I are leaving with or without you.*

Hearing my biological mother's name gave me pause, but postponing my assault in the chance the Mengh might give me another morsel of information about my mother would put me no closer to victory. It only gave them a chance to worm their way into my brain. While they continued to bicker, I shook my head and worked on expanding the shield around me so my backup would have a chance to be useful. Shit was about to get real, and I could use all the help I could get.

Hoping Kalen would wake up soon, I spared him a final look before I interrupted their squabble. "It appears we're at a stalemate."

"How do you figure?" The five responded in unison as the time-warder opened a portal behind her. They quickly resumed their arrow formation with the telekinetic wielder at the pinnacle.

I laughed hysterically when I realized they had no idea I was a borrower. Nor did they notice that everything they sent my way bounced back to them. When I started snorting, I closed my mouth and slapped a hand over it for good measure. The moment I had control of myself, I dropped my arm to my side and said, "Damn! How egotistical of me. Here I thought you wanted me for my power, but you're truly clueless. I should be interested in finding out why you wanted me in the first place, but it appears I'll have to ask you later."

"We are glad you've decided to join us. We'll answer all of your questions once we're away from here," They answered with excitement as they turned in unison and pointed to their portal.

"Join you? That's a good one," I scoffed with an extended chuckle as I made one more final push to extend the mirroring ability. When I felt stretched too thin, I pulled it back to just me and Kalen. Fuck. I'd just have to do it without them. I stopped laughing bit by bit to give myself more time before I finally spoke, "Oh, you were serious. Sorry I thought I made my intentions clear. I'm not changing my mind. No, I just meant I'd interrogate you in the dungeons later. Of course, only after I deal with the traitorous Sixers responsible for this shit show," I replied as I eyed each of my enemies with a murderous smile.

The greys' facial expressions gave little away as to what they thought as they regrouped. I knew I was working against time. The moment they discovered they had no chance of taking me with them, they'd escape using their portal and bring reinforcements. Time to put my big girl panties on and show these people who they were dealing with. Hoping I still had the element of surprise, I used Kalen's gift and pulled our friends to me at the same time Tyro attempted to use his telekinetic gift against me.

It was almost comical to watch four of the five Mengh float toward me, end over end in the air. Lyra froze their progression when they were somewhat upright and called out to Kyro, *I can't keep the portal open and the room frozen to this degree for much longer. Use one of the disruptors, so I can let the room go, and you can get us down from here! We'll try again during her trials.*

Which one, Kyro whined.

Pick something nonlethal, you idiot! Lyra shot back.

Even though I knew they were planning something, I neglected to take evasive action when I heard the words non-lethal— rookie mistake number one. Mistake number two was standing in place when Kyro pulled a glowing white marble from his pocket and hucked it at me. Staring at the thing while he rushed forward to cancel my telekinetic attack instead of doing something to stop him was mistake number three. Although blinded by the very ball, staring at when it detonated into a brilliant white light had to be the biggest rookie mistake in history.

The place erupted into a whirlwind of activity as Lyra released her hold on the occupants of the room. Without my eyes, I had to rely on my sense of sound and smell to guide my attacks. I let loose an arsenal of defensive tactics and prayed more than a few hit their mark. The ear shattering squeal of the diabolitum told me we'd have at least one less thing to worry about. Pushing my hands forward, I let Parthyn's electrical whips flow from my hands as I used Kiso's ability to lock the lab down. As a precaution, I pulled on Natashia's time-warder gift and closed the Mengh's portal as I tried to get my bearings.

Onyx started wailing as the smell of burning hair and flesh reached me. It made me a little happy that I couldn't see the massacre in front of me. Only a little. Not enough to refrain from using Annalise's gift of healing. If I could return even a portion of my eyesight, it'd be better than nothing. When I felt flames pass inches from my head, I dove left and coated my skin in diamond plating. I breathed a sigh of relief when I hit the ground, and my eyesight started making a comeback. All I could see were shapes, but it was enough to give me a target. I fired off a couple of fireballs and pushed myself to stand up. I caressed the diamond suit and couldn't help the grin that crossed my face. Who said armor couldn't be sexy as fuck? I couldn't see it, but I had a good imagination. There was no way I would survive a magical war just to be taken out by a sword or something normal like that. I know the Mengh indicated they wanted me alive, but I wasn't willing to take any chances.

I lost my breath when what felt like a brick wall slammed into my right side, dropping me to the ground. Even with the hardest armor in the world, I still struggled to catch my breath. I would have been dead without it. Whatever hit me knocked the wind out of me, for sure. I rolled to my back and used my feet to push myself out from under the slab of rock Onyx used to hit me with. Once I was clear, I shot off an electric chain of energy in multiple directions and gave myself a mental pat on the back when Onyx cried out, "My hair! Oh, you'll pay for that, bitch!"

"What are you going to do about it, hag?" I replied cockily as I mentally listened for the location of the greys. I was ninety-nine percent confident they had their hands full with my back-up.

"It's not what I'll do to you, miss fucking queen bee. It's what I'll do to your king! What can I say? I'm a poor loser. One thing's for sure, you shouldn't have revealed your weakness. If I can't have him, neither can you!" Onyx screamed to my right.

Her threat, no matter how weak, was genuine. In all the confusion, I had no idea where I'd left my love. How far away had I gone? Shit! Did my borrowed mirroring ability still cover him? For all I knew, she could be standing next to him now with a blade of onyx. Fat luck a magical deflective shield would protect him from physical damage. Fuck! I turned in the direction I thought I heard her voice and gave her a final warning, "You kill him and you can kiss a quick death goodbye. I'll make you wish for death by your diabolitum! I'll bring you to the point of death every day, and then I'll heal you so that I can do it all over again the next day!"

"Thanks for the warning. I'll make sure to take my life when I'm finished with him!" Onyx promised.

I swung my head in her direction just as she slit Kalen's throat. "No!" I screamed as I watched Kalen slump forward.

Onyx gave me an evil grin as she wrapped her hands around her throat and then changed her arms into sharp blades, slicing through her neck. The crazy bitch cut off her head. I rushed to Kalen and dropped to my knees, tears streaming down my face. With a shaking hand, I felt for a pulse. It was faint and fading, but he was still alive. Hovering over him, I tuned out the chaos around me and put everything I had into healing him. As the last of my energy passed into him, I slumped forward onto his chest and everything went black.

Chapter Thirty-Seven

I came to slowly and sighed. There was nothing better than the feeling of freshly laundered sheets. I stretched out and cringed. Damn! I was stiff and sore in places I didn't even know existed. It must have been one hell of a binger. What the hell did I do last night? Propping up on my elbows, I opened my eyes, then everything over the past few days came rushing back. "Kalen!" I croaked, looking about the lavish room. It was the same one I woke up in on my first day here.

Pushing back the covers, I squealed in surprise when two strong hands wrapped around my hips and pulled me back down. Kalen nuzzled my hair and groaned in my ear, "Where do you think you're going?"

I twisted in his arms and burst into tears when I found his aquamarine eyes staring back at me. "Is this real? Are we alive?" I whispered.

He studied my face for a moment as he wiped away my tears. Leaning forward, he placed a soft kiss on my lips and said, "Yes, we're alive. Thanks to the Borrower Queen."

I dropped my head onto his chest and groaned, "Ugh! You heard that? I thought you were comatose?"

Kalen placed his finger under my chin and raised it slowly. When I met his gaze, he said, "Oh, I was out of it, alright."

Looking at him in confusion, I frowned. "Huh. Then why'd you call me that?"

"Figured I'd join the masses," Kalen replied with a grin.

"What are you talking about?" I queried, tilting my head to the side.

"You're a bit of a celebrity around here," Kalen chuckled.

"For what? Are you sure you're alright?" I asked, holding the back of my hand to his forehead, checking for a fever.

"I feel better than I ever have, but I know how you can make me feel even better," Kalen replied with a wink.

"Really? That's where your brain is at right now? Concentrate! Let's get back to the part where you tell me what the hell is going on? What happened? The last thing I remember besides Onyx offing herself, which I'm still pissed about by the way, is healing you. What happened after I passed out?" I whined.

"Let's see, where do I start?" Kalen teased.

I slapped his chest, and he captured my hand, kissing it before he spoke, "So impatient for a woman that just saved the kingdom."

When I opened my mouth to complain, he placed a finger over my mouth and answered me, "The second you became unconscious, the surviving Mengh were able to portal out. They took their comrades with them. We have Adira and Kema in the dungeons now. Jaleal is interrogating them."

"Wait! How do you remember anything? Adira said the potion she gave you would erase your memories of me," I gasped. Pushing back from Kalen, I clutched the sheet to my chest and sat up. Turning to face him directly, I waited for his response.

Kalen pushed himself up and leaned against the headboard before he answered, "Well, that would probably be because she lied. The potion knocked me out, but I didn't lose my memories. I think Adira wanted me to know how fucked up Onyx was, even if it meant she faced treason charges for poisoning her king."

"She only did it to save her sister. Why would we charge her for treason? It's not like she purposefully set out to poison and destroy you. She did it under duress," I argued.

"Which means her punishment will be lenient, but she will receive something. Uh-uh, let me finish first," Kalen responded, holding up a finger when I moved to argue. "She had a choice Jade, whether you see it or not. She could have come to me or any of my guards and reported it. She took matters into her own hands and needs to learn a lesson."

"What about her sister? Onyx said she was already aboard the Mengh's ship," I asked, my heart breaking for Adira. I couldn't imagine how she was feeling. I'm sure fear paid a large part in her decision, but I could understand where Kalen was coming from.

"Unfortunately, we might never find her. Which is another reason Adira's punishment will be lenient. She's well aware she made the wrong decision. If she had spoken to one of us, we might have been able to save her. We'll never know, though, because she didn't give us a chance," Kalen replied, tucking a strand of hair behind my ear.

"I could…" I began only to be cut off by Kalen's growl. "Don't you dare mention going back in time. You'll never leave my side again!"

I smiled in response to his alphaness and replied, "I was going to say I could try and find her using Fansa's gift. Trust me, after my last excursion, I don't plan on going anywhere or any time, for that matter, without you. Speaking of Fansa, what happened on that front? Did we capture Bastian?"

"Bastian escaped, but not before killing the doppelganger," Kalen responded with a snarl.

"Did we lose anyone in the battle?" I asked quietly.

"There was loss on both sides today. However, nothing cut me as deep as Fansa and Clary's betrayal. I've worked with them for centuries and had no clue they were plotting against me. I've yet to interrogate them," Kalen answered with a frown.

"Well, maybe they'll have similar stories to Adira?" I posed, hopefully.

"Those hopes shattered when they murdered a couple of the guards sent to apprehend them for questioning," Kalen revealed with a far off look in his eyes.

"I see. I'm sorry, Kalen. We should talk to them. Maybe we'll garner something useful. Something that will help us track down the Mengh that escaped or give us an idea of how they communicated with each other. Maybe we could intercept the communication or something," I replied, scrambling to my knees.

"We will. Right now, we have something better to do with our time," Kalen replied, pulling me into his chest.

I melted into him and took a deep breath. It felt like it was the first time I could breathe deeply since I went back in time. It would be so easy to sink into us and forget about everything for a while, but then I remembered what I overheard the Mengh say. With a deep sigh, I pulled back and told Kalen what I heard, "I know where we can find the Mengh."

Kalen groaned. "You're killing me, Jade. Alright, fine. You win. Tell me what you know, and then I want you to forget about it for the rest of the night. Whatever it is can wait until the morning, but I won't last much longer," Kalen finished, stroking his cock slowly. Giving me no doubt of what was on his mind.

Biting my lip, I stared at his cock before I spoke, "They said if they weren't successful in taking me with them, they'd capture me during the trials. From the sounds of it, they were working off of insider information."

"Fuck!" Kalen roared, launching himself from the bed, and began pacing. "I knew your ability as a borrower would put you at risk, but I thought we'd have a few years before they started making threats against your life!"

I approached Kalen and placed a hand on his arm as he passed me. When he stopped and looked at me, I spoke, "They didn't know I was a borrower. I mean, they probably do now, but that's not what they wanted me for. I didn't get a chance to find out the real reason, but they said it was because of my mother. I should have killed them before they had a chance to escape, but I wasn't expecting that bitch to try and off you."

"Glad you had your priorities straight," Kalen replied with a slight smile before adding, "I wish you would have killed them too. I'd rather keep your gift a secret forever, but I know that's not possible. We'll add extra security and set a trap for them. With any luck, they haven't reported you to their commanding officer."

"Wouldn't it be better to postpone or at least pretend to cancel the trials? I'd hate to lose a participant in the crosshairs of their plans," I declared passionately.

"Do they know you were eavesdropping on them?" Kalen asked with a frown.

"No. Not that I know of. I liked the advantage it gave me. I never said anything that would lead the Mengh to believe I could hear them," I replied, running my hands through my hair in thought.

"Then I think we should use that to our advantage. There are too many chances for our plans to leak if we pretend to cancel. I think they'll get suspicious if we postpone. No, the safest bet is to move forward with the trials," Kalen replied with a nod.

"I suppose you're right. Does that mean we'll be using me as bait?" I asked out loud, deep in thought.

Kalen flashed to my location and wrapped me in his arms before he growled, "Maybe I haven't made myself clear? You will not be attending the trials in any capacity. There is no need for you to compete for a position in the army. Your position is next to me!"

I tilted my head back to look at him before I gave him a seductive smile and answered, "Show me."

Epilogue

"Jaleal, I'd like you to pick someone you trust to lead the next mission. Let me know by the end of the meeting who your choice is," Kalen announced from the head of the council table.

"Sir," I replied from behind him.

"What is it, Tanen," Kalen replied, sparing me a glance over his shoulder.

"I'd like to volunteer," I stated, swallowing the lump in my throat.

"Volunteer for what?" Kalen answered, swiveling in his seat to face me.

"To lead the mission, my lord," I answered, unable to look him in the face. I kept my gaze on the wall behind him. With my hands behind my back, I waited for his response.

"Really? I thought you'd want to stick around. What with a new mate and all," Kalen replied, pushing himself out of his chair to stand.

I met his gaze and replied, "Cynosis hasn't exactly accepted our bond yet. She's adamant about competing in the trials. So regardless of if you let me lead this mission or not, I'll be following after her!"

To be continued

In Cynosis and Tanen's Story:

Siren's Call

Made in the USA
Monee, IL
03 August 2021